Book One of THE LEAF'S KEY SERIES

THE WHITEASH KEY

WRITTEN BY

HEIDI LOUISE WILLIAMS

Gem-in-Eye Publishing

To my precious daughter, my brother Paul and sweet Willow
This book is dedicated with all my love.

DREAMS DO COME TRUE. KNOWLEDGE IS THE KEY.

Acknowledgments: Much appreciation to the lovely Rosita Gaston, my first editor, and to my draft readers: Judy Rust who was absolutely marvellous, Marilyn Barry, Rachel Wallace, Michael John Kellough and Sheila Hoeman for all their feedback and positive suggestions. Thanks also to Carol Corbridge for saving me from myself when it got technically complicated, and to Rab Caw for his generosity and tech savvy each time I wore out a computer.

Titles in THE LEAF'S KEY SERIES:

CONTENTS

PRELUDE

The eerie fog pressed heavy against the tinted windows of the unmarked van. The masked men waited with bad intentions for the old lady to leave her house.

Ten minutes later they saw her emerge from the dense white cloud, dressed in a leotard and rainbow leg warmers, looking like an over-aged film extra from 'Fame'. She climbed into her car and headed off down the almost invisible road in the direction of her Thursday night yoga class.

The three men got out of the van, taking a bag of tools with them. Hidden under the heavy shroud of vapour, balaclavas and black outfits, they broke the lock on the front door.

Grammy, in her Mini Cooper she called Sally, pushed in the CD. She pressed play on the song that always gave Sally and Grammy an ample boost of British courage to face dangerous driving conditions with less trepidation. Grammy sang along with Wilson Pickett, knowing all the words to Mustang Sally.

Her thoughts were sidetracked for a moment, thinking about the upcoming party. Bernadette Latoure (A.K.A Grammy) had waited a very long time for her granddaughter, Leaf Golden, to turn ten. It was going to be a memorable night, a night that would change Leaf's life forever after Grammy revealed her lifelong secret. Grammy could hardly contain her excitement, but she told herself to focus on the half-hidden road in front of her.

Meanwhile, the burglars were rampaging through Grammy's Victorian townhouse. They had to be thorough and look everywhere, but they also needed to move fast because if the old woman got home early, or turned back due to the fog, they would have to kill her. Tonight that would be inconvenient as the commissioner had dinner plans in an exclusive restaurant with his wife and children. He had not planned on burying a body and lying to his wife about why he was late. He had told his men that if all went according to their plan, they would come back to finish off the old woman and her granddaughter, especially if they had what he and his men were looking for.

The commissioner's cold grey eyes with snake-like pupils darted to the clock on the wall. It was time to get a move on. He closed the wine-coloured curtains of the front room's sash windows.

Prelude

They overturned drawers, spilled everything out onto the floor, pulled all the books from the shelves, yanked clothes out of cupboards, checked all the pockets, smashed lamps and ornaments in case it was stashed inside them.

It was a disastrous mess that, on returning, made Grammy wish that her wobbly yoga legs had carried her into the wrong house. If her arthritic knees had permitted her to carry on with her Wednesday night Kickboxing class, she might have wished she'd come home to find the robbery still in progress so she could give the intruders a good hiding, but at seventy-one she was no longer the kick-ass granny that she used to be.

At ten thirty-five she called the police in a calm state of shock. The forensic unit found no fingerprints, and because no money, jewellery or any of the antiques had been stolen, the officers suspected that whoever had broken into the house had been looking for something in particular.
Grammy was silently confident that they would never find it.

Chapter One

GIFT OF THE KEY

Leaf's mother was at the red front door welcoming the first of the guests. Before all the other people arrived, Grammy wanted a moment in private with Leaf, a very important life changing moment. She was waiting, posed by the fireplace. Grammy often looked posed, which was a side effect of her modelling days in the sixties. Smiling, shoulders back and neck stretched, Grammy beckoned to Leaf.

"I have something to show you. Come with me," she whispered. Leaf followed her to the hall and quietly slipped past Mum at the door and up the swirling two flights of stairs.

The stairs, with the ornate banister which Leaf loved to slide down, made the house look grand, like the home of a film star. Grammy was like a film star. She held herself tall with elegance and poise, and despite her usual hippy attire, she always seemed somewhat regal. Even at seventy-one her beauty was still the envy of all her friends.

They entered the old woman's colourful bedroom. Leaf thought of it as the rainbow room. The walls were white but all the furniture, paintings, bed and ornaments were in vivid colours. This was the room where Grammy had slept alone since the death of her husband five years ago. Leaf knew her grandmother missed him terribly but Leaf hardly remembered her grandfather. She had been only five when he died.

Leaf slipped off her shoes and climbed onto the bed between all the colourful cushions. She spun the dangling crystal that

9

hung above the bed. It caught the light from the lamppost outside the large window and made rainbows dance on the white walls.

Grammy opened the large built-in wardrobe, got down on her arthritic knees and pushed all her animal-print and crazy-coloured pairs of flat shoes to one side. Climbing further in, between her large collection of hanging T-shirts and long colourful skirts, Grammy started tapping on the back wall.

Leaf, curious to see what the old woman was up to, lay on her back, her head hanging off the bed, looking upside-down into the cupboard at her grandmother. Thud, thud, thud and then there was a hollow sound. Grammy pressed that part with her right index finger. One side of the wall pushed in, and ten centimetres along the other side of the wall came out. Leaf rolled over on her front, intrigued. She got up and went to the cupboard to get a closer look. To her amazement, Grammy literally turned about a metre squared of the back wall round. The wall turned 180 degrees to reveal a shelf on the other side with a rectangular black box on it.

Taking the box, which was seven centimetres long, Grammy spun the wall back to its original side to hide the shelf. Leaf's eyes were wide with excitement and curiosity.

Grammy shuffled bum first back out of the cupboard and stood up grinning with mischief.

"What's that Grammy?"

"For over four hundred years, this has been passed from grandmother to granddaughter through the generations of our family. It is always given to the first granddaughter on her tenth birthday. Now it is yours until you have a ten-year-old granddaughter of your own. Happy Birthday, Leaf! I could not be more proud of you, my love!"

Gift of the Key

Now Leaf was bursting with curiosity. She carefully opened the box. Lying on a bed of red velvet was a pretty silver Key, five and a half centimetres in length. Its slender cylinder was shiny silver. It had tiny teeth on the end. The ornate head of the Key, worn over time, had become matte silver, curled inwards on both sides in almost a heart-shape with side tails, separated at the top with a curvy letter W and below it an A. It looked very old fashioned but well preserved and Leaf thought it an elegant key.

Leaf looked to her grandmother for an explanation. Grammy smiled her knowing smile. She sat down on her neatly-made turquoise bed and patted for Leaf to sit next to her.

"This Key is what the burglars were looking for. The people who broke into my house are called Lockers, members of a secret society who search for this Key and you must keep it hidden from them. For now we will keep it in my hiding place," Grammy told her.

"Why are they looking for it? What do they want it for?" Leaf asked confused, "Why do you have it?"

"This is a Whiteash Key. You must never tell anyone about it, and you must never let the Lockers find it, Leaf. This Key is yours for the next half a century and only you and I are meant to use it, but you are the next Guardian of this Key."

"Your whole life is about to change, Leaf, because this is the Key to wonders, and with it all your dreams can come true. With this Key you can go anywhere you want to, in any dimension of time. But you cannot visit yourself. Never! That is extremely important."

"I can go anywhere? Which door will it open?" A cheeky smirk played on Leaf's lips as she did not believe any of this to be true, but she listened because usually there was some sense or fun to Grammy's madness.

"Any door with a lock can be opened with this Key, and it will take you to wherever you want to go. You can go into the past, present, future, somewhere real or imaginary."

"I am not sure that I believe you," Leaf admitted.

"I will show you," Grammy said with an excited grin on her face, taking the Key back from Leaf.

"Where would you like to go, Leaf? You can say anywhere in the entire universe in any era of time, but be careful, think first, and don't say somewhere you know to be dangerous."

"I can go somewhere in the past?" Leaf asked with a confused and disbelieving frown.

"Well, it is your birthday. Avoiding the past is recommended to prevent the consequences of accidental changes in history, but I am here to teach you and make sure you don't make bad choices. So yes, even the past, as long as there will be a door there for you to get back or you will have to make a temporary door."

"Make a door?"

"I will teach you that on another day."

"I wish I could have gone to the Katy Perry concert. My best friend Sarah told me about it. Her cousin went and said it was amazing. It was in Birmingham on May the thirteenth this year," Leaf told her after a moment of thought.

"At the LG Arena?" Grammy inquired.

"That's the one!" Leaf was impressed by Grammy's knowledge of concert venues.

"What time did it start?"

"Around nine-thirty, I think," Leaf guessed.

"It is now seven-thirty, remember that because we must come back five minutes after the time we left. Try to be precise about your instructions to the Key: the time, the place, the date, the address and exactly where you want to be in case you end up stuck in the middle of a wall or in a toilet. It usually gets you where you want to go with little instruction but try to be precise, just to be safe. Although, after a while the Key gets to know you and where you live and you can just say "Home" or "My house" and it will magically transport you there. I often wonder about that, I really don't know how it does it, but it does. Here, this notebook is for you," Grammy said, retrieving a small pad from her bedside drawer.

She gave Leaf a notebook with a Quikid World picture on the front cover. A drawing of a big-eyed blonde girl, who looked a lot like Leaf, wearing a dress covered in graffiti- style artistic tags, holding a blue Great Dane on a lead and standing fashionably in front of the Eiffel Tower in Paris. It had the words **Quikid Ones in Paris** written across the top in a small graffiti-style font. It was part of a collectable series. There was a small sharp pencil slipped into the curly binder and a string attached so you could hang it round your neck in the absence of a pocket. Leaf loved the notebook. Quikid World was her favourite brand and she had lots of their posters hanging in her bedroom that came free in the monthly Quikid World magazine.

"COOL! Thanks Grammy." Leaf gave Grammy a hug.

"You should always take a small pad of paper everywhere you go to write down times and other important things. Write down seven thirty-one so we don't forget what time we left. Okay, here we go then!" Grammy walked to the end of her bedroom, closed the door to the en-suite bathroom and placed the magic Key in the lock.

"In the audience of the Katy Perry concert at the Birmingham LG Arena, nine-thirty at night on the thirteenth of May 2014," Grammy seemed to be instructing the door, and she turned the Key in the lock three times to the left.

"You have to hold my hand for us both to get through the

door together," Grammy said, grabbing Leaf's hand. Leaf was smiling, still thinking it was all just one of Grammy's games. Her grandmother turned the handle and opened the door. Leaf's mouth fell open as she and Grammy stepped through the bathroom door and into the very loud audience of a Katy Perry concert.

The screams of the audience were deafening. The arena was quite dark except for white lasers beaming across the ceiling and low light on the centre stage.

Leaf followed Grammy through the sections of seats packed with an enthusiastic audience until they found standing space at the back with some other people. She looked around to see if she knew anyone.

The audience was split into many sections all around the stage and up above. People had their phones held up above their heads taking photographs and videos of the dancers who were flying above the stage on illuminated spears dressed as Egyptian slaves.

A large pyramid opened centre stage, lit-up with colour and surrounded by shooting smoke. Katy Perry dressed in a skirt and crop top of mirrors rimmed with light tubes, rose out of it singing 'Roar'. Futuristic gladiators danced around her and the audience sang along to the well-known words.

The audience screamed with delight. Grammy had to cover her ears. Leaf loved it.

"IF I HAD KNOWN IT WAS GOING TO BE LIKE THIS I WOULD HAVE WORN SOMETHING COOL," said Grammy in her loudest voice, trying to shout over the music, bopping away with her fingers in her ears, wearing a fitted orange dress and tiger-striped pumps. As she looked around, Leaf decided her shocking-pink dress was passable.

Gift of the Key

Everyone was so happy and colourful. The whole concert was a wonderland of excitement, colour, lasers, strobe lights, mind blowing visual effects, props and outstanding costumes.

The crowds were dancing in their seats and having a great time. Leaf and Grammy jumped up and down waving their arms and elbows around. They laughed and danced until their sides hurt.

"THANKS GRAMMY," Leaf yelled.

"HAPPY BIRTHDAY, LEAF," Grammy yelled back.

When Katy Perry had sung 'Birthday' Leaf felt as if she was singing it just for her. It was the best birthday ever.

The last song was 'Firework'. Most people in the audience put on rainbow star-diffraction glasses they bought before the show started, which magnified the visual effects. Grammy and Leaf did not have these but the effects were amazing without them. The whole stage was exploding in colours. Projected fireworks were going off and raining down over the stage.

Katy, wearing a ball gown with a firework print, walked through the audience on a long runway as she sang. At the end Katy Perry disappeared back into the pyramid and the concert ended in a deafening round of cheering and applause.

Everyone started to leave and the noise level slowly began to die down. Grammy told Leaf to stay put. People pushed passed them heading for the exits.

Finally the Stadium was almost empty of people. The last stragglers were heading out of the door. Grammy and Leaf felt small in the arena that now seemed twice as huge.

"Come! Quickly, before the staff get back. We have to find a bathroom door. There will only be toilets out the front so we will

15

have to go backstage."

"Grammy, we can't go backstage! We will get in serious trouble!"

"We have to if you want to get home tonight, Leaf. We have been gone almost two hours."

"Mum will be freaking out! She probably has all the guests out looking for us. She might even have called the police," Leaf said in panic, worry burrowing frown lines across the youthful skin on her forehead.

"If we get back a few minutes after the time we left, they will not know that we have been gone because time will not have passed for them, but right now your poor mother is probably worried sick. I was irresponsible and used poor judgement on this occasion," said Grammy, frowning.

"I should have told your mother that I was taking you out for a bit and we should not have left when your party was starting. I did not realise we would be gone so long. I thought we would stay fifteen minutes or so, but you seemed to be having so much fun that I seemed to have lost my head for a moment and so we watched the whole concert. Anyway, I hope you will learn from my terrible mistake and be a much more responsible Guardian." Grammy looked quite cross with herself but really she had planned this mistake to teach Leaf an important lesson. Although she was now feeling terribly guilty for all the worry and inconvenience she must have put her daughter and all the guests through. She scolded herself. It was really quite unacceptably rude!

"Oh well, too late to worry about it now, but we must not let it happen again," she stated and strutted off towards the stage. Leaf ran after her.

"Leaf, even though we are about to go back to only five minutes after the time we left, you and I have still aged two hours. You must not use the Key too often, twice a week is plenty or you will age too fast. I am probably about five years older than you think, after all the time I used up Key Jumping." Leaf was not happy knowing her grandmother was actually seventy-six. The thought of Grammy dying of old age often distressed Leaf.

"You should keep a journal and write down all times and for how long you used the Key so you know how much you have aged, Leaf. Even if you return to the same time you left, your body has still experienced living extra time. So don't overuse the Key or you could end up looking sixty at forty, no matter what anti-wrinkle cream you buy."

"You can also die before you were meant to in reality. It does not matter if you go into the future, the past, present, real or imaginary, because your mind and body are experiencing the time, plus the extra stress that Jumping through space and time puts on the body," she said in a hushed voice. Now that the stadium was empty it was eerily quiet.

Grammy took Leaf's hand and gave her a mischievous smile.

"Come on! Let's do this!" Grammy whispered with a tone of determination. Leaf laughed. Grammy was always so much fun.

They were hidden behind the left side of the stage. Grammy gave Leaf a bunk-up with her two hands cupped together. Leaf put her foot in Grammy's hands, hoisted herself up, her hands pushing down on Grammy's shoulders. Grammy's arthritic knees felt like buckling. Leaf was the wrong way round so with both her feet in Grammy's hands she made a wobbly turn to the right, getting her bum in Grammy's face. She almost sat on Grammy's head.

"Watch it!" Grammy cried.

"SorrRrrY" Leaf said, almost toppling. She tried to grab the

17

top of the stage but could not reach.

"I know I don't look it but I'm an old lady. I am supposed to be careful, not performing circus acts and not juggling people. OWW! Don't kill me! Hurry up and get off me, Wormy," she cried, using the nickname she called Leaf.

"Step left," Leaf instructed her grandmother, who tried to take one step closer to the stage and balance her grandchild at the same time. Leaf stretched up, managed to grab the top of the stage this time and scrambled up the side onto the platform using her feet. Not very elegantly one might add. She knew Grammy had seen her knickers, but at least it was only Grammy, who had hitched her own dress up. She had bright blue tights on.

Leaf lay on her tummy and slid one quarter of her body over the edge, her long hair dangling in Grammy's face. Grammy tried to escape from beneath the fallen golden curtain, like a person fighting their way out of a dense jungle of vines.

Hanging upside-down, Leaf grabbed Grammy's hands. She quickly pulled herself back to heave Grammy up. She had to do it super fast to make it work. Grammy's scrawny blue legs tried to speed-walk up. It was a manic struggle. Leaf's face turned dark pink with strain. She could see Grammy's eye-bulging ascent over the edge and it was making her laugh.

The strain and determination had turned Grammy's face positively puce because she usually held her breath when she was concentrating. She kept bursting into fits of giggling every time she remembered to breathe. It was not helping Grammy to get her bum onto the stage. She kept slipping, old skinny blue legs flaying in every direction, and she had to point her toes at the same time to keep her shoes on.

Straining, Leaf lay back and hoisted her grandmother on top of herself. They knew they looked ridiculous and got into another fit of the giggles. The two of them rolled around on the stage laughing and Grammy almost fell off the edge.

Trying to be quiet and stop giggling, they swerved between the gigantic pyramid, speakers, decorated gang planks, the metal frames and screens. They headed to the back of the stage and ducked under the big black No-go curtain.

It was bustling with life backstage. The grips and crew were running about starting to take down the set and lighting. Men were carrying heavy equipment in and out of doors.

"Just look like you belong, like you work here or at least like your parents work here," Grammy instructed under her breathe in a low, almost ventriloquist's voice, as they slipped past the people all busy doing their jobs.

A man in a purple suit with a clipboard was screaming, "Does anyone know where Katy is?"

Assistants were talking into headsets and the wardrobe girls were pushing rails of costumes back to the props room. Hairdressers and make-up artists were busy packing their supplies into black box-shaped cases.

"I think Katy went that way," Grammy told the man in purple and pointed down the corridor to the left. He gave her a quizzical look and strutted off down the left corridor.

Leaf quickly followed Grammy down the empty corridor on the right.

"There will be a bathroom in here," said Grammy, pulling Leaf into a room with a big gold star on the door.

The room was filled with costumes and bright coloured clothes thrown over rails and chairs.

In the middle of the room was a table covered in make-up, hairspray, nail polishes and vases of red roses. There was a faceless head with a short black bobbed wig on it. Above the table was a mirror surrounded by light bulbs, a photo of a man was tucked into the top right corner of the mirror but Leaf did not have time to see who it was.

"Quick, in here," said Grammy, pulling Leaf's arm. She shut the door of the bathroom just as the door with the star on it opened. In the last second Leaf caught a glimpse of Katy Perry entering the room.

Grammy hurriedly took the Key from her pocket and placed it in the lock of Katy Perry's bathroom door.

"My bedroom, 12 Wicker Lane, Hampstead at seven thirty-five at night on Sunday the fourteenth of September 2014," Grammy instructed the door and turned the Key three times to the left.

They came out in Grammy's bedroom and quickly shut the door behind them. Leaf opened it again but it was just Grammy's en-suite bathroom on the other side.

"That was so amazing!" Leaf exclaimed, falling down exhausted onto Grammy's bed.

"The Key belongs to you now, Leaf, but I will hang onto it until you fully understand how to use it. I will need to tell you a lot of things so that you do not get yourself into trouble with the Key. I will come and see you tomorrow after school and we can start going over what you need to know. Don't worry it will be much more fun than having to read an instruction manual." Grammy kissed her on the forehead, pulled her to her feet and they went downstairs to enjoy the party.

Chapter Two

THE PARTY

Leaf's mother was still at the red front door welcoming the first of the arriving guests. Mum's friend Harriet, and her overly chatty daughter Scarlet, were ten minutes early.

Scarlet was a year younger than Leaf, very small for her age, covered from head to foot in freckles and had fixed braces on all her teeth which she sometimes wore attached to a head brace. Her red hair was always in two plaits that stuck out from her head like they had wire in them. Not only did she talk non-stop, but she stared and was incredibly nosey. Scarlet reminded Leaf of a creepy doll from a horror movie that wouldn't stop talking or following her around the house. Leaf tried very hard to be nice to her, but it took effort.

Leaf said a quick "Hi" and she and Grammy slipped past them into the living room. Mum took Harriet's coat. Scarlet was still talking one hundred miles an hour to Mum about choosing Leaf's present herself and all the things they had nearly bought Leaf, but didn't.

Grammy had insisted that this year Leaf's birthday celebrations were to be held at her house, which was great as her grandmother's house was huge in comparison to the two bedroom one bathroom rented house that Leaf lived in with her mum. They had no garden space at home, only a slate path up to the front door and a driveway for Mum to park her blue Seat Ibiza that Leaf's father had bought her in 2005, the year after Leaf was born, and the year he left Mum for another woman. Leaf presumed it was also due to the unexpected stress of being a first time parent. She blamed herself a little but she also felt partly abandoned and was appreciative that her mum had not left her. Due to the circumstances she was always closer to her mum than her dad.

This year Leaf had been able to invite her whole class from school to her party, not that they all came. Leaf was not that popular, but six of them did come and that was fine by Leaf. Her dad and his girlfriend were supposed to come but he was not feeling well.

Grammy had invited several of her friends to the party who turned out to be fun and not old and boring at all. Leaf had more fun talking and dancing with Grammy's friends than the kids from school, except for Sarah of course, who was her one true friend outside of the family.

George, an old black man with white flecks in his tight afro, had brought his saxophone and he played along to all the songs. Millicent was an old skinny hippy swallowed up by her oversized flowing dress. She loved to dance, a whirlwind of brightly-coloured materials. Mabel, aged eighty-two, dressed very conservatively and had a short neat haircut, spoke in a very posh voice but told the rudest jokes. Old Humphrey staggered in on a cane but spent most of the evening hogging the dance floor doing 'The Shuffle', his cane lay abandoned on the sofa.

Apart from Leaf's best friend Sarah, the five other children from her school stood around looking bored at first, until Grammy got them all up dancing to James Brown's **I Feel Good** accompanied by George and his saxophone.

Even when she was dancing, Scarlet did not stop talking to

anyone who would vaguely listen. Today her subjects were her sick dog that kept throwing up on everything, how she was in love with everyone in the band One Direction and the lime green her dad had just painted her bedroom, which matched the million and one lime coloured things in her room.

After dancing they played Pin the Peace Badge on the poster of the hippy, which was made by Grammy who was a bit of a hippy herself.

Marie, Leaf's mum, who looked so pretty in her knee-length blue dress that complemented her blue eyes and soft blonde curls, pushed the dark red sofa out of the way and all the children sat on the soft cream carpet in front of the screened fireplace. They played Pass the Parcel which Mum had wrapped full of really cool gifts: earphones, glow in the dark pens, lip gloss and nail polish in great colours. One of the boys swapped his nail polish with one of the girls for a set of pens. In the centre was an MP3 player. Sarah won that and she was thrilled.

While Grammy got everyone up dancing again, one of the boys sneaked through the archway to the big wooden table in the adjoining dining room and prematurely stuffed himself with so many coloured cupcakes, sweets, and fizzy drinks that he made himself sick. Mum showed him quickly to the bathroom before he threw up and she had to call his mum to come and collect him early.

Grammy played Mustang Sally on the black grand piano that stood elegantly at the far end of the living room. Two of Leaf's classmates were sitting in front of the fire with Mabel between them, giggling their socks off to Mabel's naughty jokes. George tried to teach some of the children to play the saxophone but they could only make farting noises, which Mabel thought was hilarious and clutching her sides she snorted like a smartly dressed pig in a wig.

Scarlet was on the sofa chatting away to old Humphrey, not realising he had nodded off to sleep. So Millicent, Mabel, Grammy and Scarlet's mum escaped to the conservatory before Scarlet realised that her hostage audience of one - Humphrey - was no longer captive.

On the dining room table, Mum had laid out homemade fun food and bright coloured drinks, sweets, colourful cupcakes and the coolest birthday cake which she had spent all day mixing, cooking, shaping and icing to look like a 1920's microphone. Leaf, who wanted to be a singer, loved her cake.

There were a few snacks for the adults on the glass coffee table in the conservatory. The room overlooked the garden and Grammy had illuminated each side of the grass, from the house to the weeping willow tree, with white candles in tall glass vases.

The Conservatory, an enclosed extension of the dining room, was a safe space away from the main action. The adults sat on the two comfy mint green sofas with the big pink pillows, under a ceiling of glass panes, through which the night stars could be seen between the leafy vines of ivy. It was Leaf's favourite room because it made you feel like you were outside when inside. Leaf went to see if the elders needed drinks.

Precisely placed on a metal tripod, a golden telescope was aimed at the moon. Grammy told a fascinated Millicent that

24

The Party

years ago she had read an article which stated that the moon is actually hollow and that two Russian government physicists had claimed that the moon was an artificial Earth satellite created by alien intelligence. Millicent rose to her feet and pressed her eye to the telescope, questioning the skies.

BANG! Something landed on the glass roof. Grammy almost shot out of her skin. She had been jumpy since her home had been broken into. This shock silenced the group, who had placed the pink cushions on the floor to make room on the sofas for Humphrey. He had been woken by Scarlet's constant natter. George had also joined them, now that all the children were in the dining room getting drunk on sugar and completely ignoring the sandwiches and carrot sticks with hummus dip.

Meeeoow! It was the neighbour's black cat on the roof. It looked down at them with piercing black eyes, snarling and hissing. It bared its teeth, back arched with all hairs standing up on end. Looking up through the glass, they could see past its sharp fangs right to the back of its mouth.

Humphrey raised his arm and prodded the glass roof with the end of his cane and the cat jumped into the darkness.

Grammy exhaled and laughed with relief. The other adults responded in a tension releasing fit of the giggles. They all asked Leaf for stiff drinks after that. Trying to remember what each person wanted, she went to tell Mum.

Mum had helped Grammy tidy up the day after the break- in. It was not a small house so it had taken several hours to put everything back into place. Grammy was still a bit shaken by the thought of strangers in her private domain, yet confident that even if they returned they would not find what they were looking for. However, knowing the Lockers would come back if

25

they still suspected her of having the Key, Grammy installed extra security locks on all the doors and windows, an automatic porch light, an alarm system and a security camera in the hallway.

Mum was now busy serving drinks, mopping spills and collecting dirty paper plates. Leaf helped her to move all the presents to the Flying Horse Table in the kitchen so that they would not get ruined by the over-excited children. Leaf could open the rest of her presents later when they went home. Mum had said they were safer in their boxes and wrappings for now.

Her school friends had given her Loom Bands for making rubber bracelets, coloured hair chalks, colourful Orbeez that swell in water and Humphrey had given her a travel scrabble set.

"Mum, look what George gave me!" Leaf exclaimed, reaching into the gift bag containing the presents she had already opened. She retrieved a slim silver instrument and blew a loud, screechy note on the harmonica. Mum rolled her eyes and Leaf laughed.

"Give me time. I only just got it!"

The collapsible Flying Horse Table, on which the presents had been placed, was special. At least it was special to Grammy who was the one that claimed it was a flying horse. It was something to do with her Shamanistic beliefs. Although Grammy said strange things, told almost unbelievable stories and often behaved in a way that seemed quite bonkers, she was a woman of infinite wisdom and experience. Bernadette had travelled far and wide across the globe and had learnt a great deal. She was a woman with a huge heart that was full of patience and generosity, especially for Leaf and her daughter Marie, but she usually knew how to use her head when it came to

The Party

making decisions. She was quirky, eccentric and liked to be diverse. Her excuse was "I'm old! I'll get away with it!"

The party was over and most of the guests had left. Grammy was standing by the stone fireplace, looking unusually conservative in her fitted orange dress. She normally dressed like a hippy, but she always looked clean and somehow even elegant under her favoured charade of colour. Grammy could present herself well at any social soirée; she had made an effort for Leaf with the conservative orange dress but she usually preferred to wear baggy trousers from India or long colourful skirts. She always had shocking slogans on her bold coloured T-shirts, such as her rainbow T-shirt which read:

I WISH YOU WERE BEER

Grammy often wore her silver hair in a long plait with feathers and beads but that night it hung loose and feather free, framing her wrinkled yet still beautiful face. Grammy's hair was long thick and straight like Leaf's, and it had once been the same dark golden colour too but the years had streaked it into silver and white blonde strands.

The flames of the fire illuminated Grammy's hair giving her a spiritual aura. From her collapsed position on the sofa, Leaf looked her Grandmother up and down, trying to take her all in. Grammy never ceased to amaze her, and now this whole business of them being Key Guardians was quite overwhelming.

Grammy had taught Leaf many things in the ten years of her life, including how to speak eloquently, about deportment and how to walk gracefully. How to stand straight, chin raised, shoulders back and down. Despite Leaf being a shy person, Grammy had taught her how to strut with confidence.

27

THE WHITEASH KEY

"It does not matter what you wear, it is how you wear it!" Grammy always said.

Leaf was now slouched on the sofa, exhausted. She gave Grammy a tired smile and Grammy returned it with a knowing wink. Leaf thought her grandmother was very beautiful, but Bernadette never let anyone take photos of her anymore, unless it was of her left profile with her neck stretched to make her look younger and less wrinkly. She always stretched her neck when she let Leaf draw her. Leaf often called her Turtle which Grammy hated and in return she playfully called her Wormy because Leaf was long thin and blonde. It made Leaf laugh. She enjoyed her playful banter with her grandmother.

"Well that was very pleasant. Did you enjoy your birthday, Leaf?" Mum asked, when she returned from seeing the last of the departing guests to the door.
"It was the best birthday ever! Thanks Mum. Thanks Grammy."
Leaf's mother had already cleaned up during the last half hour of the party, so she got their coats and all the presents which she'd placed in a large paper carrier bag she had found under Grammy's sink. After hugging Grammy again, they went out into the moonlit night.

On the way home Leaf stared out the back window of the car thinking about the Key.
Seeing her face reflected in the window pane she wondered if she looked any older now she was ten. She smiled at the thought of all the adventures to come.
One thing was for sure, everything had changed.

Chapter Three

INITIATION

Leaf had drifted off in the car and Mum had guided her to bed still half asleep. The next morning she got up half an hour earlier than usual, so that she could open the rest of her presents before school.

Grammy had given her a Weird Science chemistry set for making magic potions and crystals, and a silver telescope for looking at the stars.

Mum had given Leaf a Sia album and the Pharrell Williams CD with her favourite song 'Happy' on it and a pair of white Heelys so she could skate around the supermarket when they went shopping. Heelys trainers, even with their wheels still tucked into the sole, were not allowed in school, but she could wear them afterwards.

Mum, hearing that Leaf was awake, came into the room.

"Good morning, Pinky," Mum said cheerily, affectionately using Leaf's nickname.

"Pooky, look what I got. I can make crystals!" Leaf, who was sitting on the floor surrounded by colourful crumpled and torn wrapping paper, exclaimed excitedly.

"Thanks for my Heelys and the really cool CD's," she said, getting up from the floor and kissing her mum. She put the Sia compact disc in her disc player and started dancing madly around her room to the song **chandelier**.

"You still have one more present to open. That one there in the silver paper," Mum reminded her, as she scooped up all the discarded paper and revealed the small shiny package lying on the carpet. Leaf picked up the gift from Sarah and carefully removed the wrapping. Inside a pink box was a silver necklace, a heart hung in the middle engraved with BEST FRIENDS FOREVER. They both smiled and Mum helped Leaf put it on.

"You are my best friend really, Mum. Sarah is my second best friend, the same as Grammy." Mum kissed her on the top of her head.

"I'm honoured. And you will always be my best friend too," Mum said with a smile, feeling very proud. She continued picking up bits of wrapping paper. Leaf got dressed in her uniform and went down with her mum for a quick breakfast.

At school a few of the other children in her class occasionally spoke to Leaf, but the rest just ignored her. Leaf always thought it unfair how the bossy and not very nice children seemed to have the most friends. At least she was not bullied like poor Duncan.

Duncan was small and skinny for his age and he came from a poor family. His uniform was shabby hand-me-downs from his older brothers. He never had new stuff and because of this some of the other children made fun of him and called him Dirty Dung-can. Leaf always tried to be nice to him whenever she had the opportunity, but even Duncan seemed to ignore her. Maybe he was just shy like she was.

She did not think he looked dirty, despite his uniform being a bit worn. By the end of the year her uniform usually looked quite shabby too, but Mum or Grammy always bought her new shirts for the start of each year. Leaf thought that Duncan always looked so sad and Leaf wished she knew of a way to make him smile. She had invited him to her party but he didn't come.

Leaf was a kind and considerate girl, a bit shy, maybe

slightly on the skinny side but pretty. She was loyal and devoted, yet only Sarah was her one true friend, apart from Mum and Grammy.

Sarah was also a bit of a loner, she liked it that way. Sarah was very clever as she loved to read. She was a perfectionist and, like Leaf, she was a highly moralistic girl. She was never going to drink, do drugs, or even swear when she got older. None of the things that could make you look ugly.

Sarah had short bobbed brown hair, the front strands always falling in front of her big blue eyes, which she was constantly tucking behind her ear.

Sarah was not shy, like Leaf, she spoke her mind, asked lots of questions, and delivered reasonable solutions. She considered herself big-boned and always said Leaf was lucky to be skinny, have such beautiful long blonde hair and be gifted with artistic abilities. Leaf was very good at drawing and had an amazing singing voice. Sarah said it wasn't fair that Leaf had everything.

Leaf did not think she had everything. She also did not see anything wrong with the size of Sarah's bones and thought Sarah's blue eyes were stunning. Leaf often wished she had blue eyes like her mother and she wished that she was more like her friend, who wasn't afraid to speak to people. Sarah was logical, had a great sense of humour and was always ready with a comeback, and Sarah did not come from a broken home. Her parents were still together after eleven years of marriage.

Leaf resented that she and Mum rarely had money, but Leaf was used to her parents living apart now. She got her mum all to herself which made them even closer.

There was chatter before their teacher arrived and a couple of the children were talking about how Toby threw up at Leaf's party.   Duncan wished Leaf a belated happy birthday. She thanked him and then he went back to staring out of the window.

At five o'clock that evening, Grammy turned up wearing a fisherman's hat over her two long silver plaits, a full-length green skirt, typically with an inappropriate T-shirt, which read:

KISS ME QUICK BEFORE MY BOYFRIEND GETS BACK

She told Mum that she needed to borrow Leaf for a few hours to help her sort through some old tea-chests she had found in the attic.

The attic was above Grammy's bedroom.   It was a long room with a slanted beamed ceiling which Grammy used as an art studio, her latest painting usually perched on an easel by the small window. There was a paint-stained pine table covered in used mixing pallets, brushes in pots of murky water or white spirit which gave the room a pungent smell. The other end of the attic space was full of stored memories and hoarded old junk.

Leaf had spent many happy hours in the attic room with Grammy, learning to draw and paint or rummaging through the hordes of Grammy's memorabilia, each piece wrapped in a story to preserve it from being buried and forgotten under the dust of time.   Being in the attic with Grammy was like sauntering down memory lane on a summer's day.

"As long as she gets her homework done and you feed her. She has to be back by nine as it is a school night," Mum insisted, as Leaf put on her dark blue school duffel coat over her jeans and jumper.

"Okey dokey," Grammy replied, giving her daughter a hug. Mum waved goodbye from their blue front door as Leaf and Grammy drove away in Sally. The Union-Jack was emblazoned across Sally like a garish full-body-tattoo. Mum said the gaudy Mini Cooper made Grammy look like a well over-aged spice girl. She teased Grammy and called her Old Spice.

Leaf put the stereo on and the sound of Jimmy Hendrix's voice and electric guitar burst out at full volume.

Grammy parked by the lamppost outside her house and Jimmy Hendrix fell silent. Grammy lived in a three-story Victorian town house. A cement path, like a grey still river, ran through a small rose garden leading to Grammy's doorstep.

"Right then, I'll stick the kettle on, you grab a plate for the biscuits and we can get started."

"Come on then, I'll race you to the front door," Leaf goaded with one leg already out of the car.

Grammy had spotted a large black van parked across the street. She could not see the driver through the dark tinted windows but had an ominous feeling that she was being watched. She shook off the paranoia.

"Bet I beat you," Grammy cried, making a dash for the door, but not even bothering to try and run. She just watched Leaf and smiled.

"YEAY! I WON!" yelled Leaf, crashing into the red front door. Turning she saw Grammy still wandering up the path.

"GRAMMY, YOU DIDN'T EVEN TRY," Leaf complained.

"Thought I'd let you win, my Treacle Pie. I didn't want to make you look bad, what with my super speedy, faster than light legs," Grammy joked, rubbing her arthritic knees. Grammy could not run fast any more. In fact she could hardly run at all, but there was still so much spirit in the old woman that she made Leaf want to skip and dance whenever she was with her.

THE WHITEASH KEY

Grammy looked suspiciously back at the van as she turned the keys in the lock and pushed.

The red front door opened onto the large hallway painted in pale magnolia with a gilded gold mirror on the wall. In the centre of the hall a circular mahogany table, which Bernadette had inherited from her parents, supported a vase of realistic yellow sunflowers.

To the left of the red front door, mahogany double doors opened into the living room. The walls, painted in cream, were contrasted by the wine-red sofa in front of the large grey stone fireplace from which Grammy hung their stockings at Christmas. Wine- coloured heavy velvet curtains hung on both sides of the large panes of glass in the sash windows that looked out onto the street.

"I almost forgot, first we need to go out into the garden and perform the Key Transference Ritual to transfer the ownership of the Key from me to you. Then we will come back in, have a cup of tea, and begin your training," Grammy told her. She sounded exhausted already.

The conservatory sliding doors opened onto the rectangular garden, a stretch of lawn edged by ivy covered walls. Rose bushes and potted herbs led to Grammy's feather tree, a large weeping willow that swallowed the end of the stretch of green grass.

The sky had turned grey, preparing for the onset of night. A cold wind spun through the curves of Grammy's metal wind sculptures that decorated the four corners of the long rectangular lawn. Leaf was glad she still had her coat on. She zipped it up, pulled the hood over her head, tucked her chin into the collar and wedged her hands into the pockets filled with bits of paper, hair bands, her Quikid World notebook and two half-eaten packets of chewing gum.

Along the sides of the grass there were long candles in tall glasses to stop the wind from extinguishing the flames. Grammy lit the candles with a silver clipper lighter.

"You stand on the right side. I'm on the left," Grammy instructed and handed her a long white robe from a small trunk of dark wood sitting on the grass to the left of them. The grass was not trimmed neatly like the Parker's grade one grass next door. Grammy preferred to cut her grass rather than mow it. Her grass was not extremely overgrown, but it grew unruly in all directions like a rock singer's hair.

"Just put it on over your coat. These robes, the instructions for this ceremony and everything else you will need, you'll find in that trunk, waiting for the day when it will be your turn to transfer the Key to your own granddaughter. So pay attention Leaf!" Grammy said, while struggling to get the robe over her own clothes.

"I keep the trunk hidden behind the wall in the cupboard, where I hide the Key," Grammy whispered and glanced to the neighbour's upper windows. Mrs. Parker stepped back behind the half drawn curtain.

"Now, Leaf, this may seem strange but it is just a prayer to give thanks to those who have given us knowledge and protection." Grammy raised her arms into the air and began to chant to the darkening skies in the most dramatic performance.

"Praise be to the Ogdoads from the ocean of Nun who gave us life.
Praise be to the Anunnaki who gave us knowledge.
Praise be to the square throne of Amoun, our door between the physical and the spiritual.

35

THE WHITEASH KEY

Praise be to Hathor who gave us magic.
Praise be to Osiris and Isis who protect us under the constellations of Orion and Sirius.
On the lines of Saint Michael and Mother Mary who shelter us.
In the eye of the father Elias Whiteash and those who guide us in wisdom,
Bestow upon us fullness in our need."

"Follow me," Grammy said, and disappeared inside the weeping willow. Leaf pushed apart the dense drooping branches and entered the hidden magical space. The circular green area was filled with mystical light that broke in through the twigs and leaves. A rope swing hung from a thick-shouldered branch. A wooden bench, which Grammy had made, curved around the trunk of old Mother Willow whose protective inner space felt so nurturing and private. The sagging branches were so dense that no one could spy in. From there the house could not be seen, lost to an outside world.

Whenever Grammy had sadness or a problem she hung another feather on the outer branches of the tree so that the wind could air them out and blow the problems away.

It was getting darker inside the tree. Grammy lit the candles that had been arranged in a large circle.

Tonight, there was something else that was unusual in the inner space of the green willow, a golden bowl supported on a metal tripod. Resting on the bottom of the bowl was a centimetre of water and two tablespoons of pink Himalayan salt which Grammy had told her was two hundred and fifty million years old. Leaf was wondering how long Grammy had had the salt. As if reading her mind, Grammy laughed and informed her she had bought the pink salt from the local health food shop that week.

"Three years ago I brought back a sack of this rose coloured salt from the Himalayan Mountains myself, but I have used it all up. It is very good to use it on food, very alkaline. Still, this is the same stuff from the same place but I didn't have to travel by yak to acquire it."

Grammy indicated for Leaf to stand on the right. She placed the Whiteash Key in the bowl. It settled upon the bed of pink salt, almost completely submerged by the water.

"Elias Whiteash maker of the Keys, we your daughters come hither with pureness in our hearts. With your blessing I, a crone of the bloodline of Bethany Tailor, bestow upon a maiden also from the bloodline of the granddaughters of Bethany Tailor, the sacred Whiteash Key and I transfer the honour and responsibility to safeguard it until such time for it to be transferred upon the next granddaughter. I, Bernadette Latoure, do on this day give the Key to my granddaughter, Leaf Golden, Guardian, defender and protector of the Key from this day on."

Grammy pricked her finger with a thick silver needle and let a few drops of her blood drip onto the Key in the bowl. It spread out, making pretty patterns on the surface of the water.

"I need to prick your finger now, Leaf. It will be quick and won't hurt. Then read out loud what is on this piece of paper," Grammy said and handed her a small piece of paper. She reached for Leaf's finger but Leaf withdrew it.

"It will hurt!" Leaf looked petrified.

So far this ceremony had been nothing but creepy.

"I promise it will be quick and over before you know it,"

37

Grammy assured her.

"Please Leaf, it must be done willingly." Leaf held out her trembling finger, tears forming in her eyes. There was a quick sharp prick and a drop of blood surfaced.

"Oww!" Leaf yelped really loud.

"Oh really Wormy, it didn't hurt!" Grammy frowned. "Yes, Turtle, it did!" Leaf retorted.

"Squeeze a few drops of your blood into the bowl over the Key and then read the words on the paper." Leaf did as she was told.

"I, Leaf Golden, bloodline of Bethany Tailor, do swear to follow the rules of being a Guardian. I will guard my deeds, defend and protect the Whiteash Key and the passages of time to the very best of my abilities," said Leaf, reading the words. Grammy raised her arms and chanted.

**"Each shade and light,
Each day and night,
Each moment in kindness,
Grant us Thy Sight**."

Grammy bowed her head and Leaf did too.

"The Transference Ceremony is complete. Congratulations, my love." Grammy gave Leaf a big hug and then she poured the salt water in a circle around Mother Willow's trunk, wiped the bowl with a cloth, took off her robe and put the Key into the pocket of her jean jacket.

Leaf blew out the twelve candles and carefully placed them, still in their slender glass holders, into the cubical slots of a box as Grammy had instructed. It grew eerily darker inside the weeping willow with each flame that Leaf extinguished. After

38

having called upon who knows what kind of spirits, for the first time Leaf did not feel safe under Old Mother Willow and could not wait to get out. She picked up the box of candle holders and headed towards the streak of moonlight breaking in through the drooping branches.

Carrying the bowl, the stand, the needle and the Key, Grammy pushed through the tear-drop leaves of the weeping willow and led Leaf back to the trunk on the grass. Leaf placed the box on the shabby-chic lawn, pulled off her robe, and blew out the twelve candles along the grass while Grammy packed everything back into the trunk.

Waiting for her to finish, Leaf sucked on her sore finger, squeezing it to make more blood come out and showing it to Grammy.

"A brave warrior like you surely will not faint at the sight of a drop of blood?" Grammy encouraged, as she packed the things into the trunk.

"Who is Bethany Tailor?" Leaf asked, changing the subject. She wanted to ask who the other people Grammy had mentioned were too, but she could not remember their strange names.

"Bethany Tailor was the first Guardian whom Elias Whiteash gave this Key to. We are descendants of her bloodline, from my English grandmother's ancestry, my mother's mother who became a Jew to marry my grandfather. I get my fabulous hair from her, and so do you," Grammy stated stroking Leaf's blonde head.

"In 1577, Bethany Tailor worked as a seamstress and came from a long line of tailors. Bethany was a kind woman who often made clothes in her spare time for orphans or the homeless. Elias Whiteash saw that she was kind and believed she would do great good with the Key. She did. She made clothes for poor people in need all over the world. We must honour her Leaf, and continue to follow her example and do some good for the planet," Grammy replied, without giving away any more information than Leaf needed to know for the moment.

The Parker's black cat shot them a disdainful look as it strutted home for its dinner along the wall between the two gardens. Mrs. Parker pulled her curtain across the rest of the window and went downstairs to tell her husband what the weirdo woman at number twelve had been up to now.

When everything was neatly packed up, Grammy carried the trunk through the back door into the kitchen and Leaf followed, wondering what was next.

The kitchen was warm and homely and smelt of gingerbread. There was the arch on the left of the kitchen that led through to the dining room, the backdoor that led to the garden, the door to the hall, and another door on the right side of the kitchen which opened onto thin stone steps leading down to the cellar where Grammy kept coal and wood for the fire, a large freezer, and a collection of fine wines. Leaf didn't like it down there, she found it creepy. It was cold, damp and badly lit. Leaf suspected it was full of spiders and maybe ghosts.

Grammy put the kettle on and then leaving through the door that led to the hallway, she took the trunk back up to her bedroom. Leaf stayed in the kitchen and placed homemade ginger biscuits from the tin onto a plate. She took them to the long table with the fold down flaps which apparently became a magical flying horse in the spirit world. Sometimes Leaf found some of Grammy's Shaman beliefs a bit unbelievable, but most of the things she said were wise and beautiful.

Initiation

Grammy returned and finished making the tea.

"I must first warn you and explain six very important rules to being the Guardian of the Whiteash Key," Grammy said, putting the cups on the table and suddenly looking very serious.

"The Whiteash Key is a magic key, but it comes with many rules, and can only be kept well by a responsible person. I will teach you the main rules and give you lots more advice, and teach you how to be responsible with it. I know you will do well and be worthy of this Key, my darling Leaf."

"RULE NUNBER ONE: PASSING ON THE KEY.
The first rule is that the Key must be given to the first granddaughter on her tenth birthday by her maternal grandmother. So when the first daughter of your daughter reaches ten years of age you must pass it on and explain to your granddaughter the rules, teach her your knowledge, and tell her that she must also in turn pass on the Key to her granddaughter on her tenth birthday."

"What if I don't have a granddaughter? What if I do not have any children? Then what will happen to the Key when I die?" Leaf's questions tumbled over each other but Grammy was calm in her reply.

"The women of our family have always been magically blessed with daughters and then granddaughters ever since the Key was first forged in 1577 by Elias Whiteash, a blacksmith from Somerset, and blessed at Stonehenge on a lunar eclipse of the winter solstice. You will have a daughter and she will have a daughter. It is destiny, so you don't have to worry about that, sweetie," Grammy told her.

"The Key must always skip a generation of women. The

person who is skipped can never be told, so you cannot tell your mother. Ever! And you can't tell your daughter when you have one and that is really hard. Your mother is a wonderful woman but she will not understand this. She will try to stop you using the Key for your own safety. So you can never tell her. Do you understand?" Leaf nodded and promised, although she did not like keeping secrets from her mum.

"I hate making you keep secrets from your mum, I really do, but now that the Key exists it is our duty to protect it and use it wisely. Don't give your mum reason to suspect you. Don't be away so long that people miss you and you cause them worry. Be on time for appointments you have made, like the time your mum expects you back. You must learn to be a moral Guardian that only tells lies when it is completely necessary. I am not teaching you to lie, Leaf, lies are very bad, but I am teaching you to fulfil your duty to protect the Key at all costs." Grammy looked deadly serious.

"To tell the truth this is scary for me too. You must promise me you will be responsible. If anything happened to you I would never forgive myself, but I cannot deny you this great honour even if I wanted to, which I don't, but I do worry for your safety." Worry made Grammy look older.

"I must trust in you. I do trust you, but be safe, Leaf. Please don't do anything stupid with it or go anywhere that you know would put you in danger. Learn about the world. Keep the Key safe. Never lose it and it will be your escape. Use it correctly and your life will be amazing, and sometimes you get to use the Key to help others, but never in the past or you will be changing the future."

"RULE NUMBER TWO: NEVER VISIT YOURSELF.
If you do you will explode with the energy of a million atom

bombs. You should always write down the place and date to remind yourself to not go there on that day, so as not to meet yourself. Remember to write down the time you leave. Return from the Key Jump five minutes after the time you left to avoid being early and bumping into yourself leaving, but if you forgot to write it down and can't remember the exact time, then guess a bit later, half an hour or so to be sure. Not too late or you will have missed too much time and that will end up having some mental effect too. By not coming back to more or less the same time you left can also have consequences on the future. If you miss doing something, meeting someone or whatever might be significant, the consequences could be dire."

"RULE THREE: PROTECT THE SECRECY OF THE KEY. The Key must be kept a secret, be kept safe and hidden from all others at all times."

"Where will I hide it?" Leaf asked.

"I used to find that keeping it with me was the safest. Keeping it in plain sight diverted suspicion. I simply hung it on my key chain and everyone presumed it was just a decoration. Just don't wave it around and make a show of it. If anyone asked me about it I would say I found it in an antique shop. If I felt the presence of a Locker or suspicious people watching me then I would bury it in the ground or in a wall. Our Key has been hidden in my wall since the seventies," Grammy told her.

"But I haven't got a key chain or any other keys or a secret wall or a garden to bury it in!" fretted Leaf with a disappointed look.

"In that case you shall have a set of keys to my house and then you can come and go as you please. This old house will belong to you and your mother one day, so you may as well have the keys to it. I gave your mother a set since I changed the locks so you can have a set too. I will get them cut for you next week,

43

my love."

"Thanks, Grammy."

"For now we will keep the Whiteash Key in my hiding place. I cannot give you this magic Key straight away Leaf, not for a long time. Not until you are ready, but one day I will hand it over to you. After that, if you ever feel a need to hide the Whiteash Key you know a good place in my wardrobe. It seems the Lockers now suspect us so the Key is best kept hidden."

Leaf was overwhelmed with disappointment. The Key was a transporter of some sort and that was just about the coolest gift Leaf had ever been given, but now Grammy was taking it back. However, Leaf wouldn't have felt brave enough to teleport by herself. She fretted that she would do it wrong and send her four limbs in the four different directions.

"Don't look so disappointed. We are still going to open plenty of doors with this magical Key, but you need training and at first I will guide you. We get to experience it together. It is going to be great fun!" Leaf could not wait to see what was going to happen on the next Key Jump, to know what entertaining card Grammy had up her sleeve, but first she had to learn the rules.

"RULE NUMBER FOUR: DOORS.

Doors are important. Whatever door you go in, you must use the same type of door to return home. They do not have to look the same, but if it was a kitchen door that was used, then you must use a kitchen door to return. You cannot use the door you just came out of which usually on the other side is not the same as the one you went in through. So you cannot just turn back if you do not like what you see on the other side of the door. Once you have stepped through you must search quickly for the same type of door you used to get in so you can get out. This means

44

Initiation

you must also pre-think about the type of door you are using. Is there likely to be the same type of door where you are going?" Grammy paused and took a swig of her tea.

Leaf thought about the eras of time that would not have doors and in eras with doors, what type of doors would be the most likely to be found. With all these rules, Leaf felt it was like stepping into a computer game.

"If you go to a place without locks in doors then you must pre-think and take a lock with you. Mobile locks, such as padlocks, can be used as locks as long as they don't have a really tiny lock that the Whiteash Key can't fit in, and you must use the same padlock to return. Mobile locks are not to be used constantly but they are an option in an emergency. Every time you use a mobile lock it will corrode from the force of the magic, it damages the lock a little. A well-made padlock will last about ten uses and then it will start to fail you. Locks in doors withstand the magic better for some reason, but having to change all your locks every five years is still a bit of a nightmare."

"RULE NUMBER FIVE: ONLY THREE DOORS.
You can only use the Key to open a maximum of three doors during twenty-four hours. You must use the third door to go home or you will be stuck inside for twelve hours before the Key will work again. The Key was given this cut-off point to stop us overusing it and killing ourselves from the stress to our bodies and too much information to our brains. Using this Key will have physical and sometimes mental effects on you, so try not to go places with it too often, once or twice a week is plenty."

"Can you not get me out, Grammy?" Leaf felt frightened.

"When I eventually give you the Key you will be responsible

for yourself. With this Key comes great responsibility and danger, so you must use it wisely and that is why I cannot give you the Key straight away. I will have to hang onto it until you know how to use it properly."

"RULE NUMBER SIX: DON'T MAKE CHANGES.
This last rule is so important. Do no harm in the past. Never visit yourself in any time frame, and never change anything in any time zone, but especially not the past. Never kill plants or insects in the past, the effects of which could be devastating. Never leave anything from the future behind in the past."

"If you are just Jumping from one place to another without a time difference you can stay and you don't have to return so soon unless expected, but if you are Key Jumping into the past or future, then you must return as quickly as possible. It is not just the effect time travel has on you and your carbon footprint that you leave behind, you also need to consider the effect the time is having on people in your reality of present day and how much of their lives you will have changed when you Jump back. Whatever you do using the Key should be done with thought and caution. Always be careful, Cupcakes, because you could be changing the past, present and future by your actions. Take care in all you do."

"I will try my best, Grammy. I promise."

"I know you will, Pumpkin," Grammy replied, kissing Leaf on the top of her head.

Grammy picked Leaf up on Wednesday, and again on Friday afternoon for more training sessions. Leaf practiced going from Grammy's house to the supermarket and back with the Key. Leaf put the Key in the lock of the downstairs toilet door which was in the hallway next to Grammy's office. Grammy had told

46

Initiation

Leaf that toilet doors and front doors were usually the easiest to find.

Leaf checked the time and date on her phone and wrote them down in her Quikid World notebook hanging around her neck. It was six-thirty on Wednesday the 17th of September. Leaf gave the instructions and turned the Key three times to the left.

"Inside the supermarket, Brent Street, five o'clock in the afternoon, Friday 31st of October 2014."

They found themselves stepping through the toilet door and out of the manager's office door into the main part of the supermarket.

As it was Halloween, the shop had a Last Day Sale on the festive Halloween stand which was decorated with cardboard pumpkins. They bought a real pumpkin reduced in price and a selection of Halloween sweets: Gob-Stopper eyeballs, jelly fingers, edible fanged teeth, vampire bubble gums with strawberry blood in the middle. Grammy also needed some milk, cheese and a stick of French bread.

"We can make pumpkin soup for dinner with bread and cheese. Good thing we went a month into the future and not a month into the past or the milk might have been off by the time we got home," Grammy stated, laughing.

She paid for the items and then asked the spotty gum-chewing teenage girl at the cash register if there was a toilet she could use. The girl gave her a key and told her it was down in the parking area. When the girl was getting a bag and not looking, Grammy put the key back beside the register and gave the man behind her in the queue a mind-your-own-business smile.

Leaf followed Grammy down to the parking lot. The toilet was to the far right. Leaf put the Whiteash Key in the lock.

THE WHITEASH KEY

"In the kitchen at Grammy's house, 12 Wicker

Lane in Hampstead, at six thirty-five p.m. on Wednesday the 17th of September 2014." She turned the Key three times to the left and they walked back into Grammy's nice warm kitchen.

Grammy made Leaf write down how long they had been gone, which was twenty minutes in this case. Then they scooped out the pumpkin together. Leaf carved a jack-o-lantern face while Grammy made a yummy home-made pumpkin and dill soup with warm, buttery, garlic bread.

"Remember that you must not go to that supermarket at that time on the 31st of October because you would meet yourself. The merging of the now and then would destroy both in its independent time and space, probably causing anti- time and anti-space and resulting in neither event occurring and you could implode or be sucked into a time wormhole of anti-existence. You could end up in a black hole or trapped in a parallel universe. Therefore it is important to write down where you go and at what time, so you can remember when and where you have been."

"When you start to venture alone on Key Jumps it would be best to write a note saying where you went before you leave and hide it somewhere for me. Put it in your pillow case." Grammy suggested. Leaf nodded. She was listening, but she was also thinking about something else.

"Do ghosts really come out at Halloween, Grammy?" Leaf asked. Grammy shrugged her shoulders, but when they were seated at the table, soup spoons at the ready, Grammy began to tell Leaf about the origins of Halloween.

"On the 31st of October, after the crops have been harvested the days have a chill in the air. The skies are dark and grey, the leaves have fallen from the trees, the flowers are dormant and the earth is dead, this is the time when the veil between our world and the spirit realm is the thinnest. This is the time when it is the easiest to communicate with the deceased."

"It is called Halloween by the Christians who used the festival to honour any saint that did not already have their own day. All Hallows Eve became known as Halloween and November the first is called All Saints Day. Originally it was named Samhain by the Pagans, a time to honour our ancestors. Samhain lasted three days with rituals and feasts each night to give thanks and pay respects to the Goddess who on the night of Samhain entered her incarnation of the old crone. She was Old Mother Earth, the wise one who taught us sometimes we need to let go in order to move on." Grammy dipped her spoon away from herself as she had taught Leaf was the correct way, sipped her thick orange soup, wiped her mouth on a serviette and continued.

"During Samhain the pagans also paid respects to a god, the horned one, who represented the hunted stag they ate and the grains and corn they harvested. This is why now during the Christian Halloween we dress up as witches who misrepresent the old crone, and devils misrepresenting the horned one. Most new religions make the old religion out to be evil so that people will follow them into the new religion," Grammy told her. Leaf thought this was all fascinating, and the soup and bread were delicious.

Even though tonight was not really Halloween as they were only in September, it was still special and she planned to share all her new information with Mum on the 31st of October and make this yummy soup again.

Leaf did not eat the sweets that night as the Key Jump had

caused her a headache and made her feel a bit sick, so Grammy drove her home. On the way, she thought about all the places she could go with the Key. Despite feeling queasy, she was excited about the future. She knew exactly where she wanted to go first. She just had to talk Grammy into it.

Chapter Four

BEHIND BARS

On Friday the 19th of September, Grammy told Leaf stories about her own Key Adventures. Interesting and amazing stories, including the time Grammy was twenty-five and she had travelled back two thousand years through a door woven from reeds into the jungles of Peru, where she had seen naked pale pink aliens sixty-one centimetres tall. They had tiny faces, large slit eyes, only holes for ears, long jaws with serrated fish- like teeth in elongated heads supported on necks that could extend like periscopes.

These aliens ran like birds up on three long toes, the same on both feet. Dangling long arms ended in three long fingers. Their left hands were implanted with reconnaissance microchips in round metal plates. The aliens ran around touching specimens of plants, trees, rocks, insects and animals. The DNA information of each object was stored on the microchip implants in their left hands. Implanted in their right hands they had round detectors that alerted them to the presence of monatomic gold.

One of these aliens saw Grammy hiding behind a rock and reached out to touch her with its three very long bony fingers. Grammy, having been terrified, ran away. Once she reached safety, she wove herself a door from reeds and quickly went home, believing she never would return.

Leaf marvelled at this bizarre story that Grammy insisted was true. It filled her mind with all types of questions and wonders.

"Be careful where you choose to go and try not to use the Key more than three times a week. Give yourself a couple of

51

months once in a while when you do not use the Key at all. Excessive use of the Key can make you very ill. It can even kill you, Leaf. Don't ignore your body's warning signs. Do not use the Key if you are not completely well or you will get sicker. Using the Key will affect your immune system and make you prone to colds and viruses. Make sure you keep yourself healthy at all times, eat well, sleep well and take regular exercise," Grammy insisted.

"Most importantly, keep your mind calm. Using the Key, you will go through enormous transitions in a matter of seconds. This can have a big impact on the mind, Leaf. It can make you tired, moody and depressed in the days that follow, but meditation helps calm this. You must not let it have a negative effect on your personality. You must shake it off and feel happy. Every day is a gift. Make good choices and remember Knowledge is the Key!"

"When can I have the Key, Grammy?"

"Not until you are twelve. I am sorry Sweetie, but those are the rules. I know it seems a long time, but you have a lot to learn before then. You will get to go on plenty of adventures in the meantime. I have a big surprise coming up for you. I am not ready to tell yet, but soon. Just be patient," Grammy said, smiling.

No need to get up early for school as it was Saturday, lie-in day. Yet Leaf had sprung out of bed wide awake at seven-thirty. She knew exactly what she wanted to do. Today she wanted to go to the zoo.

Leaf loved animals and a day at the zoo was a perfect way to spend a Saturday. Mum couldn't afford to take Leaf on these types of day trips unless it was Leaf's birthday. Leaf would feel awkward asking her Mum knowing Grammy always had to pay, even if Grammy could more than afford it, but that was not the point. With the Key she could now get into the zoo for free. Leaf sent a text on her mobile phone to Grammy.

LET'S GO TO THE ZOO TODAY. CAN YOU MEET ME OUTSIDE SARAH'S HOUSE AT TEN WITH THE KEY??? REMEMBER IT IS THE ONE WITH THE WHITE FRONT DOOR.   DON'T LET ANYONE SEE YOU, ESPECIALLY MUM. STAY HIDDEN UNTIL MUM GOES INDOORS.

She got a text back from Grammy:

OKEY DOKEY C U THEN Xxxxxxxxxxxxxxx :)
P.S. WHY ARE WE SHOUTING???

Leaf's mother was already in the kitchen making pancakes for breakfast. The kitchen was spacious and homely and Mum loved to cook, but the rest of their house was much too small to entertain more than three people.

"Mum? Would it be okay if I went to Sarah's house today? She invited me to come over at about ten. Can I go?" She did not tell her mum that she was going to the zoo with Grammy because Mum would want to come too, and then they would not be able to use the Key and Leaf wanted to practice. If Mum came too they would have to drive, deal with traffic jams, stand in a long queue, and Grammy would have to pay. It was just easier not to tell Mum.

"Sure, as long as you are back for lunch at one-thirty," Mum answered, stirring the pancake batter. Leaf ate her breakfast in silence. She was thinking about the consequences of her mum finding out that she was not at Sarah's. Although, Mum would not know if she came back at the time she left that morning, but then Leaf would have to repeat a whole day, she would be tired and probably hungry. If she came home at one-thirty the time would have passed from the time she left to the time she returned and she could have lunch. She would have to get Sarah to cover for her just in case her mum called Sarah's house and spoke to Sarah's mum. Leaf swallowed the last gulp of her orange juice, put her plate and glass in the sink, and then went back upstairs.

"MUM? CAN I CALL SARAH TO TELL HER I'M COMING OVER?" Leaf shouted down to her mum.

"OKAY!" Mum yelled back from the kitchen. Leaf used the landline phone in her mum's bedroom.

"Hi, it's Leaf! Can I speak to Sarah please? Hi Sarah, listen, I need you to cover for me. My mum may call your house just before one-thirty so could you make sure it is you that picks up your house phone. She will probably just tell you to tell me to come home as she thinks I am going to be at your house. You only have to say okay. If she asks to speak to me just say I am in the bathroom."

"I hate lying, Leaf! Where will you really be going?" Sarah asked, concerned.

"I am making a surprise gift for my mum's birthday. I have to go shopping, but don't worry I'm going with Grammy. I'll be safe," Leaf said, starting to feel hot and flustered. She was planning to get her mum a special gift so that wasn't a total lie. She felt bad lying and hated not being able to share her secret with Sarah or her own mum, but she had to keep it a secret and she had not worked out how to do that yet without telling a few porky-pies.

"Okay, I'll answer the phone, but you better be home by one-thirty or we will both be in trouble" Sarah warned her.

"Thank you! Love you!" Leaf replied.

Behind Bars

"Do not get me in trouble," Sarah said crossly and put the phone down.

Leaf went into her own bedroom and picked out a pair of jeans and a long sleeve black and white tie-dye T-shirt, a black hoodie and a thin waterproof jacket with a hood in case it rained.

She got out the leaflet of the zoo that she had found in the school library. Leaf had been using it as a bookmark for the past year. It showed pictures of some of the animals and had a little map on the back showing exactly where the zoo was located.

Leaf got out her rucksack and put the things she needed for the day into the bag and then she went downstairs.

"Mum? Can I take some of those small Madeleine cakes and juice boxes for us to share?"

"Okay, but only one Madeleine each or it will spoil your lunch," Mum told her. Leaf took two Madeleine cakes and two small juice cartons from the cupboard and put them in her rucksack.

It seemed ages before the clock read five to ten and Leaf could tell her mum she was leaving. She kissed her mum goodbye at their gate. Mum watched her while waving frantically, and repeatedly yelling, "I love you, Pinkie!" until she reached Sarah's gate.

Leaf smiled. She did not get embarrassed by her mum like her friends did with theirs. She was proud to hold her mum's hand in the street. Her mum made her laugh. Most of the time they were like cool sisters, and Leaf knew she was doing her best to be a responsible single mum at other times. Mum tried not to yell and instead respectfully reasoned with Leaf in a way that made Leaf moralistically consider her actions and want to do better, to once again be the daughter that received praise and made her mum proud. Her mum worked hard and loved hard and Leaf was more than happy to have her.

Leaf saw her dad on alternate weekends and half the holidays. He was now living in Finchley with his girlfriend in a four-bedroom ground floor flat that had a small garden. Leaf's dad was half German on his mother's side and his girlfriend was Russian. They made her eat brown bread and broccoli, Yuck! Fortunately, Mum never gave her broccoli or mushrooms and Mum didn't like brown bread. Mum always made healthy meals but at home Leaf got to eat the yummy thick white slices and go to bed half an hour later than at her dad's.

Sarah only lived five doors up the street from Leaf and her mum, so Leaf was allowed to walk there on her own, but Mum like to watch, wave, blow kisses and shout out silly things that made Leaf laugh.

At Sarah's white gate Leaf turned and waved. "I LOVE YOU TOO, POOKY!" she yelled down the road to her mother. Her mum waved, blew kisses, stuck out her tongue, pulled a silly face and went back inside.

Grammy popped out of a nearby bush, scaring the wits out of Leaf. Hand in hand, they quietly crept down Sarah's pathway towards her white front door, but they did not knock or go in. They went down the side of the house to where Sarah's dad kept birds in a tall cage.

"I presumed there would be cage doors at the zoo for us to use to get home," Leaf whispered to Grammy, who nodded approvingly.

Leaf's cheap mobile phone showed the time to be nine fifty-eight. She wrote down zoo and the time they were leaving in the notebook in case she changed her mind and decided to return five minutes after they left.

Grammy gave her the Key and Leaf placed it in the lock of the cage door. Not wanting to get caught in the zoo before they opened its doors to the public, she instructed the door to be a portal into a viewing area of the zoo at eleven o'clock. Leaf turned the Key three times to the left and holding tight to Grammy's hand, she opened the cage door.

They came out of a wooden door, half hidden under leafy vines, both relieved that they had not ended up in a lion's den. Parents and children were walking along a path, passing from cage to cage, looking at each of the animals.

Leaf and Grammy started at the huge re-enforced glass wall encasing a compound with a large expanse of grass. Two black panthers lay sunning themselves on a rock. Leaf thought they were sleek and elegant.

In the next glass cage, there was a big old lion asleep on the roof of his concrete den. The sign on the cage said his name was Samson, and that at four o'clock every day he gives out a tremendous roar, but the rest of the time Samson sleeps.

They went along a path to a reptile house. Inside it was dark and scary. Around the room were windows to illuminated glass tanks full of huge snakes and little snakes coiled around branches or hidden in the corners under leaves.

There was a large glass tank with two meter green iguanas, small dinosaurs that were gentle when well treated. Leaf knew Duncan in her class at school had one and it travelled on his shoulder as he rode his bike through Hampstead. He brought it to school once and the teacher went mad and made him lock it in the cupboard until the end of the day. It was the only day

Duncan was popular at school. He was warned by the headmaster never to bring it to school again, but the iguana went everywhere else with him, even into the shower. Duncan told the class that the iguana loved the water, its fat pointy tongue trying to catch the falling drops. It slept on his pillow at night and it scared the life out of his mother's guests.

Leaf thought the iguanas in the vivarium, perched prestigious and prehistoric on the thick branches, looked sad and lonely. They each needed a Duncan to love them.

There were many other types of reptiles, lizards and turtles in different sized vivariums. Leaf absolutely loved turtles and tortoises. Giant sea turtles made her want to become a marine biologist, almost as much as she wanted to be a famous singer.

In another building, a specialist told them about arachnids (insects with eight legs) and how spiders have fangs that inject venom. Leaf held a tarantula, which was not as terrifying as she thought it was going to be. She had been told that someone had milked the tarantula of its venom that morning, though she was relieved when it was put back in its tank. She held a stick insect, which prickled and tickled, and then a large praying mantis that Leaf decided was the coolest insect on the planet. She wanted to take him home.

Grammy took her along to see the gorillas in their encampment. A big Silverback shook his fist at Grammy. Grammy showed she wasn't scared of him by shaking her fist back at him. He rudely showed Grammy his bottom.

"Grammy, don't you dare!" Leaf threatened, before her grandmother could retaliate.

Behind Bars

There was a poster that informed them that at twelve-thirty there was to be a talk and slide-show in the showroom about Dian Fossey and her work with wild gorillas. The poster showed photos of Dian hugging the huge gorillas.

"I would very much like to go to that. I met a woman who knew Dian Fossey. She was a fascinating woman apparently." Grammy declared.

It was almost twelve-thirty according to Leaf's phone. Leaf ran to one of the zoo maps which were posted around the grounds. She looked for the show room and saw it was not far.

They ran up a path to the right, past polar bears and penguins, down a path to the left and at the end Leaf found the show room as indicated on the map.

Inside people were choosing seats. It was very much like a cinema with a stage in front of the screen. They found two empty seats in the fifth row and made themselves at home, ate a Magdalene cake each and drank a juice to wash them down.

When everyone was settled, the lights dimmed down, an old woman stepped into a spotlight on the stage. She introduced herself, and told the people in the audience that she had worked with the late Dian Fossey. Leaf thought that meant that Dian Fossey was going to come but was running late. She was very upset to find out that the word "late" in this case meant dead. Dian Fossey had been murdered.

The woman told them what an amazing person Dian had been, her dedication to the gorillas and her courage in standing up to the poachers who shot gorillas, cut their hands off, and sold them on the illegal black market for lots of money. Some people bought them as ashtrays. Leaf and Grammy sobbed into tissues from Grammy's handbag.

THE WHITEASH KEY

The talk lasted about an hour and while the woman spoke, beautiful photographs of Dian Fossey and the gorillas were projected onto a large screen above her. Leaf hung on every word and loved every photo. She felt inspired and very sad about the Dian Fossey story and all she had learned about the gorillas.

Leaf wept when she heard that Dian's favourite gorilla named Digit had been slaughtered by poachers. Then eight years later Dian herself had been killed. Leaf would have loved to have met such an incredible woman and to have seen those gorillas up close. Leaf suddenly had a realisation that if she really wanted to, she could.

Leaf had been listening carefully so all the information was still fresh in her head. Dian had started a conservation camp in Rwanda which she named Karisoke because it was in a rainforest half way between two volcanoes, Mount Karisimbi and Mount Bisoke. She had joined the two names of the volcanoes together to make the name for the camp.

"Grammy, let's go and meet Dian Fossey." Leaf was standing by an empty cage. She reached out her hand for the Key. Grammy took a moment to consider the dangers of this Key Jump, but she too really wanted to meet Dian Fossey and she had got out of worse situations, like the time she had been kidnapped in Turkmenistan. Not much fazed Grammy these days so in a moment of weakness she gave Leaf the Key. Leaf put it in the lock of the cage door.

"Camp Karisoke, in the rainforest between the volcanoes Bisoke and Karisimbi in Rwanda, March 1978, at four in the afternoon," Leaf said, hoping she had pronounced the names correctly and they didn't end up in Timbuktu. She knew that Dian had usually checked on the gorillas in the early morning hours and again around four p.m.

Leaf thought she must ask Mum where Timbuktu is. Mum would surely know because every time they got lost while driving she always said, "Oh dear, I've done it this time, we are well and truly in Timbuktu!"

Leaf turned the Key, opened the cage door, and started to ask Grammy about Timbuktu when she found herself crawling, and pulling Grammy with her, into a much smaller cage in the middle of a rainforest. Grammy almost rolled into the small space and the cage door shut behind her.

"NO! Trust this to be the one in a thousand times the doors get to be the same on both sides," Grammy cried. The cage had two exits, bars on one side slid up but it was locked with a big padlock, and the cage door they had come through had shut behind them and locked automatically. A key was needed to open both exits.

Leaf looked for her Key, emptied her pockets, searched the ground, but it was gone. She must have dropped it because she could not find it anywhere. Leaf pushed and rattled on the bars but could not get the cage door open. She realized that they were trapped inside like animals. She started to panic and that was not helping her search. She'd only had the Key two minutes and she had already lost it. Grammy was going to kill her. JUST GREAT!

"Grammy, I can't find the Key," Leaf mumbled and searched again. She could feel panic setting in.

"GRAMMY, I CAN'T FIND THE KEY!" she cried, when realising she really could not find it.

"Okay, keep calm, it must be here somewhere. You didn't leave it in the door did you?" Grammy asked, looking around.

"No, I definitely took it with me. HELP! HELP!

THE WHITEASH KEY

SOMEBODY PLEASE HELP US! WE ARE LOCKED IN A CAGE. CAN ANYONE HEAR ME?" Leaf yelled out. There was nothing except huge trees, giant leafy plants, biting monster mosquitoes and a snake that slithered away into a bush. It was all so very humid and hot.

"HEEEELLLLP!" Grammy shrieked as giant ants crawled towards her. Leaf wrapped her thin raincoat around Grammy's legs to stop them biting her.

There was a little rustle behind a bush and out came a baby gorilla. The little gorilla sat down and stared at Leaf and Grammy with curiosity.

"It seems very tame. I bet it is one of Dian's gorillas. Can you help us? Dian, do you know Dian?" Grammy asked the gorilla baby. The gorilla jumped up and down shrieking.

"WHOO WHOO HAA WHOO WHOO WHOO!"

"Dian, DIAN, do you know her? Do you know where Dian is? Can you get Dian? Get Dian," Grammy instructed, shooing the infant gorilla away. The little gorilla bounded away on all fours into the bushes.

About half an hour had passed and Leaf was about to start crying, believing the mosquitoes and giant ants were going to win and eat them alive. Grammy blew hard on her forehead.

"Sorry. It was a big mosquito and I could not kill it. Make sure you do not kill any insects Leaf, it can have dire consequences on nature between now and present day. We could get back and find that Hampstead Heath is no longer there. Watch what you are sitting and stepping on," Grammy warned her.

"This situation, in which we have landed ourselves, is an example of why you must give precise instructions of where you want to end up and always carry a padlock with you. Typically I left mine at home today," Grammy informed her.

A tall well built dark-skinned man wearing black boots, an olive green T-shirt and combat trousers was following the excited baby gorilla through the jungle, and they suddenly burst out through the big-leafed banana trees.

"My, my! What do we have here?" He laughed at poor Leaf and Grammy trapped in the small cage.

"Can you get us out?" Leaf pleaded, forgetting her shyness with strangers as she was being eaten alive by mosquitoes. The baby gorilla sat next to the cage, looking at them with sad empathetic eyes. He put his fingers through the bars so that Leaf could hold his hand during her time of incarceration.

"What are you doing in the rainforest? You should not be here disturbing the gorillas. It is dangerous!" He looked quite cross now.

"Well? How did you get here?"

"I don't think you would believe us if we told you," Leaf said, looking quite apologetic and at the same time falling in love with the cute baby gorilla.

"Somehow I can believe that." He laughed, trying to believe the pitiful and unlikely sight of an old white lady and a white child cramped up in a small cage in the furthest, deepest, almost unreachable parts of the rainforest. Then he looked cross again.

"Are there more people with you? Do you have a team of porters with your supplies and gear? Dian is going to be furious to find out you are up here. It is a protected area. At least it should be. It is dangerous for both you and the gorillas."

"We came alone. I'm sorry, we didn't mean to disturb the gorillas," Leaf told him.

He really could not understand how a child and an old woman had got out there alone. Maybe they had run away from a horrible situation, but why into the rainforest unless they were looking for a much worse situation.

"Come on, let's get you out then." He unlocked the cage and helped them out. Leaf crawled out, stood up and stretched. Grammy's legs and her back were so stiff from having been cramped up so long inside such a tiny space that she remained stuck, bent double for a minute or so. Trying to smile with her bottom stuck up in the air, Grammy was cursing herself for her lack of judgement in allowing Leaf to bring them here.

"What are your names?" he asked.

"Bernadette Latoure," Grammy told him, holding out her hand as she unfolded herself. He shook it as Grammy stood up straight, neck stretched, returning to her regal self.

"Leaf Golden," Leaf told him, shaking his hand, shyly.

"My name is Benjamin. So Bernadette Latoure, are you a medicine woman or a chicken? Did you fall out of a nest and into my cage?" he said, referring to the feathers in Grammy's hair.

"I am a Shamana actually," Grammy replied.

"I bring the feathers of a rooster when I travel into the unknown," Grammy gave as an explanation. Medicine men or women were highly respected by Benjamin's tribe and around all these areas. He just nodded at Grammy as if he understood her, but then frowned disapprovingly at her T-shirt. She was wearing her MONKEY MAGIC T-shirt from the awesome Japanese martial art drama she used to watch on television. Grammy had told Leaf that she might one day be lucky enough to inherit such a super-cool T-shirt, if she hadn't worn it out by then.

Benjamin looked as if he did not know whether to like the T-shirt or hate it. This woman was taking the serious Mickey seeing she really should not be there, let alone casting monkey magic about

64

the place. This was no place to be joking around. This place was a severe test of survival.

"Where are you from?" He questioned, sternly.

"England. We wanted to meet Dian and hopefully see some of the gorillas. Sorry if we intruded. We meant no harm," Grammy told him.

"Are you sure you came alone? From England?" Benjamin disbelievingly asked again, disturbed at the thought of others turning up to frighten the gorillas.

"Yes."

"Well you cannot see Dian! She will have you sent away before harm comes to you or the gorillas. You two are crazy to come up here!" He could not let Dian find out they were up here, but how to get them out? He could not just send an old woman and a child unequipped back into the jungle, but how did they get here? He was amazed and confused.

"We are not sure how we got here, but we did," Grammy told him, not giving anything away.

Benjamin could not believe an old woman and a child had made it into the middle of the rainforest on their own with no supplies and survived. The child was not offering much information and neither was the old woman, so he decided to get it out of them over a hot beverage.

"Come. I will make you a cup of tea."

He led the way through the rainforest to his fire that was two meters from his tent.

"This is where you live?" Leaf asked.

"No, this is where I camp. I don't stay up here for long. I come and go with supplies. Dian has a permanent cabin up here. She calls it the Mausoleum," he told them, laughing. He opened a fishing stool for Grammy to sit on and placed it by the fire. Grammy smiled. Leaf did not know what mausoleum meant, so she just smiled politely and sat down on a tree stump by the small fire smouldering in a circle of large stones. It had a metal stand over it supporting a small saucepan that Benjamin had dipped into a bucket of rain water.

"Dian is on her rounds. She has gone deeper into the forest and will be gone for a while. I know of a small pack of female gorillas that often come without the silverback to a clearing nearby. While the water is heating up, would you like to see if they are there?" Benjamin asked them. Springing to their feet, they replied that they would love to, and followed Benjamin down a path into the thick foliage.

"This is not the type of Key Adventure I should be encouraging you to go on," Grammy whispered to Leaf.

"We are putting ourselves in too much danger on this Jump," Grammy stated, but she secretly loved every moment of the excitement.

"The small gorilla you met at the cage was one of Digit's sons. Digit was the big silver-back, the leader of the group. Another silverback has taken over the group now," Benjamin mentioned as they walked through the dense jungle. Leaf knew what had happened to Dian's favourite gorilla Digit in January of that year. It was so sad that she did not say anything. Grammy gave a heavy sigh.

They broke through bushes and ducked under massive spiders. Benjamin stopped suddenly and put his finger to his lips so Leaf and Grammy knew to be quiet.

"Over there! Look!" He pointed through the trees to a clearing where two mother gorillas, five toddlers and two babies were assembled.

"I know them, but still you must move very slowly. Always let them come to you. Sit down behind me about ten metres away and pretend to eat leaves. If one of the mothers tries to scare you off DO NOT RUN! NEVER RUN! They might want to investigate you, just let them. If you do as I say they won't hurt you." Benjamin moved into the clearing and sat down where the gorillas could see him. Leaf and Grammy followed very slowly and sat down a distance away.

The mothers stared but didn't move. Benjamin moved backwards slowly towards Grammy and Leaf. One screamed at Benjamin for bringing strangers but ignored them after a while, and the mothers went back to feeding their youngest babies. The older children were curious and one by one they came over. They sniffed at Leaf and jumped back. Then they came forward and touched her hair, her clothes, and one even pulled on her nose. Benjamin moved closer. One of the toddlers sat down in Benjamin's lap and he tickled her. She seemed to like that and clung to his T-shirt smiling at him. They knew him and trusted him.

The other four were playing with Leaf and Grammy like they were their new toys. Leaf loved every fun and scary moment of it. She knew hardly any people had ever been up this close to these gorillas. She touched their hands and stroked their heads. One stroked Leaf's face, laid its head on her shoulder and hugged her. It was a touching moment.

All of a sudden there was a crashing sound behind the foliage. They could hear the breaking of tree branches and something very large heading their way. The two mother gorillas jumped up and started screaming. The infant gorillas ran back to their mothers.

"COME! We have to go quickly before he sees us. Edge back slowly behind those bushes...then...RUN!" Benjamin grabbed Grammy's arm, pulled her backwards behind a bush and started running. Leaf ran, terrified. Grammy ran petrified.

They could just make out something huge smashing its way through the leaves. Leaf and Grammy tried to keep up with Benjamin but Grammy was repeatedly tripping up on the plants, and big leaves smacked her in the face.

Behind them the tops of large plants were disappearing into the collective leaves as they were torn from their roots. Then the sound of ripping and crashing through the undergrowth suddenly ceased.

They were close to Ben's tent when they stopped running. Grammy was so out of breath and hobbling on her painful arthritic knees.

"The male of that group gets very protective and he would not have liked to find you near his children," Benjamin explained laughing, but out of breath too.

"He must have caught the scent of you down wind. Only run if a gorilla has not seen you yet. That was a very close call. We are safe now. Tea? I'm sure the water has boiled."

Grammy and Leaf collapsed onto tree stumps near the fire. Ben made tea in metal cups.

"No milk or sugar I'm afraid. It is Rooibos tea made from the Rooibos root. It is good." It was hot.

While they waited for it to cool down, Leaf thought about the time spent today on this Key Trip, first at the zoo and then to Rwanda. They had been gone for hours. She planned to return to normal time at one twenty-five, just in time for lunch. According to Grammy's wrist watch, which was still on English time, one twenty-five was in ten minutes so there was no time for tea.

"Benjamin, we need to get out of here. My mum will be so worried if I'm late for lunch."

"Where is your mother exactly?" he asked, finally getting

68

some information out of the child.

"In Hampstead, North London," Leaf replied matter of fact. Grammy shot her a look.

"How did you plan to get there by lunch time?" He was amused.

"We need to get back to the cage. Can you show us how to get back to it?" Grammy interrupted before Leaf said too much. Benjamin looked very confused but said he would show them.

"I will have to provide you with basic supplies for your trip back through the rainforest. I do not have much but I will give you what I can spare," Benjamin said.

"Thank you, but we do not need your supplies. You keep them. You need them more. Very kind of you to offer though. We just need to get back to the cage." Benjamin thought they were bonkers but took them back to where he had found them.

"I use this cage for injured animals to keep them safe until they are better. What do you need to come here for?" Benjamin asked.

"We know the way back from here," Grammy replied. Benjamin frowned.

Leaf looked around on the ground for her Key. She checked in her empty pockets again. There it is! She had searched by the cage three times before but now saw it poking out of the dry leaves on the ground. She was so relieved. She picked it up and subtly showed Grammy.

"Goodbye and thank you, Ben. It was really wonderful to meet you. If you wouldn't mind, would you turn away and not look for three minutes," Grammy said to Benjamin, who was looking more confused than ever but politely did as he was asked. Leaf put the Key in the lock of the cage door.

"Goodbye, Ben" Leaf said. Grammy knew Ben might turn and would see them disappear but she did not know any other way to get home.

They had not seen any other cages or doors around these parts. It was not like there were loads of people around for him to tell, and they probably would not believe him anyway. Grammy decided to take the chance. Hopefully he would think they just ran off into the trees.

"Bye, Benjamin. Thanks for the tea. Keep up the good work and, don't tell anyone we were here. Now could you please stick your fingers in your ears," Leaf said to him, and he complied smiling, thinking that this was a joke.

"In the hallway of my house, 6 Springfield Road, Hampstead in North London, England, at 13:25 on the 20th September 2014," Leaf instructed in a whisper, turning the Key three times to the left.

Taking Grammy's hand, and pushing the cage door open, Leaf crawled back in through the front door of her house back in Hampstead North London, England. Grammy crawled on her hands and knees into the hallway behind her. They both quickly stood up, feeling foolish. Grammy shut the door quietly behind them. She gave Leaf a quick kiss and a hug goodbye.

"See the trouble you can get yourself into if you are not careful and I am very cross you came back at lunchtime. I told you to come back five minutes after we left this morning. You must not miss so many hours of your natural life," Grammy whispered crossly to Leaf. She gave Leaf another hug, and told her to do better next time.

Grammy took the Key from Leaf, opened the door again, and sneaked off to her Mini Cooper (Sally), which was parked under the trees round the corner and not at all subtle with its Union-Jack paintwork.

Behind Bars

"Oh there you are, Pinky. I was just about to call Sarah's mum to remind you the time for lunch." Mum said as Leaf walked into the kitchen. Mum was scooping hot homemade stew into bowls.

"Hi Mum." Leaf gave her a kiss, and took a full bowl and spoon to the table.

"Did you have a nice time with Sarah?" Mum asked.

"Yeah, it was okay. We played cards and dominoes," Leaf lied and looked away. It made her feel sick in her tummy when she lied to her mum. She was bursting to tell her mum about her time in Rwanda, about the baby gorilla and the big scary one. She used to tell her mum everything. She hated this situation.

"What did you and Grammy get up to last night? Did the two of you, mad pair that you are, have a nice time?" Mum inquired, smiling. She sat down at the table to eat.

"A great time, very educational," Leaf replied, having thought of a way to be able to half share her experience with Mum, but without giving away the secret that she had actually spent that afternoon with Grammy in Rwanda.

"What do you mean?" Mum said, laughing.

"We watched a documentary on Dian Fossey and her gorillas in Rwanda. It was really interesting and very sad."

"Ooh, I loved the film they made about her, Gorillas in the Mist. I haven't seen it in years. After we have been shopping, we could rent the film for tonight. We could get a Chinese take-away, crisps and chocolate, and have a girlie night, put on face-packs and have a good cry. It is a very sad film. How does that sound?" Mum asked enthusiastically. Leaf wanted nothing more than to put her feet up as she had far too much sun and was also feeling slightly dizzy from the Key Jumps. They rarely could afford a take-away and a Girls Night sounded perfect.

"I'll make popcorn and get a box of tissues," Leaf replied

with a big smile, knowing that after watching the film she could talk to her mum about Rwanda, the poachers, and the gorillas. It had been a long time since she'd had Girls Night with her mum and she was really looking forward to it.

Chapter Five

THE WIZARDS

Grammy called while Leaf was finishing up her homework.

"Okay, I think she is almost finished her project. Okay, I'll tell her. Bye Mum, love you," Leaf heard her mum say into the phone.

"Grammy is coming to pick you up. She wants you to make biscuits with her. She will be here in fifteen minutes. You two are spending a lot of time together these days, which is good I suppose. Have you finished your homework?"

"Just finished," Leaf told her, putting her Maths book back into her school bag.

Ten minutes later Grammy tooted her horn outside, which was as loud as a fog horn. Leaf grabbed her coat and ran out to the car. Mum waved from the door. Grammy gave another blast of her horn in response, and pulled away from the curb with The Who blaring out of the stereo.

"So what's going on?" Leaf asked.

"I have some friends I would like you to meet. We have to hurry because they should be arriving at my house in ten minutes," Grammy replied, putting her foot down on the accelerator.

"Friends?"

"Just wait and see."

Grammy parked under the lamppost and Leaf bolted up to the red door with the shiny number twelve on it. Grammy opened the door with her ordinary house key.

Putting the kettle on, she asked Leaf to get six mugs from the cupboard as Grammy filled a plate with ginger snaps and homemade flap-jacks.

"They should be here any min..." Before she could finish speaking there was a loud pop and three old wizards appeared in the kitchen. Leaf stared wide-eyed in shock.

"Good evening," they said in unison. The smallest wizard named Barroton, who wore thick rimmed glasses and had the shaggiest beard, peered around as if searching for something or someone and smirked irately.

"Just typical!" he muttered. There was another pop and a fourth wizard stumbled into the kitchen.

"Sorry I'm late. I was painting and forgot the time," said the tallest of the men who had just appeared. His name was Viento and his face wore a jovial expression. He had splatters of colour on his hands.

"Oh, I thought we were wearing our dress robes for this occasion," Viento apologised again. He was wearing a yellow cloak covered in tiny stars. A yellow elongated top hat, with a symbol on it that Leaf did not recognise, was propped sideways on his head. He tried to straighten it and almost knocked the light fitting off the ceiling. Viento gave an apologetic smile from under his short trimmed beard. Barroton rolled his eyes in dismay.

"Typical!" repeated the smallest wizard, looking down his crooked nose in disapproval. Barroton was not only the smallest of the wizards, he was also chubbier than the rest, and he had a stern look in his green eyes that were enlarged behind his wire-rimmed spectacles. He had a long shaggy beard and wore an old green cloak and a hat that looked to be made of rams horns.

74

The Wizards

"Good evening, gentlemen. Thank you for coming. May I present to you my granddaughter, Leaf?" Grammy welcomed them. Leaf smiled weakly, feeling overcome with shyness.

"Leaf, this is Viento the Wizard of Air, Flamous the Wizard of Fire, Rivertos the Wizard of Water, and Barroton the Earth Wizard."

"We are pleased to meet you young lady," conveyed Barroton respectfully for all four wizards.

Flamous gave her a friendly wink and a cheeky smile, his lips almost hidden beneath his medium-length pointed grey beard. Flamous had a permanent mischievous sparkle in his dark eyes. He wore a red cloak over a dark orange robe and a pointed red hat with the symbol for fire painted on the front in sepia, which is a dark reddish-brown pigment made from the liquid in the ink sacks of certain cuttlefish.

Rivertos had the longest beard. His long hair was curly and white, and he looked the oldest of the wizards. Above his big red nose, he had watery blue eyes that matched his blue cloak and a bulbous blue hat with a Chinese symbol on it which Leaf presumed correctly represented water.

Each wizard carried a silver sceptre in their left hand bearing the symbol of their element and in their right hands each held a golden triangle.

"We are the Wizards of the Four Cardinal Temperaments: Sanguine, Choleric, Melancholic and Phlegmatic. All people fall under one of these temperaments. Sanguine and Choleric are extroverted people. Phlegmatic and Melancholic are introverted. Sanguine and the Phlegmatic avoid conflicts, the Choleric and Melancholic seek conflicts. I believe you, Leaf to be a Phlegmatic," Barroton said.

"Yes, I probably am," Leaf agreed.

"We are also the Wizards of the Four Elements, Earth, Air,

THE WHITEASH KEY

Fire and Water and the Four Directions of the Compass, North, South, East and West. Your grandmother has asked us here tonight for us to offer you our protection," Rivertos told her.

"Oh?" Leaf uttered, quite bewildered.

"My, my, you do look a lot like your grandmother did at your age, just as pretty," Flamous said. Leaf and Grammy smiled at each other and Grammy rolled her eyes. Leaf swallowed her giggle.

"We are the four elements. Leaf, now that you are the new Guardian of a Whiteash Key, you are the fifth, the element of self, the bridge between the physical and spiritual, the bridge between body and soul within the microcosm," Rivertos told her.

"You as the fifth element are the root of all existing matter and may call on us, The Four Temperaments, to assist you in your trials of life. As a Guardian, you may find yourself sometimes in danger, and we want to assure you that whenever you need us we will come to your aid, just as we did with your grandmother. Oh boy, did she get herself into some tight scrapes." Rivertos chuckled, remembering Grammy's adventures.

"We do hope you will be a bit more responsible and not need us quite as often," put in Barroton, and Grammy blushed.

"How can you protect me? And how will I call you if I do need you?" Leaf asked.

"We each possess powers to help with different difficulties..." Flamous started to answer, but Viento interrupted.

"I, for example, represent the wind in our skies, the breath of life. I am the Wizard of the East and have a connection to universal force. I represent intellect, communication and wisdom. I am also phlegmatic! I know you are shy and sometimes have difficulty speaking when you get nervous, maybe I can help you there. I can also blow away troubles and strife," Viento informed her. Leaf thought about Grammy's

76

willow tree and how she tied feathers representing her troubles to the twigs and waited for the wind to carry the troubles away.

"When you are in need of my assistance, scribble a note on a light piece of paper and let the wind carry it to me," Viento added.

"As clever as he is, he often interrupts, and Viento is terribly clumsy. He often acts like a donkey's ass so do not let him near your expensive china," scoffed Flamous, and then he finished what he had been saying before he had been rudely interrupted. Although he spoke crossly, the jovial mischief never left his eyes and Leaf could tell that this was a usual friendly banter between two close friends.

"I am a Sanguine but I protect those I care about, and in those cases I will seek conflict if need be and can be quite deadly, but in most cases I do not seek conflicts, I prefer just to be the light of the party. I am the wizard of Fire and the Wizard of the South. I bring new life or destroy the old. I can give you strong will, energy, personal power, and inner strength. I can heal you, and harm your enemies. When you need me just write me a note and burn it," Flamous told her, theatrically using expressive hand actions to accompany his words. He opened his hand. Magically, a flame appeared and danced on his palm. He blew it out and gave Leaf a wink.

"I am the Wizard of the West, and I represent passion, emotion, intuition, and inner reflection. When you feel overwhelmed by your emotions call on me and I will come to wipe away your tears." Rivertos spoke in a kind and overly concerned voice.

"Oh Rivertos, you are such a mushy Melancholic," Barroton smirked. Rivertos ignored him and continued.

"When you wish to call on me, just throw a note into a body of water, a river, a lake or an ocean. Here is a bottle of holy water which might come in useful. Holy water is ordinary water with salt in it, so you can make more when this runs out. You can throw it on demons or unfriendly spooks or on Flamous when he outstays his welcome." Rivertos told her. Leaf stepped forward and said thank you when Rivertos presented her with a full litre and a half plastic bottle. She put it safely on the Flying Horse Table. Leaf was thinking how life is often bizarre and unexpected.

"I, Barroton, Wizard of the North, am the element of terra firma. I am a choleric, and I can ground you, connect you to life and family roots. I represent fertility and stability. I was there at your birth, I shall be there at your death, and I shall direct your rebirth. Earth Wizards live two hundred years so I shall outlive you all."

"Leaf, I shall not neglect you through this life. If you need me, write me a note and bury it in the ground, and I shall come to your aid."

"We have a gift for you, Leaf," revealed Rivertos. "You see that each of us carries a triangle, pointing in different directions, they represent the four elements. When these four triangles are laid on top of each other in their correct position, they form a pentagram which is used for protection against evil. We have a silver pentagram necklace for you, to keep you safe from harm."

"We all prefer a bit of notice with the note form of communication, but if you are in serious jeopardy and do not have time or materials to write a note then hold the necklace and call the name of the wizard you need and he will be by your side instantly." Barroton told her.

Flamous stepped forward, laid his sceptre and triangle on the Flying Horse Table, reached into his pocket and took out a silver pentagram on a chain. Leaf lifted her long blonde hair and he fastened it around her neck.

"Thank you." Leaf smiled bashfully, pleased with the pretty necklace.

"Oh gosh, I forgot to make the tea," Grammy cried.

"No matter, Bernadette, we must be off now, important work to be done!" Barroton stated.

"You just want to get back to weeding your garden," Flamous chuckled.

"Well it is a full moon which is the perfect time to plant my Artemisia Annua," replied Barroton.

"Yes, we must be off. I personally have a flood to clean up in Indonesia." Rivertos frowned.

"I wouldn't mind one of those ginger-snaps before we go" said Viento, having spied the plate of biscuits and he almost knocked the plate to the floor as he reached for one. Flamous, who had magically beaten Viento to the biscuits, managed to catch the plate and all the biscuits before they hit the floor.

"It was nice to meet you all." Leaf said politely.

"Thank you all for coming," Grammy said again.

"Goodbye," said Flamous kissing Grammy's hand. Viento just raised his hand as his mouth was full of flap-jacks. Then with a loud pop they all vanished as quickly as they had appeared.

"Wow, Grammy, you never told me you knew wizards!"

"I haven't told you lots of things," Grammy replied. "All in good time."

"Grammy, is your story about the aliens in Peru really true?"
"Of course it is! Do you think I would fib to you, my love? If my imagination was that good I would be a writer instead of a painter."

"Can you show me?"

"Not tonight, Leaf. I must get you home. I will ask your mum if you can spend the weekend with me and we will go then. Did you want a quick cup of tea before we go?"

"No, I'm fine," said Leaf, grabbing her coat, and a few flap-jacks for Mum so she would believe their cover story of a simple night baking biscuits.

With the passenger window open, Leaf sang along to Gloria Gaynor's **I Will Survive** all the way home.

Chapter Six

OUT OF THIS WORLD

Grammy picked Leaf up in her little car called Sally, late Saturday morning. They both sang along dramatically to Queen's Bohemian Rhapsody on the short journey, which always ended in them head-banging and having the giggles.

When they were comfortably seated at the Flying Horse Table with tea and biscuits, Grammy continued with Leaf's training.

"I have so many exciting things to tell you that I don't really know where to start. I cannot possibly tell you everything I have learnt to do and *what not to do* with the Key over my sixty-one years of experience of being the Key Guardian. I will try to think of the most important things you should know. The rest I can tell you when I remember it or when it seems relevant and you can ask me questions whenever you like."

Grammy continued to teach Leaf who listened carefully as she munched on a homemade biscuit.

"Never go back and try to change what has happened in the past because you could change an unending series of things in the future. Even if you feel you cannot cope with what has happened you must not risk the future by changing it. You must accept this, Leaf. For example, say someone you loved died and you wanted to go back to save them, they will most likely die again in another way very soon after, but instead of that person slipping and falling in the bath tub, they might die three days later in a car crash and kill a whole family in the other car. By changing the past you would have changed the fates of the whole family that died and all their loved ones and all the future things they were meant to do, when really it was only meant for one person to die. You must accept life as it has played out."

"Use the Key to enjoy and experience life but never to change history. For life to be as it is now, and we don't really want to change what we know and have become accustomed to, every single event that has occurred through time has been perfect in creating us, the lives we lead, and the futures we hold. If you change the past it is very likely that in some way it will change you, maybe even everyone and everything you know. So think wisely. Weigh up your risks," Grammy advised her.

"Make wise decisions, and don't go stepping on bugs, because you never know if that was the ant that carried the seed to where it grew into the first sunflower which released its seedlings into the wind and pollinated hundreds of fields of sunflowers that the locals used to make oil and toasted seeds which created income to save a hungry town. Okay, so I am making it up as I go along, but you get the point that all bugs in the past helped in the evolution of today as we know it. When you kill an ant or any creature you take away the part it was born to play in the evolution of our planet." Grammy took a sip of her tea.

"Remember not to talk to people about where you have been or they will think you are mad, lock you up and throw away the key. That happened to my maternal grandmother, Doris from Brighton, the one who converted to Judaism in order to marry my Jewish grandfather. She was the one who took Judaism the most seriously. That often happens when someone is a newcomer to a religion. They can become overly fanatical in order to prove their devotion to themselves and others. She was very strict with my mother and insisted that my mother was to be very strict with me," Grammy said, running her fingers through

82

her long hair.

"Anyway, she went on what she intended to be a quick Key Trip into the past. The people at the Inn, where she was eating in London, were suspicious of strangers and wanted to know where she was from. Being an honest woman, and assuming they would take it as a joke, she told them. She said she had time travelled from the year 1953. They told the authorities who arrested her and locked her in the Bedlam madhouse. The word Bedlam means chaotic, mad, which she was not. They took away all her possessions including the Key. She was stuck in a mental institution from 1929 until 1939, a terrible time for inmates of mental institutions. They were places of torture," Grammy said and sighed deeply.

"Eventually they released her and she got the Key back when they returned her suitcase of possessions. Time had not stopped in the present so our family had thought her dead when she disappeared for ten years. It must have been terrible but none of us can remember it now."

"Granny Doris did not want to miss a day of her loved one's lives so returned to the time she had left, but she looked dramatically older than when we had seen her the day before, and our family, although unaware of it, had to repeat ten years of our lives, even though Granny Doris never got to see it." Grammy's eyes welled with unshed tears.

"A month later, on the day of my second and very different tenth birthday, she passed the Key on to me. She taught me as much as she could, but she died soon after, bless her soul. She was very naughty changing the past like that, although it was the future to her, but she had to give me the Key. It changed the lives of my whole family. I cannot remember the life I was leading before her return but I am sure it was not as exciting as the life I am leading now. I only know about it because Granny Doris told

83

me, but you must learn by her mistakes. You must not talk about the Key to anyone except me," Grammy insisted again. Leaf thought the story of her great-great grandmother was terribly sad.

After a lunch of bread and cheese, they went out into the garden so that Grammy could teach Leaf how to weave long reeds into a door. Grammy said there would be no doors where they were going on their alien hunt so she had collected reeds from a pond on Hampstead Heath to make the door. She said they would also have to use a padlock. Leaf was a little nervous of padlocks and hoped it did not fail and leave them stranded in Peru with scary aliens.

After forty minutes, Grammy stood their improvised door between two garden chairs, hooked the large padlock between the reeds and placed the Whiteash Key into the lock.

"In the Peruvian jungle 2000 years ago," Grammy said and turned the Key in the lock three times to the left. She opened the door, and holding Leaf's hand they stepped through into the leafy wilderness.

Everything was so green and lush. A toucan watched from his sturdy branch as a family of capybaras disappeared into a bush. Red monkeys leapt from tree to tree overhead and colourful parrots squawked between the leaves. The trees were so high that Leaf felt dizzy when she looked up to their tops.

"As beautiful as it all is, we must not stay long. The jungle is a treacherous place. Be careful where you step. There are snakes and plenty of things that will eat you given half the chance. First sign of an alien and we are out of here!" Grammy insisted. Leaf screamed as a spider the size of her hand crawled over her converse trainer.

"Ok, let's go home!" she exclaimed and kicked the spider off. It went flying up into the air and landed in a bush,

"Nope, we came here to see aliens and we are not leaving until you are convinced I was telling the truth." They did not have to wait long. Running down the path towards them, long arms waving above its head, was a meter high naked alien with a big, almost heart shaped, head and a small skinny grey body with no genitalia. Leaf screamed and dived into a bush.

"Oh thank the merciful masters of the universe! You have to help me!" cried the alien, hysterically. Grammy was frozen to the spot, her eyes wide in terror.

"Do you speak English? Vous parlez français? Sprichst du Deutsch?" the alien asked.

"Yes, I speak English and French and a bit of German," uttered Grammy in a state of shock.

"Oh thank the merciful! That saves me going through the ninety-nine earth languages I know. You have to help me! I was in Hawaii last week, just heavenly, but then I came to Peru and got lost in the jungle. I have been wandering lost in this horrific place for five days. I almost got swallowed by an anaconda yesterday and this morning I was almost torn limb from limb by a leopard. Please say you will help me. I have to get out of here but I lost my phone and can't call home." His voice was of low tones and Grammy presumed he was a male alien.

Leaf, overcome by curiosity, ventured out from behind the bush, thinking that if the alien was going to kill them with a laser beam he would have zapped Grammy by now, so she spoke up bravely.

"But how can we help?"

"I was left here on a recognisance mission to find monatomic gold, of which we are now in short supply on my planet. I was supposed to call home when I wanted them to come and get

85

me, but as I said I lost my phone, a very rude monkey stole it."

"You can use my phone if you like" offered Leaf kindly, pulling it out of her back pocket.

"Dear smaller person, if you have not noticed, we are in the middle of the jungle two thousand years before cell phones were even invented, so I doubt we will get reception on it. I had a phone that didn't need those ugly towers you cover your planet with. What year are you from?"

"2014," Leaf was glad she knew the answer to that one after the berating he had given her over the phone reception.

"I thought so, judging by your clothes and technology. 2014 is close enough. If you could kindly give me a lift to 2014 and then my brother could pick me up from there. Please take me home with you," he pleaded, sniffing through the two small slits that served as his nose.

"Oh I don't know..." Grammy started.

"Oh please don't leave me here. I'll die! I can't stand the heat for one, and then there are all these creepy-crawlies to contend with."

"We can't just leave him here, Grammy!"

"Oh, come on then. If we all gather reeds we can get out of here." Grammy sighed convinced this was a bad idea. What if Mrs. Parker at number fourteen caught sight of their guest?

"Don't you have a spaceship or a time machine?" The alien was flabbergasted.

"No, so if you want to get home start collecting reeds." The alien, not needing to be told twice, started running around collecting reeds, his long arms oscillating, his mind racing with reasons for why they might need the reeds. Were they going to burn them in some kind of magic transporting ceremony? Grammy and Leaf, sweltering in the heat, wove them together and slowly created a door.

Out of this World

"I thought you said they had three fingers on each hand and ran around like birds?" Leaf whispered, having noticed this alien had ten long, skinny fingers and did not fit Grammy's previous description. The alien, who must have had exceptional hearing, shouted to them through the undergrowth: "Those dudes are from another planet, completely on the other side of the galaxy from where I live. They were here also looking for monatomic gold. And Tequila! I gave them the mathematical coordinates of Mexico in 1959," the alien told them, really giving a party emphasis to the word 'Tequila' and a perfect Mexican accent on the word 'Mexico'.

"I would have hitched a lift with those guys but they already seemed considerably drunk, definitely over the limit."

An hour later, Grammy stood the shabby door with the padlock on it between two trees and gave the instructions and time for their return journey home.

"Just a door? That's it?" he pondered, "How ingenious!"

"Hold my hand," Leaf reluctantly instructed their new cling-on friend. His hand was cold but his skin was smooth and not unpleasant. Grammy whispered the instructions to the Key in the padlock and the three of them filed through the reed door back into Grammy's kitchen.

"Oh isn't this cosy. Bless you both, I owe you my life."

"Take a seat. Are you hungry?" Grammy asked, being hospitable but wondering what the hell was she going to do with the alien in her kitchen. If this plan to get him home did not work would she have to keep him?

"Just some water please."

"What is your name?" Leaf asked, taking a seat next to the alien.

"I think you would have trouble pronouncing it or even

hearing it, but here goes..." The alien let out a high pitched sound that shook the vase of wild flowers on the Flying Horse Table.

"Can we call you Ernie?" Grammy asked, handing him a glass of water which he grasped in his elongated fingers.

"Why Ernie?" Leaf asked, laughing.

"Ernie the alien was the first thing that came to mind," Grammy replied.

"Ernie. Yes I like it!" the alien exclaimed. The tiny slit pupils of his big round eyes enlarged with pleased approval. Leaf thought he was so cute.

"Where do you come from, Ernie?" Grammy asked.

"A planet three billion light years from earth called Zorgatronion. It is the year 299019290121102 there."

"How are you going to be able to call your family?" Grammy inquired curiously.

"If I could use a computer or tablet and connect it to a radio, find the right frequency and then I can call FRB 121102."

"I have a tablet and you can use that old radio over there" Grammy said, passing the tablet to Ernie who connected it to the radio on the window still and started listening carefully to the channels of static.

"Is there waste ground near here or a deserted park? Somewhere I could tell my brother to land?"

"If we did it in the very early hours of the morning we could use the heath. Tell them Parliament Hill on Hampstead Heath, North London in England at four in the morning." Grammy suggested. Ernie typed something into the tablet and spoke in a high frequency voice. The pitch was so high that Grammy and Leaf had to cover their ears. The vase on the table exploded. Then they heard a reply from the other end, which thankfully did not break anything but was deafening just the same. Ernie gave a quick confirmation that resulted in one small crack in the window.

"He is coming! He said he can make it by four in the morning your time. He has the latest Spinflash craft. It can move at five hundred million light years per hour, but he will be paying it off for the rest of his life. Anyway, I cannot thank you both enough. Your human kindness is overwhelming. I am so sorry about your vase and the crack in the window. Here let me pay you in monatomic gold," he said, pulling a hemp pouch out of his invisible pocket.

"Do you have a small pot with a lid I can put it in?"

"That is okay, you do not have to pay me. It was an accident. Really, do not trouble yourself dear," Grammy assured him.

"Please, I insist. If you mix this with avocado and lemon juice, and then leave it in the fridge for twenty minutes, you can use it for fifteen minutes as a face-pack and it works absolute miracles on wrinkles. Don't overdo it mind, only quarter of a teaspoon once a week in a face pack or mixed in a glass of water to drink. Also, mixed into a cream and applied externally can also be used to heal wounds." Grammy went to the cupboard above the sink. She found a little pot she had washed and kept from the Chinese take-away chilli sauce. Ernie poured until it was half full.

"Thank you very much I shall use that tomorrow night on my face. I've got an avocado in the fridge," Grammy said.

"Remember only a tiny bit once a week. Give it time to wear off otherwise people will be wondering how you suddenly look seventeen," Ernie warned. Grammy laughed and could not wait to try it out.

"Be careful because too much can also burn your face off," he added.

"Okay, I will ration myself," Grammy promised, feeling

slightly less enthusiastic. She'd planned to tell everyone she'd had good plastic surgery. Explaining away major burns as a face peel gone wrong did not seem so great. She still wanted to try the face pack, but carefully.

"Now, we have to wait until four in the morning so what would you like to eat?"

"Do you have pizza? I love Pizza. I had it last time I came to earth and enjoyed it so much that I still crave it. We do have pizza on Zorgatronion but it comes out of a machine and it is not quite the same as Earth pizza."

"I love pizza too!" exclaimed Leaf.

"I think I have some frozen pizza. Bacon and mushroom, is that alright?"

"If your oven is broken I can fix it for you."

"No my oven is fine. I will heat it up for you," Grammy laughed. "Right then, non-frozen-pizza for everyone coming up," she said, and headed to the big freezer down in the cellar.

"Ernie, what is monatomic gold?" Leaf asked.

"It is a powdered white gold, the colour of silver, which has only two dimensions. If you consume enough of it you will gain super brain power and be able to move through other dimensions. It heals, and enables you to live much longer and even shape shift. When you eat enough of it your body becomes luminous. My people are known to you humans as a species of Greys, but when we have enough gold to go around we all shine like the sun."

"Do people from other planets come to Earth often?" Leaf inquired.

"You have people from other planets living among you here on earth who are a species of taller Grey's from the constellation of Draco. They are descendents of the reptile races and here on earth they usually hold high positions of power such as presidents and royalty. They use monatomic gold to disguise themselves. They have many secrets and keep so much information hidden from the general masses of common folk." Leaf wasn't sure she believed everything he was saying. She found it hard to believe that Prince Harry was a big user of monatomic gold so as not to look like a taller version of Ernie.

Ernie was entertaining and it was interesting to learn things about Zorgatronion from someone who actually lived there. You don't get that opportunity every day. They spent several pleasant hours chatting and laughing and getting to know each other. Ernie turned out to have a very courteous nature and was extremely funny. They laughed until their sides hurt.

At twenty to four, bleary eyed and yawning, they set off to Hampstead Heath. Ernie was wrapped in Grammy's black hooded coat. Luckily, the streets and the heath were deserted.

At exactly four a.m. they saw lights appearing in the distant sky. The spinning craft grew nearer at a breathtaking speed. It was silver with many tiny windows that cast immense light over the heath. Ernie hugged them goodbye, gave Grammy back her coat, and with tears in his eyes said that he would never forget them.

"We will not forget you either," Leaf assured him.

"Farewell, Ernie. Have a safe flight home." Grammy bent down and kissed him on the cheek. He raised his hand in a farewell, his thin grey lips quivered, and a tear fell down his face which brought tears to Leaf's eyes too.

The spacecraft landed in the clearing with a tremendous force of wind that bent the tops of the tall trees and almost took Grammy off her feet. A drawbridge was lowered and Ernie's older brother appeared at the top of the gangway. He looked like Ernie but older and fatter.

91

Shouting goodbyes, Ernie ran on his little legs towards the craft, up the ramp and hugged his brother, who hugged him back and then punched him in the arm and hugged him again. They waved goodbye and then disappeared inside the ship. The bridge retracted into the craft. In a flash of light and a blast of wind it was gone.

"Well that was unusual. So, do you believe me now?" Grammy asked. Leaf said she would think about it. Grammy laughed, said it was time for bed, and they headed back across the heath.

Chapter Seven

THE LOCKET

Leaf's mother's birthday was on the 12th of October and that was in only thirteen days. Leaf had been so busy on her adventures that she had not had time to properly plan her mum's surprise. She wanted to get Mum something really special to show how much she loved and appreciated her. Mum worked hard every day, she did all the shopping, cooking, cleaning, and still had time for hugs and moral advice.

Marie was more than just a mum, she was also like a big sister, whom Leaf could trust with all secrets that had nothing to do with the Key. Mum was always ready to give advice with the best for Leaf in mind. She had a wonderful sense of humour and made Leaf laugh all the time. Mum was great at telling stories on the spur of the moment, and she was always positive no matter how hard life got.

"Things that go wrong are leading you to what is right," Mum would always say.

Despite Marie being hard working, they always seemed to be broke. She spent all her money on food, cleaning products, school supplies and new clothes for Leaf when she needed them. Mum sometimes only ate one meal a day if there was not enough food left at the end of the month, but she made sure Leaf never went without and had at least three meals every day plus snacks.

Apart from items Grammy sometimes bought her, all Mum's clothes were second-hand. Not that you could guess as such because Marie always looked well presented when she went out. Inside their house, which did not often see visitors, Mum looked like she had fallen out of a tree with wild untamed curls. She plodded around in scruffy T-shirts and tracksuit bottoms, either working all hours on her illustrations for children's books, scrubbing out the bathtub or the oven, mopping floors, washing up or spending time with Leaf. She gave everything she had to Leaf, almost never treating herself, so Leaf wanted to get her something beautiful for her birthday because she truly deserved it.

Her mum liked silver lockets. Sadly, she had lost her own the year before when she had taken Leaf on their first ever holiday, camping in the Lake District, so Leaf really wanted to buy Mum a new locket for her birthday.

On Sunday evening, Leaf was at home watching a programme about London. They showed the weekend market in Camden Town. It seemed an extremely quirky place full of strange and colourful people, where you could find all kinds of jewellery and lots of unusual things. Leaf phoned Grammy and asked if she would go with her to Camden Town in the morning before school, so that they could go shopping for her mum's birthday present.

"With the Key we can make it Saturday and I can get back before Maths starts, just a quick shopping trip. Pleeeeeeeeeeese Grammy?" Leaf persuaded her.

"Okay, Leaf. I will wait outside your school at ten to nine. Be there or be square! See you mañana, Wormy," Grammy said, and hung up.

Monday morning, Mum dropped Leaf off at the school gate, blew her an extra kiss, declared her love for her Pinky, and drove off. Grammy jumped out from behind the big recycling bins, scaring Leaf half to death.

Grammy and Leaf entered the building and walked quickly down the almost empty school corridor. Most of the children would not arrive until nine.

"We need a toilet door as those are usually the easiest doors to find," Grammy reminded Leaf. Grammy was feeling nervous. She did not want to get caught on school property without a reason, especially as she had dyed the bottom of her hair pink last night. She said her pillow cases were ruined. Her long silver hair tinged at the bottom with pink, hung loose except for her long fringe that was pulled back at the sides and made into a thin plait at the back of her head, garnished with two small turquoise feathers like a squaw. Grammy was wearing a pale blue Care Bears T-shirt on which Love-a-lot Carebear was giving the peace sign. Leaf hoped it was the peace sign, it was hard to tell with his stubby little fingers and you could never tell how outrageous Grammy was going to be, her clothing an expression of her most colourful life.

Grammy was very moralistic person, but she was a rule breaker. Schools, teachers, and people of authority made her nervous. She had told Leaf she was an Ubermensch and that Leaf should grow up to be one too.

"What is an Urbermensch?" Leaf had asked.

"You must read Nietzsche, Leaf, he was a fabulous philosopher. Ubermensch is the highest form of man that creates his own values and moralities to live by," was the reply.

Leaf and Grammy were making their way down the corridor trying not to attract attention. Two teachers were coming down the hall towards them and Grammy was starting to panic.

"I don't look like I belong here, Leaf. Quick find a door before they have me arrested for looking like the bad granny drug

95

dealer or they think I am trying to break into classrooms to steal computers or graffiti something. Just stick the Key in any of these doors," Grammy said, pushing Leaf down the corridor. The next door was the headmaster's office, not a good choice but the teachers were getting closer and would stop to question what Grammy was doing there. Grammy was cringing.

"That won't be an easy door to find but go on quickly before we get caught. QUICK!" Grammy pushed her towards the door. Leaf stuck the Key in the lock, turned it to the left and said, "Camden High Street, before the bridge on the side of the market, last Saturday the 27th of September, at eleven in the morning." They opened the door and walked out into the bright colours of Camden Town, closing a shop door behind them.

The high street was lined with different coloured houses and interesting shops, selling souvenirs, Doctor Martens boots, bags, postcards and a million other things. There was a massive converse shoe on the wall above a shop. Leaf thought it was so cool.

The adjacent shop was painted black with Gothic designs up the sides and a huge silver angel at the top of the façade. A huge dragon dominated the adjoining wall of the neighbouring shop. Grammy said the look of Camden had changed a lot since she had last been there in 1993 but the atmosphere was still the same.

The pavements were heaving with shoppers. The people were mostly bizarre and amazing. There was entertainment for Leaf's eyes in every direction: people with blue hair, pink hair, purple or green hair, sticky-up hair and no hair, people with high spiky hair, chains hanging from their jeans and noses, colourful hippies, elegant ladies, and girls in mini-skirts with bright coloured DM boots, and so many tattoos. People of all kinds but most of them were quirky. Grammy blended in with ease. Leaf stuck out like a sore thumb in her school uniform on a Saturday.

At the end of the street, market stalls sold all kinds of wonderful items. The stalls were pitched mostly around the lock by the blue wrought iron bridge with big yellow letters on a green background, spelling CAMDEN LOCK.

Grammy showed her the way, professionally whizzing through the crowds of people. They looked at all the stalls. Grammy tried on colourful scarves and looked at T-shirts. Leaf found a stall that sold lovely antique necklaces. Among the jewellery Leaf spotted the perfect silver locket. It was even prettier than the one her mother had lost. It had leaves on a vine delicately engraved along one side. There was one leaf that was larger and stood out from the others as it curled towards the centre of the locket. Perfect!

"There is a shop called Ziggy Letters in the covered part of the market across the road which does nice engraving if you would like to write a name or message on it," suggested the gypsy woman stall holder who had dark almond shaped eyes and wore an emerald green headscarf over her thick curly dark locks. She put the locket in an orange tie-string bag for Leaf. The bag was for free and Leaf was delighted.

Leaf had £22 to spend on her mum's gift. It was what she had left from the £50 her dad had given her for her birthday. The locket had cost £8, so they followed the woman's directions, across the road and down into a tunnel that was the throat of the labyrinth going down into the belly of the underground part of the market. Leaf wanted to see how much the engraving cost.

A bell rang as she opened the door below the words ZIGGY

THE WHITEASH KEY

LETTERS.

"What can I do you for?" asked a gigantic, big bearded man in his fifties, wearing a skull and cross-bone bandanna on his head, black jeans and a biker's waistcoat over a Metallica T- shirt. His huge bare arms were covered in tattoos. He looked Grammy up and down with slight confusion, decided she was an aged hippy, a bit wacky way out but still good looking.

There was not much space between the door and the high counter behind which he stood, and he seemed to fill most of the room. Behind him was an open door to the machinery room where the engraving was done.

Leaf felt nervous and shy as she spoke, "How much would it cost to engrave this with, I love you Mum?"

"£2 per word, so that is £8 for four words!" he answered in a voice too soft for his size.

"Okay then. Write it on the front please," Leaf requested, giving him the locket and hoping he would give it back. He looked dodgy.

"What kind of writing do you want? Choose from these," the man said, pushing a sheet of laminated paper towards her which had lots of different writing fonts on it. Grammy pointed out the best ones and from them Leaf chose a joined-up style that was pretty but clear to read.

"Come back in ten minutes. There is a photo booth in the entrance of the underground station if you want to make a photo of yourself to put in the locket." He gave her a ticket with a number on it for her to reclaim the locket. It was the number **One Hundred and Eleven**. This made Grammy smile. Leaf did not know yet what that important number meant to Grammy but within a few months that number would become significant to Leaf too.

The Locket

They raced up the Camden High Street, swerving between the people and out of the way of a big red bus.

A young man, wearing a dark suit, a black three-quarter length wool overcoat and mirrored sunglasses, gave Grammy a double take as he walked past. He looked her straight in the face for a long moment so that his face recognition sunglasses could register Grammy's features. The commissioner had given each of his men a pair and told them that it was the latest technology out of China.

The man had tried to hide his initial surprise of seeing Grammy, but she was quick on the uptake. He just kept on walking, pretending neither to know nor to have noticed her. As Grammy watched him walk past, she noticed that behind his ear he had a black tattoo of a circle of flames that formed a sun and in the centre was a cross above three small nails.

Grammy pointed out the bricked building of the station. Inside to the right of the doorway was a shabby old photo booth. Leaf climbed in, sat on the splitting plastic stool and pulled the dirty beige curtain closed so no one could see her. It was £4, so she put the money in the metal slot and tried to stay still and look pretty as the camera flash blinded her three times.

She pulled Grammy in for the last shot. The flash went off as Grammy was falling in with a look of surprise and Leaf was laughing. They pulled back the curtain in a daze and got out.

It was required to wait two minutes for the four photos to be developed and drop down into the box on the outside of the booth for collection.

They watched the odd looking people coming and going. A

teenage boy in tight green jeans with a shaved head dropped a lit cigarette near Leaf before he went down to the trains. Leaf coughed and stamped it out. She heard the line of photos drop. The second one was the best one of Leaf. At least you could not see the gap where her milk tooth fell out three days ago. The last photo of the two of them was so funny.

Leaf and Grammy pushed politely through the people and returned to the engraving shop.

"Sorry, I made a bit of a mistake. I wrote I love you Ziggy on the locket," the big tattooed man said through his beard. Leaf hoped he was not serious. He chuckled at the expression on her face and then she knew he was joking.

"I can cut the photo you want down to size and put it in the locket for you if you like," he offered.

"Thanks Ziggy," Leaf said with a cheeky smile, handing him the strip of photos.

"Please can you put the second one on the inside right and the last one on the inside left. Thank you. I think that's best," Leaf told him, feeling very grown up and in control. Since having the Key in her life Leaf was feeling more confident. It seemed that she was getting better at being able to talk to strangers.

Ziggy chuckled through his thick beard when he saw the last photo. He cut the pictures with a small guillotine, rounded them off with sharp scissors and placed them perfectly. The locket was better than Leaf had hoped.

"That'll be £8 then please. Actually, you can have it for £6 as it is for your mum," he told her. She gave him the money and a big smile. She had decided that he was not dodgy, he was nice and she had misjudged him.

"I like your T-shirt," he said to Grammy who stretched her

neck a little and tried to act cool.

"Bye, Ziggy," said Leaf.

"Bye, Kiddo. Your mum will love the present," he assured her, and waved goodbye.

"Bye, Ziggy." Grammy smiled.

"Bye, Carebear. Thanks for caring," he replied and gave Grammy a wink. Grammy blushed and gave him a peace sign. At least Leaf hoped that was the sign she gave him.

Leaf and Grammy wandered around Camden Town for a while, looking at the shops and trying on DM boots. Grammy bought herself knee high black ones with roses up the side, and the original up to the ankle DM's in purple for Leaf.

"I'll hold onto the boots and then bring them over to you tonight. I'll just say I bought them when I went shopping for my own," Grammy told her, because it would seem odd to Mum that Leaf went to school and came back with brand new boots on.

With her last £4, Leaf bought a packet of Cola bubble gum and a key chain that said I LOVE CAMDEN in rainbow letters. She hung it on the key chain that Grammy had given her the week before with two keys for Grammy's house. Dad had then given her one for his flat and Mum was going to get one cut for their house. Leaf would not need other keys once she had the magic Whiteash Key but she still had to wait two years for that.

Grammy had told her that the Whiteash Key was able to open any locked door as long as you said when, where, and what was supposed to be on the other side of the door. Opening a door in the here and now as if it was simply a normal key did no harm at all to a Guardian's body because they were not making a Jump through time or space, but Leaf liked having simple keys too for the important places in her life. Now she had a colourful key chain and cool boots as reminders of her wonderful day in Camden Town.

Grammy noticed the man wearing the mirrored sunglasses outside the shop on the other side of the road. He was pretending to be looking at postcards on the stand but was watching them in the reflection of the window. He raised his wrist to his mouth and spoke into the tiny microphone hidden in a silver bracelet that projected a computer, phone, and G.P.S onto his arm.

"Let's go. We need to move fast. We are being followed. Stay close to me," Grammy instructed in a serious toned whisper. She took Leaf's hand and they set off at a fast pace into the flow of the crowd. The man followed. They swerved back into the underground part of the market, past Ziggy Letters.

"RUN!" yelled Grammy. They ran through the tunnel and out the other side.

"I think we've lost him!" Grammy said, but they did not stop running. Grammy kept bumping into people as they raced through the crowds. Leaf apologised over and over as disgruntled people turned to give them dirty looks.

Getting back to school was not going to be easy. They had to find a headmaster's office door which was probably was not the best door to have chosen. Grammy stopped her hobbled running and tried to seem composed as she asked a few people about schools in the area, pretending she had just moved to Camden and was considering a school for her granddaughter. Leaf smiled innocently but kept looking back over her shoulder. Her heart was beating through her chest. She was so scared that the man with the mirrored glasses would reappear.

No one seemed to be from that area and no one knew where

the schools were. They ran through the back streets of Camden for over an hour before they found a school. Leaf had a terrible stitch and by this point Grammy was really hobbling on her arthritic knees. Leaf imagined them looking for her back in her own school. They might even have called the police by now and phoned her mum.

They walked in through the Camden school gates. It was quiet as all the children were at home for the weekend. Grammy opened the front door with the Key. They wandered along corridors and even stopped off at a toilet they found before coming across the door that read, Headmaster's Office. Leaf quickly and quietly put the Key in the lock.

"My school, Joan of Arc elementary, in the corridor outside Maths class today, October the 1st at 9 a.m." Leaf turned the Key three times to the left and then the knob on the door. Luckily, she didn't visit the Headmaster who was in his office doing paperwork despite it being a Saturday. Instead they stepped back into a corridor in Leaf's own school, and Leaf joined her classmates on the way to Maths class. Grammy put the Key in her pocket, waved to Leaf and slipped away out the main door.

Mum cried with joy on her birthday when she unwrapped the present from Leaf and she ate three pieces of the cake that Grammy and Leaf had made for her. They had a jolly good time and the giggles while playing Trivial Pursuit, their faces smeared with yummy chocolate.

"Did you know that Trivial Pursuit was invented by two men sitting on a beach in Spain? They asked friends in their local bar in Nerja to invest in the idea but no one would. Now the game is worth millions," Grammy told them.

"I would have invested if I had had some money. Yet, even

though I never seem to have any, I am still the richest woman ever because I have the best mother and the best daughter in the whole universe," Mum replied giving them both a kiss on the cheek and long hugs.

"Thank you for my locket, Leaf. I love it and I really love you," Mum said, making Leaf beam, knowing that she was the heiress to an endless fortune of unconditional love.

Chapter Eight

THE ENCHANTED MAZE

Bernadette Latoure (Grammy) had been born in Paris, France, on the 28th of July, 1944. She came from a Jewish family, her mother half English, her father was fully French.

Bernadette began her life in the attic of a house belonging to a Christian widower who had known Bernadette's father all his life, and he had been a good friend to her grandparents. The widower had allowed Bernadette's family to all hide from the Nazis in his attic until the end of the Second World War in 1945.

On the night of Bernadette's birth, after the waters had broken their sleep, her mother was tied to the wooden pillar that served as a support for the pointy wood-beamed ceiling of the attic. With clenched teeth, her big brown eyes she stared up at the small window-frame in the left slope of the roof beams. She searched the skies for a merciful God in the window of framed hope, a painting of stars on an endless royal blue canvas.

During the daytime, this small window also served as their daily clock. Watching the light of the sun passing them by was their only sense of an outside world, apart from hearing the German soldiers shouting in the streets, where the Jewish family no longer ventured. Everyone's hearts jumped each time a shot was fired.

Bernadette's mother had a strong contraction and tried not to scream. She was gagged with a rag by her loving husband, Joshua Latoure who cried profusely, wishing for freedom and homely comforts for his suffering wife and for the birth of his

105

second child. His wife's eyes bulged with pain as she tried not to cry out. Being tied to the pillar stopped her from making noise by thrashing in discomfort.

Baby Bernadette did not cry and no one smacked her to breathe. Every sound was a luxury they could not afford as the price would be all of their lives. Baby Bernadette took her own deep breath and then proceeded to suck her thumb. The family all exhaled with relief.

Bernadette would spend her days happily marvelling at the new and interesting attic-world around her. Twice a day the kind Christian would stand on a chair, and with the long pole of his mop he would beat a tune on the newly plastered ceiling.

When the tune sounded in thuds on the floorboards the family hid behind the tea-chests and stored furniture. Joshua lifted the plank in that part of the floor and reached down through the slit to the Christian's outstretched hand. He retrieved small packages of brunch or tea, sometimes small bits of boiled chicken or dairy, never both. Because they were Jewish, these two food sources, meat and dairy, could never be in the same meal. They never ate pork as it was completely against the Jewish faith to do so. As all things were in short supply during the war, most days they lived on bread, boiled potatoes, mushrooms, and raw carrots. Baby Bernadette survived on her mother's milk. She was overfed to keep her quiet and grew into a chubby baby. Her mother became very thin.

The first year of Grammy's long life was spent in the silence of that one room. Bernadette quickly learnt not to cry or make sounds, but she rarely wanted too. She was used to the silent smiles and warm hugs in the tight attic community consisting of four grandparents, a doting mother, a gentle father, and a loving brother.   During that time her brother became a very astute chess player as it was the main family pastime.

The eight of them rarely communicated verbally for fear of being discovered, but the children never doubted the unspoken love that presided with the members of their family.

After the war ended in 1945, Grammy's father bought a flat in Paris.   From an early age, Bernadette received lessons in the Torah (The Jewish Bible), piano lessons, and elocution lessons to help her progression of speech which was slow due to that muted first year in which babies normally learn through copying their parents.   She responded well to the lessons and learned to pronounce French and English perfectly.

Grammy was ten when her maternal grandmother died. Soon after, the family moved to England. Bernadette attended a Jewish school and also went to a summer school camp every August until she was sixteen. This had been the dying wish of her late grandmother, Granny Doris from Brighton who had attended the same camp in her youth.   Granny Doris had left money and instructions in her will to pay for the seven years of the expensive summer camp in Somerset.

Bernadette's father was a salesman but his work was not bringing in enough money. He had a cousin in South Africa who offered him a job as manager in his car factory.

On the first day of September 1960, the year in which Bernadette had turned sixteen, her family moved to South Africa and she attended a college there to complete the exams she had missed in her final year of school.

The move was short lived, and they left after thirteen months of Apartheid, living in a nice house with servants and well-kept gardens. South Africa was a beautiful country, but Johannesburg on the other side of the high garden walls felt hostile and violent to Bernadette.

She had made friends with a few people from a local tribe but she had been banned by her uncle from visiting them.

She was unhappy. Bernadette needed to feel free and also she had never been very studious. Her concentration always wandered and her grades rarely rose above a seven. She found it hard to make friends with the South African Christian girls from wealthy families who attended the same college after returning home from years at posh boarding schools in Switzerland, Paris or England. Her brother was also unhappy and unable to find work. Bernadette's mother hated the heat.

Much to the delight of Bernadette, when she was almost eighteen the family moved back to Paris and she bloomed into a fashion model. Bernadette was nineteen when her family moved again, this time to Miami in America, to live with another uncle. Bernadette continued to be a model for magazines and catwalk shows, and she got a dancing job in the chorus line of the Moulin Rouge. Grammy had never been shy.

Around this time, Bernadette started painting and sculpting and was very good, she was becoming well-known and making a good living, but then in 1965 when Bernadette was almost twenty-one, she packed it all in to go to Greece to live on a hippy commune.

When Bernadette left her family to go to Greece, she left behind most of her Jewish practices. She had never liked being a Jew with its hundreds of rules, like her mother having to wear a wig even on hot days as her hair could only be seen by her husband and no other man. Bernadette did not want to be hiding her hair from the world. Her beautiful hair was considered especially non-kosher in her family as she had inherited it from Doris, her English grandmother.

Bernadette had known Judaism to bring plenty of pain and danger to her family, and what she considered unnecessary labour to her mother who needed a kitchen with two of everything so as dairy and meat were never prepared or cooked using the same utensils. However, her mother never seemed to mind, she was happy in the Jewish faith and saw only the good things that came with the Jewish community.

Much to the despair of her parents, Bernadette had been a rebel from an early age. After she left home, the only Jewish tradition that Bernadette kept up was the lighting of the eight Menorah candles over eight days to celebrate Hanukkah, the festival of light that starts on the twenty-fifth day of Kislev which may occur any time from late November to late December according to the Gregorian calendar. At this time of year Grammy would bring Leaf and Mum gifts and delicious homemade jam doughnuts.

On the commune in Greece when she was twenty, Bernadette started to study Shamanism and it suited her better than Judaism. Having found inner peace, she drifted back to America six months later to spend three flower-power months on another commune in California where she learnt to surf, despite not being a particularly strong swimmer.

A year later she flew to Australia and surfed the Gold Coast, where she met her first husband in a bar. He was a rich Australian oil tycoon who was always away on business.

Two years later she divorced him for being unfaithful.

THE WHITEASH KEY

Bernadette got a lot of money in the divorce, so she banked it and went back to surfing along the Gold Coast.

After two months of surfing, Bernadette met her second husband.

Albert Trail, an English banker who was in Australia on a short term contract, also had a passion for surfing and he liked to say he met Bernadette on a wave. They surfed together, hung out at beach parties and rode the white horses at dawn.

One early stormy morning, Bernadette had a surfing accident. A huge wave swallowed her whole and then spat her out on the rocks. Then another wave tried to eat her but again she was projectile vomited onto the rocks. She must have been foul-tasting because the third wave was so angry that it smashed her unconscious. Albert was the one that pulled her out of the water and gave her mouth to mouth. He saved Grammy's life but she never liked going in the water again after that. For the rest of her life she was too afraid to even go swimming in the sea, convinced that the sea did not like her.

They fell in love and Bernadette went back to live with Albert in his small flat in King's Cross in London, England.

In 1970 they bought the house in Hampstead. Bernadette insisted on making renovations. She instructed the builders to tear out the whole middle section of the house and install a lavish staircase spiralling up to the attic with two open galleries for the two floors overlooking the hall. Before the conversion there had been an ugly moss coloured carpeted staircase that lead up to narrow corridors and only a pull down ladder to the attic.

Secretly, she had the builders make a couple of other adjustments to the house. The first was a secret escape route, dug out from the cellar to the trees behind the garden wall. She

110

also made an adjustment to her wardrobe, and it wasn't just a rack for all her crazy shoes. She told no one about the two other changes to the house, not even Albert.

While they had no stairs to reach the bedrooms, Albert and Bernadette's backs managed to withstand the months of sleeping on a sofa-bed in the living room. They snuggled in front of the great fireplace. They were so happy and in love.

Soon after the renovations had been finished, they got married and then had a daughter, Marie, born on the twelfth of October of 1975. Bernadette was a very good mother.

Up until then, Bernadette's life had not been conventionally normal, especially with all the Key Adventures she had secretly been going on once a week. After Marie was born, Bernadette did not go on a Key Adventure for three years and then only once a month when Marie started nursery. She was very devoted to her child.

It was not easy for her to leave her daughter out of the biggest part of her life (Key Jumps). She always felt that their closeness was affected by that and this made her treasure Leaf even more. Bernadette had waited a long time for a granddaughter to share her secret with.

Leaf was also feeling a loss in her relationship with Mum by having a secret as huge as being a Key Guardian and not being able to share it with her, and she knew she was causing stress for Sarah. Sarah was getting understandably fed up with covering for her. Leaf did not like to keep telling Mum she was going out with Grammy all the time. Mum would feel left out, so Leaf would often say she was with Sarah.

Sarah had really saved her one night. Leaf was grateful as it had been a stressful night involving evil witches and fairies, and she could not have handled her Mum being mad at her on top of everything she had already been through. Mum had called Sarah worried because Leaf was late home. Sarah had asked Leaf's mum if Leaf could stay later to watch the end of a film as it was not a school night. This gave Leaf another hour or so to get back. Of course when Leaf returned five minutes before she was due home, her mother no longer remembered her being late and Sarah could not remember the phone call that evening, but Sarah was upset that Leaf kept asking her to lie and she knew Leaf was lying to her about where she was going. Sarah didn't like it that her best friend was keeping secrets from her.

A few days later, Sarah told Leaf on the phone that it was starting to feel wrong and she was sick of covering for her. Leaf's heart felt heavy. She really appreciated Sarah as a friend but could feel her slipping away.

On weekdays Leaf had started going to the school library during break time to do research for Key Adventures. She had found a book on Paris and sat down to read it when another book, which had been left open on the table, caught her interest. It was a fairytale book about a very beautiful but evil woman who lived in a dark part of the Boreal forest in Finland with her most ugly daughter.

Fairies of the forest had told the woman when she was pregnant that the mother gives the unborn child her beauty. The mother becomes less beautiful on the outside but twice as beautiful on the inside. Maronna was frightened to lose her beauty. She was very vain. She cast a dark and selfish magic spell so she would keep all her beauty and spared the child none. The baby was born severely ugly. The fairies knew what the beautiful woman had done and cast shame on her. So Maronna decided to get rid of the fairies. She used a spell to steal the light of the forest. All the trees grew rampant and out of control.

112

Thick roots and branches spread all around. There was a flash through the forest and then all the light was gone, the forest cast into eternal darkness.

Leaf read that many, many years ago that part of the forest had been enchanted because fairies had lived there. Now it was cursed and doomed by the witch who had stolen the light of the forest. The story did not have a happy ending. It said that the fairies were never able to get the light back and the darkness killed most of the plants and animals, and even the fairies themselves. The book said that there were less than two hundred fairies left in the whole world. One day there might be none left at all. She read that the last time any fairies were spotted in the Boreal Forest was back in 1703, soon after Maronna had stolen the light.

At four-thirty that afternoon, Leaf asked if she could go to Sarah's so they could do their homework together. Her mother watched her walk up the road to Sarah's gate and called, "I LOVE YOU PINKY!" She waved with her thumbs in her ears and her cheeks puffed out. Leaf did the same back.

"LOVE YOU POOKY!" Leaf replied. Her mum turned and went back inside. Grammy leapt out of a bush.

"So where are we off to then?" Grammy cried. Leaf panted, holding her heart.

"Stop leaping out of bushes, you'll kill me!"

"Are we there yet?" Grammy replied sarcastically, following Leaf back to her house.

Leaf turned her house key quietly in the lock, they crept back in through the front door and up the stairs to Leaf's bedroom. Luckily, Mum had Tina Turner on loud in the kitchen and was too busy dancing while doing the dishes to notice. Leaf shut her bedroom door and hid her school bag in the cupboard.

"Here Grammy, put these gloves on and this blanket around you. It will be very cold where we are going."

"The Ice Hotel in Sweden?" Grammy asked hopefully.

"Maybe one day but not today. Can I have the Key?" Leaf figured they might not have a bathroom so far into the past but with luck they would have a cupboard. She put the Key in the lock of a cupboard door.

"An afternoon in the darkest part of the Boreal Forest, Finland, 1703."

"I'm not sure I like the sound of this, Leaf!" Grammy frowned. She turned the Key three times to the left, held Grammy's gloved hand, opened the cupboard and they went through a door into a dark snow covered forest.

Luckily, Leaf still had her coat and gloves on because it was freezing. They were in a clearing in the middle of the forest. Thick branches grew over their heads blocking out the moonlight. Leaf turned around and saw the door they had just closed belonged to an old wooden shack. The flowers in the garden were all dead, presumably from the cold. Leaf felt like her blood was freezing and she could not breathe.

"I don't think I like it here, Leaf! It is so very dark and cold. I think we need to find a cupboard quickly and go home. It is way too scary to be out here on our own!"

There was smoke coming out of the chimney of the shack. Grammy wondered who lived there and if they would let them warm themselves by their fire, if they had a cupboard and if their cupboard had a lock.

Leaf would not usually knock on a stranger's door and ask to be let in but they were freezing to death outside. She heard wolves howling nearby and she knew the only possibility of a cupboard was inside this shack. Leaf wished she had used a front door. Leaf banged on the door. It opened slowly, and a beautiful woman with long black hair and mesmerizing green eyes stood staring at her. The woman was wearing a long black dress like she had been to a funeral. Leaf hoped she was not disturbing her on a bad day.

"What do you want, child?" the woman demanded. Then she noticed Grammy and her tone softened. "What is it, child?"

"We don't mean to trouble you but we are all alone in the forest and so cold. Please may we get warm by your fire for five minutes?" Grammy stepped forward and asked the woman.

"Come in! It is no trouble, no trouble at all! Come in, come in!" She stepped aside to allow Leaf and Grammy in.

There was not much furniture just a wooden table, two wooden chairs, and a rocking chair by the big black cauldron cooking on the fire which was giving off a very odd and unpleasant smell. Lots of dried herbs hung from the ceiling, a dead cat and two dead chickens hanging on hooks in the corner. Leaf tried not to look at them. Why did the woman have a dead cat? Was she going to eat it? Grammy and Leaf exchanged appalled looks between them.

There were lots of different sized pots on the shelves containing powdered herbs and spices and strange looking things floating in liquids. Leaf noticed another shelf with jars of dead insects, frogs, small snakes and lizards, all pickled in vinegar. One jar even had a human eyeball floating in it. Leaf spotted a tall cupboard in the corner with a lock on the door.

"Come sit by the fire and tell me your names," the woman said, pulling the two wooden chairs up to the fire for Leaf and Grammy. She had water boiling in a pan on a grill over the hot coals and the woman added herbs to make a type of tea.

"Here, this will warm your bones," she said, handing a cup to

115

Grammy.

"Thank you, most kind," Grammy said, taking the tea and sipping at it. She offered a cup to Leaf, who said, "No thank you." It smelt funny, a strong strange smell and it probably tasted disgusting, although Grammy seemed to be quite enjoying it.

The woman had a key on a black ribbon in her hand that she placed in a red box above the fire before sitting down in the rocking chair in front of Leaf. Her eyes were very unnerving, beautiful, but bewitching.

"My name is Leaf and this is my grandmother." They turned to see Grammy had fallen asleep.

"Let her rest a while. She must be tired. Leaf, let me introduce you to my daughter," the woman said. Without turning her eyes away from Leaf, she called out to her child.

"Ajatar! Ajatar! Come out dear, we have visitors." A door immediately opened, and in shuffled a huge frumpy girl with an enlarged head and an oversized chin. She had short black badly cut hair and tiny black button eyes, most unlike her mother's mesmerizing green eyes. She was wearing a black dress that looked shorter at the front because of her large belly.

The girl was very pleased to see Leaf and smiled a big almost toothless grin that stretched across her big round face as she unconsciously squeezed the life out of a scruffy white teddy bear whose throat she grasped in her left hand.

"This is Leaf. She has come to play with you, isn't that nice," the woman told her daughter.

"Very nice! Very nice indeed!" Ajatar looked happy but Leaf felt disturbed and confused. "How old are you?" Ajatar asked.

"Ten," Leaf answered, shifting uncomfortably in her chair.

"SO AM I! Wow! We can be like twin sisters. Can't we,

Mummy?"

"Yes dear, twins," her mother agreed. Leaf felt nervous and decided it was time to get out of here and away from these weird people. She wished Grammy would wake up.

"Thank you for your hospitality but my mum will be worried so we must go now," she said, trying to shake Grammy awake, but she did not stir. Leaf was really panicking. Was Grammy dead? Laying the "my mum will be worried" card usually worked quite well on people but it had not worked on this crazy woman.

"No child, you must stay and play with Ajatar," the woman insisted. There was something most definitely wrong with this woman and her very odd offspring.

"I'm sorry, we really must go home now, but thank you though, maybe another time." She was shaking Grammy really hard now and thinking oh please don't be dead. Leaf started to cry.

"NO, NOW!" demanded Ajatar, stamping her foot. Leaf was so afraid that she ran to the wooden front door and opened it.

"NOW!!!" screamed the woman in a deeper voice that was manlier, more demonic than before. Her eyes blazed red and her hair blew up as if someone had turned on a big electric fan. The smouldering fire burst into flames around the cauldron. The front door slammed shut and Leaf, although not wanting to leave Grammy, decided it was definitely the time to run.

She opened the door and sped out into the garden of dead flowers and hid behind a naked tree. The crazy woman stood in the light of the doorway, said something and went back inside. All of a sudden the plants sprung to life and started to grow taller, sprouting leaves and spiky twigs. They instantaneously grew together to form an immense maze. The only direction away from the shack now was through the newly sprouted spiky archway and into the foreboding looking labyrinth.

117

Ajatar appeared in the doorway of the wooden shack.

"NO! DO NOT GO INTO THE MAZE OR YOU WILL BE VERY SORRY," Ajatar shouted. Leaf thought she was just trying to make her stay, so she turned on her phone's torch and ran through the archway into the enchanted maze. The walls were high leafy green bushes and creeping vines. The pathway seemed to be made of sinking mud. She found the faster she ran the quicker she sank. When she moved slowly she could get further without sinking and realised panic was the enemy. She remembered what her mother had always taught her, "Don't be scared, just be careful!" She really wanted her mum right now. Leaf was sobbing, thinking how Grammy might be dead.

Walking fairly slowly through thick mud, trying to stay calm, she waded to the left and then took a right, then another left and right again, but that was a dead end, so she turned round to go back the way she had come but it was not there anymore. Now there was a new leafy corridor to the left. It was a short path and veered sharply to the left and left again ending in a ten metre high hedge.

The plants were still growing and the maze was changing by the second. It all seemed to be growing and changing faster and faster and the vines were becoming wicked. They hit and scratched Leaf and caught at her ankles trying to trip her up.

Leaf was so scared. She started to run, but the more she ran the more she sank into the muddy path.

"HELP! Please someone help me!" Leaf screamed, sinking above her knees.

"Keep still and think positive," said Ajatar's voice from the other side of the hedge.

"PLEASE, AJATAR, HELP ME."

"I can't! I cannot go into the maze."

"How do I get out?" Leaf cried, now up to her waist in the

mud.

"I don't know, but stay still. I am going to ask the fairies who live on the edge of the forest to help. You must stay still."

"Don't leave me! You have to get me out, Ajatar. PLEASE!"

"I cannot go against Mummy's magic but the fairies can help. Stay still, I will be back soon. Think positive and stay very still."

The ground was up to Leaf's chest now. She had her arms up, still holding her phone out of the mud, but she was well and truly stuck. If she stayed still and did not panic she didn't sink any further. So there she stayed not moving. She could not feel her legs anyway. She noticed that when she stopped moving completely and relaxed the plants stopped growing. She waited. Nothing was happening.

She was starting to feel the mud harden, compressing her ribs, when she noticed a small blue light dancing in front of her face. The light dimmed and Leaf saw it was a fairy boy.

"Hello. My name is Isetal of the Boreal Forest Fairy Clan. We heard you were in black magic trouble and came to help."

All of a sudden, six other coloured lights appeared around her. The lights dimmed and they were boys and girls, each dressed in a different colour.

"Can you get me out of here?" Leaf asked, hopefully.

"Yes, but you need to fall asleep. The maze feeds off your energy. The more you fight it, the more you lose," said a fairy girl, wearing yellow.

"I can't just fall asleep right now!" Leaf protested.

"That is where we come in. We can sprinkle you with baby blue fairy dust and you will fall asleep. When the maze is dead from lack of energy, we will sprinkle you with yellow fairy dust, wake you up and quickly get you out," a fairy boy in green told her.

119

"Okay, anything is better than being like a stick stuck in the mud!" Leaf exclaimed.

The fairies each took a handful of blue fairy dust from a tiny bottle and flew around Leaf showering her in an azure mist which made Leaf feel all light and dreamy, and she fell asleep. The maze drew back, slithering plants disappeared into the ground or withered and died, disintegrating into grey dust on the white snow.

When the maze was completely gone, the fairies sprinkled a bright yellow dust over Leaf. She fluttered her eyelashes, opened her eyes and yawned.

"Wow! That was the best sleep ever!" declared Leaf. "How long was I out for?" She was amazed and relieved when she looked around to see that the maze had disappeared, assuming she must have slept for hours.

"About three minutes," the red fairy told her. Ajatar approached.

"Hiya Leaf, I'm glad you are okay," Ajatar told her humbly, fidgeting with her dirty teddy's ears.

"What has your mother done to my grandmother?" Leaf yelled at her.

"It is okay, she is just sleeping," Ajatar assured her.

"Here, use some of this yellow dust to wake her," said a fairy in purple, coming forward and giving Leaf a handful of yellow dust.

"I cannot thank you all enough for your help. Thank you so much. Grammy and I need to go home but to do that I must find a cupboard door with a lock," Leaf said, addressing the fairies who did not think it strange that someone should be asking for a cupboard as a way home. They had met all sorts of magic folk, some who travelled by cupboard all the time.

"There is a cupboard in our kitchen in the shack, but I would have to distract Mummy for you to get in safely," Ajatar offered as a way of apology. Leaf gave her a begrudged nod.

"Before you go we would like to ask a favour of you, Leaf. Please come over there with us so we can talk more privately," interrupted Isetal. He and the green fairy boy flew over to a dead tree on the other side of the garden so that they could talk without being overheard by Ajatar. Leaf walked over to join them curious and eager to help in any way she could.

"We need you to take a jar that is in their cupboard and throw it out the window before you leave. Can you do that? It is very important to us that you do it," Isetal insisted.

"You want me to steal it?" Leaf did not like the sound of this.

"It was stolen from us. It is the light of the forest and truly it belongs to no one and everyone. Most the fairies have died since the light has gone. We are the children of the last four remaining fairy families. Please Leaf, you must help us, my mother is dying from the lack of light and the cold," pleaded the green fairy.

"What will stop Maronna from stealing the light again?"

"Once we have the light back we can cast a spell so that the light will stay forever. Our magic is stronger than hers because we work with the forces of good," Isetal replied.

"How will I know it is the right jar?" Leaf inquired.

"Oh you will know," laughed Isetal.

"COME ON!" called Ajatar to Leaf.

"We will be waiting outside the window," Isetal whispered in Leaf's ear. They flew beside Leaf as she walked back to Ajatar and the other fairies.

"Leaf, we wanted to give you this," said a pink fairy girl. Two fairy boys came forward with a bottle as big as themselves, but to Leaf it was only as big as her little finger. The bottle seemed to have appeared from nowhere, unless the fairies had bottles

121

stashed in trees. It was full of green fairy dust and had a leather cord attached so that Leaf could hang it around her neck as a necklace.

"It is green magic dust that brings healing, money, and good luck in bad events. You say the words written for you on this paper. Learn them and then burn the paper. Use the dust responsibly, Leaf, because it is a fairy law that we can only ever give you one bottle."

"Thank you very much for everything!" Leaf was very happy with her gift and hung it around her neck. It hung below her silver pentagram necklace and her best friend necklace that Sarah had given her for her birthday. She put the paper in her pocket for now.

Ajatar went into the shack leaving the door slightly open for Leaf to get in. When her mother was not looking, she took the key on the black ribbon from the box and placed it on the table so that Leaf could open the cupboard.

"Mummy, can you help me get some books down from the top shelf in the bedroom? I want to practice my spells of flight, and also find out how to grow watermelons in the snow," Ajatar called from her bedroom as a distraction.

"I need you to help me carry the old woman out and bury her in the maze mud," Maronna yelled back, following her daughter's screechy voice into the bedroom.

"I will, but help me get the books down first."

Leaf crept through the front door, threw the handful of yellow dust over Grammy and shook her awake. Grammy opened her eyes and smiled. Leaf put her finger to her lips and beckoned for Grammy to follow her quietly.

Leaf led a half dazed Grammy to the tall blue cupboard in the kitchen area. Ignoring the key on the table, she put her magic

Key in the lock saying, "Please open this cupboard right now!" Quietly she pulled open the door of the tall cupboard. The lower part was full of bound twig brooms. On the shelf above there were many different shaped jars. There was a light coming from behind the glass containers.

Leaf quietly moved the front ones aside and was instantly blinded for a second by the bright light coming from a jar at the back. Leaf took the jar and threw it out the window. Grammy started to protest and began a lecture on not changing the past but Leaf put her finger to her lips again, panic showing in her eyes. Grammy fell quiet and looked towards the bedroom door. Just as Leaf closed the cupboard and put the Key back in the lock there was an explosion of light outside the window. Everything sprang to life. Flowers bloomed as the snow melted away, and birds sang in the leafy trees. Leaf smiled, knowing she had saved the forest and the fairies. Grammy just stood with her mouth open trying to work out what was going on. They heard an enraged scream from the bedroom. Leaf quickly said her address out loud.

"Today at four thirty-five, my bedroom, 6 Springfield Road, Hampstead, North London, England." She turned the Key, opened the door, and holding hands they hurried home.

"What a nice woman. So hospitable! I wonder what she uses in her tea. It was very calming. I think I nodded off to sleep," Grammy declared, none the wiser. Leaf did not say a word. She definitely had not planned that trip well, and if Grammy knew the full story she would surely be cross with Leaf for putting them in such danger and changing the past.
Yet Leaf was glad they had gone.

Grammy crept down the stairs, passed the kitchen where Mum was practising her Tina Turner moves with the mop, and silent as a ninja she left by the front door.

THE WHITEASH KEY

Leaf looked again in the library for that fairytale book which said the Boreal Fairies were made extinct but it was no longer there. Instead she came across a book about two girls from Cottingley in West Yorkshire who took photographs of fairies at the bottom of their garden. Leaf knew she had changed history. Grammy might not have approved but Leaf felt very proud.

Chapter Nine

EVIL LIES BEHIND HAPPY FACES

All the town's children were very excited. There was a circus coming to Hampstead and it was going to be set up on the heath for two weeks. Mum said they could go on the opening night. She had already booked tickets on-line. Leaf could not wait.

On Saturday night they bought popcorn and stood in the queue for the evening's performance in the big top. There was lots of chatter as people parked themselves on wooden benches that curved in two circles around the performance ring. It was a great circus with lots of clowns, elephants, a dancing bear, lions, chimpanzees, tight-rope walkers, acrobats, bare-back horse riders and so much more.

After the show, Leaf went to the tent of mirrors while mum went in search of a toilet. The mirrors made Leaf look fat, then thin, and then very ugly. At the end there was a small labyrinth of looking-glasses to walk through to find the way out.

As Leaf was walking through the quiet half-lit labyrinth she heard the haunting sound of girl's voice singing in Polish. It was eerie and she felt frightened. She saw a young woman's face in a mirror. Leaf turned around but no one was there. The face appeared again and a whole body this time. She was reflected in all the mirrors and when Leaf turned the corner the reflections bounced off the cleverly placed mirrors, making hundreds of reflections of the girl seeming to get further and further away as they infinitely spread out in every direction. Leaf did not have a reflection.

"Help them. You must warn them. Beware the clowns," said the dark haired girl in the mirrors. Then she disappeared. Leaf could now see infinite versions of herself.

She quickly found the way out into the noise of the people and there was Mum waiting for her. Leaf told her mum what she had seen but Mum dismissed it as a visual trick cleverly set up by the circus. Leaf could not sleep that night. She was haunted by the face of the girl. She tossed and turned in bed for hours.

Sunday morning, she was brushing her teeth when she saw the girl again in the bathroom mirror.

"You must warn them," said the face. Leaf was so scared that she knocked over the glass for the toothbrushes and it smashed in the sink.

"Warn who? About what?"

"Beware the clowns," said the girl's voice in the room behind Leaf. Then she was gone.

Leaf decided she better do something about this. So after carefully cleaning up the broken glass, wrapping it in lots of toilet paper and placing it in the bathroom bin, she stuck her magic Key in the bathroom lock. She was still in possession of the Key since the trip to Finland. Grammy had been so dazed by the whole experience that she had forgotten to ask Leaf for the Key back. Leaf had been waiting until the next time she saw Grammy to return it, but now she needed to use the Key in an emergency. And wasn't it hers after all!

"The circus on Hampstead Heath, Now, Today."

She opened the door, tripped, fell and rolled out of a tent into the bustle of circus life.

A teenage boy with dark hair and a freckled face was walking about with a yellow bucket feeding the animals. He

126

tipped his hat at Leaf in a greeting.

"Practising to be a clown when you grow up?" he teased. Smiling, he went off to feed the lamas. Leaf, feeling embarrassed, picked herself up and hurried away. She walked around the tents, passed the strong man and the very tall man sitting on wooden crates playing chess, passed the fortune teller sitting on the steps of her brightly painted gypsy wagon brushing her long black hair. The beautiful gypsy woman smiled at Leaf and Leaf smiled back.

Behind the trucks and caravans Leaf saw three clowns acting suspiciously. There was a tall thin one, an extremely round one and a dwarf. They were hurriedly walking towards a caravan, whispering to each other. Leaf followed them. They went inside the caravan and shut the door. Leaf crawled into the space below the parked caravan. She stayed hidden behind two spare tires and a bucket of water. From under the caravan she could hear their voices quite clearly.

"It is all arranged for eight-thirty tonight. I will have the trucks parked out the back by the big top. They will be ready with the doors unlocked and the keys in the ignitions. Dodo, you just have to walk the elephants out at the end of act two like you always do, except this time you march Nelly and Smelly out of the big top into the back of truck number one and drive them to the meeting point. Don't wait! Toto will be five minutes behind you with the lions in truck number two. I will wait until we get the chimps back after act five and bring them in the third truck but I will not be there for about forty-five minutes. I need time to set the fire," Leaf heard the first voice say.

"What about the bear? Ringo offered us £12,000 for the bear!" asked another of the clowns.

"After the children have had their photos taken with Big

Teddy, Jerry will be bringing him along in his van," replied the first voice. Leaf was trying not to sneeze but it was very dusty under the caravan. She decided she had heard enough, rolled out from under the vehicle and ran a safe distance to sneeze without being heard.

Leaf searched around the circus grounds, looking in through the windows of mobile homes. Eventually she found a bathroom door in an unoccupied camper and put her Key in the lock and returned to her own bathroom earlier that morning.

Lying on her bed in the late afternoon she was thinking that she had to get back to the circus and tell someone. She realized that she had already used the Key twice that day. She still had to return to the circus and get home again that evening. She decided she would walk back to the circus and leave the last turn of the Key for getting home.

It was not far to walk to the heath, it took about ten minutes, but Leaf ran it in six. She had told her mum that old Mrs. Archibald, who lived down the street, had asked Leaf to walk her dog. Mrs. Archibald's dog was very old so it would have taken at least half an hour to walk it around the block.

When Leaf reached the circus, she looked for the fortune teller. She saw the brightly painted wagon with the sign outside that read Tarot and Fortune Telling £25. Leaf knocked on the little door. It was opened by the woman Leaf had seen brushing her hair. She was wearing a red head-scarf, large hooped gold earrings, a white off-the-shoulder top and a full length dark green skirt.

"Come in, dear, and let me tell you how I can help you." The woman showed her into the wagon. There were three chairs, a small wooden table with a crystal ball on it and tarot cards laid out in rows.

"I don't have any money," Leaf admitted.

"You look troubled, dear. Sit. Sit. Give me your hand." The woman took Leaf's left hand, turned it palm up and explained the lines to Leaf.

"The lower part of your hand from your wrist to where your thumb starts is your animal region and it affects your emotions. I see you are shy, but strong in spirit and your love is pure. The middle of your palm to the start of your little finger is your intelligence and how it affects you. I see you are a clever girl, probably good at Maths and you will learn many languages."

"The fingers tell us how moral and good you are. You are a very moralistic person and one day will teach these morals to many people. You are destined to have many teachers. So you can pass on all your knowledge you must listen and learn."

"The bottom of your wedding ring finger, here above the mount of the sun, tells us about the material world around you and if you are materialistic. It tells me not especially, strange considering you are a Virgo." Leaf was impressed that she knew all that about her just from a quick look at her hand.

"The middle of your ring finger shows your practical world, how the world around you works and if you are practical. It seems you have a very practical mind that will aid you to find a solution to many problems. The top of this same finger says how the world affects you mentally. The top of your thumb tells me how strong willed you are and if you are brave. You are very brave and a great adventurer. The rest of the thumb tells me if you are logical."

"You, my girl, are a problem solver." Leaf smiled, hoping she could solve her current problem.

"The bottom line of your thumb tells me about your family. I see it was broken a few years ago, split in two, but both lines are strong and life with your mother is a happy one. Your father loves you, even though he may sometimes seem cold. He cannot help it. He comes from a cold country."

"This big line around the thumb is your life line and your life is long, but you must be careful not to change this as there will be grave danger along the way, and plenty of joy too."

"This long line below the ring of Venus is your heart line. You will love and be loved by many but you will meet the man you will marry when you are very young. You will have other relationships before you marry and you will not marry him for many years, yet, when you do, the marriage will be forever. This line through the middle is your head line." The fortune teller's words drifted off as she considered what she saw. She traced all the lines again with her finger.

"You have a very adventurous destiny. You are the keeper of an important secret. You shall lead a very eventful life and help many people. Right now you are in trouble. Let me look at your cards." The woman picked up all the cards and placed them in two piles.

"Pick a pile," she instructed Leaf.

"Left," Leaf replied. The gypsy picked up the left pile and laid the cards facing upright.

"You are on a dangerous quest and many people will be hurt if you do not succeed. Evil lies hidden behind happy faces. Y o u have come to tell me something child?"

Just then Leaf noticed a photo stuck on the fridge at the back of the wagon. It was of the fortune-teller and another girl, the ghost face from the mirror.

"Who is that girl with you in the photo?" Leaf asked her. The woman looked at the photo and sighed.

"That is a sad story. She was a Polish tight-rope walker but

130

she fell to her death last year because someone forgot to check the net was secured. I should not say, but it was one of the clowns. He is drunk most the time and it was his job to check. They could not prove it but the circus is just waiting for a justifiable reason to fire him. She and I were very good friends for five years. I miss her very much," she said sadly in her Romanian accent.

"I know this will sound bonkers but I have seen your friend in mirrors and she told me that I have to warn you about the clowns," Leaf said and proceeded to tell her what she had overheard.

"Okay, say I believe you, we would still have to catch them in the act to prove it," the fortune teller stated. Leaf shrugged not knowing what more she was supposed to do.

"Come with me," the gypsy woman instructed. Leaf followed her outside and through the tents to a big silver caravan. She told Leaf to wait outside and she went in and shut the door. Ten minutes later she came out with the ring master.

"Like I said, I saw it in the ball and I saw a child overhearing their plan. Then I saw the same child walking around the grounds, so I brought her to you. Tell him what you heard."

"One clown is going to take the elephants after the second act and put them in the first of three trucks parked behind the big top. They will drive the lions away in the second truck and the chimps in the third. Jerry will make a last minute get away with the bear in a van and they will all go to a meeting point after one clown sets fire to the big top to cause a distraction," Leaf told the ringmaster.

"Well thank you for coming to tell me. You may have saved a lot of lives young lady!" He shook her hand.

"I will inform the police and the fire service and ask them to stand by out of sight. You should go home now, seems it is not

131

safe here tonight," the ringmaster told her. Leaf thought how late she must be. Her mum might go down to Mrs. Archibald's house looking for her and find out she was lying about walking the dog. Leaf asked if she could use the ringmaster's bathroom in his trailer. He showed her where it was and went back outside. Leaf put her Key in the lock of the bathroom door.

"Outside Mrs. Archibald's house, Springfield Road, at seven-thirty this evening."

She stepped out of Mrs. Archibald's front door. Just in time, as Mum was on her way down to Mrs. Archibald's house.

"Hi Mum." Leaf opened her arms wide and ran up the street. Mum too started running towards Leaf with her arms open. They ran into each other's embrace like in a scene from a film.

"Hi Pinky."

"Hi Pooky."

"Shall we make sushi for dinner?" Mum asked, walking Leaf home. Leaf grinned because sushi was her favourite food in the whole world.

The next day after school, Leaf was sitting at the table drawing a portrait of her mum. Leaf loved to draw and weekends with her mum were often spent drawing and painting together. Mum had inherited a lot of talent from Grammy. For a living, Mum illustrated books for children and she had taught Leaf lots of techniques which had helped her improve quickly despite her young age. Leaf was exceptionally talented.

Mum asked if Leaf had heard what had happened the night before at the circus. She told her it was in the newspaper on the kitchen counter if she wanted to read about it. Mum said she needed a bathroom break anyway and had a pile of ironing to do so they would have to finish the drawing after Leaf had done her homework. Leaf put down her pencil and picked up the paper from the counter.

CLOWNS CAUGHT IN THE ACT

At eight-thirty last night, during the evening performance, the four clowns: Dodo, Toto, Jerry and Dingo of THE BIG TOP CIRCUS pitched up on Hampstead Heath for the next two weeks, were arrested after being caught red-handed trying to steal the circus animals which they had arranged to sell to another circus. Dingo has also been accused of causing an accident last year which led to the

death of a Polish tight-rope walker, Paula Smitz. Dingo was caught attempting to set fire to the big top last night. He was holding the canister of petrol and a lighter when he was apprehended by the police. The clowns, if convicted, are looking at sentences of eight-fifteen years for theft of livestock, five years for intent to commit arson and possibly life sentences for the intended manslaughter of 120 people inside the big top tent. It is believed that the culprit clowns were overheard in their plotting by the circus fortune-teller and an unnamed witness.

Leaf smiled. She was so glad that her name had not been mentioned. Her mum would have gone mad. Grammy would have killed her if she had known she had used the Key alone. After pouring out a bowl of cereal Leaf went upstairs to do her homework.

"Leaf, where has the glass for the toothbrushes gone?" Mum

inquired from the bathroom.

"I'm really sorry, I broke it." Leaf called back.

"Did you wrap it up so it doesn't cut anyone?"

"Yes, Mum."

"I love you, Pinky!"

"I love you too, Pooky!"

Chapter Ten

THE CAVES OF NERJA AND
NEANDERTHAL FRIENDS

Over the weekend Leaf had to complete a project for school on Neanderthals, ordered to be a six page essay plus drawn diagrams. She did not have internet at home because her mum could not afford it, so she asked if she could go over to Grammy's. Grammy had the internet and had taken up internet surfing as a new hobby. She said it was dryer than sea surfing. Adventurous as she was, Grammy was not fond of water.

When Leaf called her Grandmother at ten-thirty on Saturday morning, Grammy said she would come and pick Leaf up in half an hour. Grammy had told Leaf to ask her mum if she could spend the whole weekend. Mum said she could. Leaf packed her toothbrush, clean underwear, a pink T-shirt and her black hoodie.

Grammy seemed extra happy as they drove back to her house. She was wearing a big straw hat, dark glasses and a mischievous grin. Her T-shirt read:

MOST OF TODAY'S WORRIES ARE LIKE PUDDLES TOMORROW THEY WILL HAVE EVAPORATED

They sang along to the song by America, A Horse with No Name, playing in Sally's compact disc player. Leaf's taste in music had been deeply influenced by the two main women in her life, Grammy and Mum.

135

THE WHITEASH KEY

Leaf stopped singing because Grammy looked ready to burst with joy her smile was so big.

"What are you planning Grammy?" Leaf prodded her grandmother. Grammy laughed and replied.

"Well, I have a much better plan than being on the internet all weekend. Last year my friend Betty from my yoga class went to the Costa del Sol to a lovely town on the coast of Malaga called Nerja. She was telling me all about these amazing caves they have there where they found pre-historic drawings, possibly the oldest ever discovered, and charcoal that was 42,000 years old. You can read the historical facts and see other remains inside the caves. Honestly, I'm just so fed up of this rain and I have been painting in the attic so much recently, breathing in lots of white spirit, so fresh air and sunshine would be good for me," Grammy insisted.

All the women in Leaf's family were artistic. Mum had taught Leaf to draw faces properly at the early age of seven. She had lots of artistic training with Grammy in the attic, and Leaf possessed her own natural talent. She had spent an hour everyday for the last three years practising by drawing and painting her friends and family. Mum liked to draw portraits, paint murals in acrylic, landscapes in oil, along with the illustrations she made for children's books.

Grammy liked to make big colourful abstract paintings and huge wacky sculptures which she would sell or destroy, saying she had no space to keep them. They decorated all the walls and shelves around her house. A huge cupboard in the cellar and half the attic stored Grammy's paintings and creations, not forgetting the four metal sculptures in the garden that twirled in the wind.

Leaf did not have her own style yet. She had been taught to

draw in so many different ways that she liked to experiment and none of her drawings looked like they belonged in a collection yet.

Grammy turned off the engine of her little Union-Jack painted Mini Cooper. Sally's stereo, which was blaring I LOVE ROCK 'N' ROLL by Joan Jet, went quiet.

"Well, what do you think, Leaf, to a weekend in sunny Spain? We'll have to go by Key of course, which you still have by the way. Got it on you I hope? And I hope you haven't been using it without me. What do you say, shall we go? Say Yay!"

"I say YAY!" Leaf laughed and they went quickly into the house to pack towels and suntan lotion.

"Right then," said Grammy, after she had taken a last pee, washed her hands, re-applied her factor 50 lip protector, packed apples, juice and slices of homemade cake wrapped in foil. She printed off a map of Nerja and its bus timetables from the internet which she placed in her green recycled shopping bag, now doubled as a beach bag.

"Nerja Bus Station, Malaga, Spain, now, today," Grammy said and turned the Key three times in the lock of her front door.

As Grammy opened the door, Leaf was almost knocked back by the light and the heat as they came out through the door of a bar and stepped onto the hot pavement by the side of the bus lay-by. That is all the station consisted of, just two lay-bys on either side of a busy road, and on the right a green ticket office box next to a sweet kiosk.

"Let's cross over and buy tickets for the bus to the caves." Grammy walked to the zebra crossing and Leaf followed. The cars did not stop to let them cross so they had to wait for the traffic to pass. Grammy strutted across the road in her big sunhat. Leaf ran in case any cars came, but Grammy walked with an air of challenge as if no one in their right mind would dare to run her down. Safely across the road, they queued in the heat behind three people.

Grammy could have transported them by Key directly to the caves but had thought this would be a nice way to see some of the town. She liked bus rides, especially in other countries.

"NERHAR CUEVAS, CAVES. DOS PERSONAS," Grammy shouted through the little slit in the glass when it was her turn.

"Las Cuevas de Nerja, muy bien. Dos ochenta por favor. TWO EITEE PLEEESE," shouted the man behind the glass. Grammy paid and gave Leaf the tickets for safe keeping as Grammy had a habit of losing things.

They took off their coats and Grammy put them in her big bag. Wearing big floppy hats and dark sunglasses, Grammy in flip-flops and a summer dress, and Leaf in jeans, the two of them sat happily down on a tiled bench to wait.

Grammy said that according to her timetable there should be a bus along in three minutes. It was November but it was still hot at midday. Grammy fanned herself with the timetable. They waited ten minutes.

The bus driver was friendly and said, "No problema! I tell you get off! Nut far! Sit ear," he said, indicating the first two empty seats at the front of the bus.

It was a quick trip through the top of the town, then along a beautiful main coastal road edged on the right with the cobalt blue of the Mediterranean Sea and dark pink bougainvillea, patches of green campo (farmland) and old stone aqueduct bridges. On the left, great green and indigo mountains reached high into the deep blue and fluffy white sky.

"LAS CUEVAS DE NERJA!" shouted the bus driver, as he pulled to a halt at a bus stop by a busy round-a-bout. No sign of any caves. The driver turned to Grammy and Leaf and gave them directions, pointing out the window to the left.

"You go, abajo de la puente, under bridge, go road up, despues parking, go in, caves there," he explained to them with plenty of hand movements.

"Gracias," Grammy replied, looking a bit confused and flustered as she hauled her bag off the bus. Leaf took the bag from her to carry it for a while.

"AHI! Over there! UP! UP! SUBE! SUBE!" the driver shouted out his window, indicating with his hand across the road going up under the bridge. They nervously ran across the road with cars whizzing left and right.

Following the pavement under a bridge, Grammy and Leaf began an assent up a hot and demanding road to a car park, Grammy complaining about her knees.

To the left of the car park there were decorative gardens on different levels and lots of trees. Views of cultivated land and sea stretched in the south, protected by woodland and mountains to the north.

They followed other people through the car park and came to a restaurant, a souvenir shop, the ticket office, public toilets, and the entrance to the stairs going down into the caves. They bought tickets and stood in a line at the doorway.

While they were waiting, Grammy read out information from the English versioned leaflet she had been given when purchasing the tickets.

"According to this we are no longer in Nerja but in the next town of Maro which falls under Nerja municipality. It says here that five local Nerja boys discovered these caves in 1959 when they went down a well looking for bats. They found a great empty cavern and inside were ceramics and skeletons. They got so frightened that they ran out and went to tell their friends, family and teachers. A doctor and a photographer went down to take photographs of what the boys had found, which began the international fame of the Nerja caves."

"Photographers and journalists came from around the world and took pictures of the five boys and their friend Ayo in the caves. Even Mussolini and Franco came to view what only one year later would be declared an Artistic Historical Monument and part of the Spanish Historical Patrimony."

"They built easier access into the caves and opened them to the public, although not all of the caves are open. Some galleries and caverns have still not been investigated or are still under investigation."

"We can see the Ghost Gallery - ooooh that sounds a bit scary. The Gallery of Bethlehem were the rocks look like the holy family, the Gallery of the Cascades, Gallery of the Cataclysm, and the Gallery of Torca. Right then, are you ready?" She squeezed Leaf's hand in excited anticipation. They gave the man at the entrance their tickets and went down the steps into the deep dark bowels of the earth. Leaf felt like she was walking into a haunted house at a funfair. She held tight to Grammy's hand as they descended and followed narrow twisting paths into a gigantic cavern trying not to step on the heels of the family in front of them. There was an echoing sound of water dripping slowly.

"WOW!" Leaf was spellbound by the enormity and beauty of the cave interior. She felt very small compared to the space around her which resembled something from a fairy-type world.

The ceiling, decorated with dangerous looking stalactites,

loomed high above. They followed walkways and bridges and steps through the gigantic cave, featuring intriguing secret nooks and crannies everywhere formed by the stalagmites that towered up all around them. It was truly magical and lit most atmospherically. Leaf and Grammy were thrilled by the caves, and Leaf got lots of information written down for her school project.

In one gallery they saw cave drawings of seals discovered in 2012. These are the first artistic representations known to humanity of the oldest drawings on the planet dating back forty-two thousand years.

It was almost two in the afternoon and the caves were closing for the siesta period, open again at four. Leaf and Grammy followed a line of other people to the exit and out into the light.

"Let's go to the beach!" Grammy cried, raising her arms to the blue sky and breathing in the warm air.

They twirled and danced across the car park and began their descent down the hill to the bridge by the round-a-bout.

There was an English looking woman standing by the bus stop. Grammy asked her for directions. She was in fact from Belgium but spoke perfect English and she told them how to get down to Maro beach as that was the closest.

Passing through the charming little village of Maro, they stopped at an open doorway where an old woman was selling tomatoes, avocados, and oranges. Grammy bought four of everything and put it in her big flowery beach bag. Then Grammy nipped into a bar and bought a long loaf of bread called a barra, like a French baguette but fatter, filled with Jamon Serrano.

"Jamon Serrano is a thinly sliced cured Spanish ham," Grammy explained to Leaf.

"But, Turtle, you are Jewish!" Leaf faked a look of shock.

"Not when it comes to delicacies like these, Wormy," Grammy replied, tickling Leaf for being so cheeky. Wormy wriggled and falsely laughed in an uncontrolled manner when she really felt like screaming, but she managed to break away. Grammy promised not to tickle her anymore, placed an arm around her shoulders and off they went down towards the sea, across rural land and along wild country lanes.

Nearer the beach in such a lane, hippies had built makeshift housing or were squatting in sweet little country ruins. Grammy said it reminded her of her days on a Greek Island in the Sixties. They smiled and said "Hola." (In Spanish the letter H is not pronounced.)

They found a small cove edged with boulders and large rocks with a backdrop of cliffs and greenery. They had it all to themselves. Grammy was sure they must have taken a wrong turn and that this was not the main Maro beach but the privacy was perfect in this little cove. So they stripped off their clothes and splashed about in their underwear. Grammy's tiger stripped knickers and matching bra were outrageous for her age. Leaf was thinking hallelujah it is not a thong.

Leaf went swimming. Grammy stayed where she could still keep her feet on the sand. The day was hot but the clear water was freezing. They sat on a warm rock and ate a picnic and drank warm bottles of lemonade through straws that Grammy had also got at the bar. Grammy tore the long roll in two. Leaf thought the Jamon Serrano was delicious.

"Grammy, I need more to write about for my project. Don't

142

you think it would be cool to actually see what this place was like 42,000 years ago?" Leaf suggested in her most convincing voice.

"Think about it, Leaf, how would you find a lock to get back? Even doors were not invented that long ago."

"Couldn't we use a mobile lock on a door made out of reeds?" Leaf replied.

"I do happen to have a spare padlock in my bag. If we use the padlock to get there we can use it to get back too. Come on then, we have some reed weaving to do. I don't want to stay for long, Leaf, it could be very dangerous and we must not get close to the Neanderthals. Plus, it is quite irresponsible for us to let them see us as we are people from the future. They could be violent people. I don't know, Leaf. We have already used the Key once, now this would be twice, so to get out of there we would have to go straight home. I was just starting to enjoy myself in this glorious sun." Grammy did not sound up for it now.

"We have all weekend! We could use the third turn to come back here to have more time in the sun. We can stay here the night in a hotel and then when twelve hours have passed or later if we want, we can use the Key to go home. How does that sound?" Leaf persisted. Grammy mulled it over in her mind. It was a lot of hours to use up on a Jump but they had Jumped to Spain in present time so it wasn't so bad. She was desperate for a short holiday and she decided it was worth it.

"Okay then."

They packed up their stuff, got dressed and went back up the dirt track to where Grammy had seen reeds, canes and long grasses growing. Leaf and Grammy picked lots and set about making a door frame from long branches and weaving reeds between them, covering holes with long grasses. Grammy told

143

her the door didn't have to be perfect, just as long as it could function as a door. They stood their shabby creation between two trees. Grammy found a small length of chain in her bag, threaded it through a hole and hung the padlock on the makeshift door, fastening the two sides of dangling chain together. Grammy put the Key in the lock.

Leaf wrote down in her Quikid World notebook the time and date they were leaving.

"Right here on this beach, in the afternoon, 42,000 years ago," Grammy said, turning the Key three times to the left. She pulled the door towards her and held it open for Leaf who, taking Grammy's hand, went through to the other side.

Leaf, who had been looking at her phone to double check the time, noticed her phone lost reception. Not much had changed really but the sky was overcast and the weather had turned cold. Grammy stepped through behind Leaf, removed the padlock, and pulled the door closed.

"Always remember to shut the door behind you, otherwise you are leaving an open wormhole that anyone could fall into," Grammy told her, trying to make sure the door was properly shut. There was a lot more foliage and no houses in sight. They heard a rustle in the bushes and saw a big pair of eyes staring at them through the leaves. Leaf got closer. A girl about her age, dressed in animal skins, flew out of the bush with fright. Grammy caught her by the arm.

"It is okay! We will not hurt you," Grammy told the girl in her most soothing and reassuring voice. The girl just stared at her bewildered. She kept looking at their clothes and the top of their heads. Leaf noticed the size of the girl's forehead. It was really big compared to that of anyone else Leaf had ever seen. She was smaller than Leaf in height but much bigger in bulk and bone structure. Her skin was light brown and her hair blazing red. Not how Leaf had expected cave people to look. She had thought they would be dark and hairy and look more like apes. Apart from her long red hair and thick red eyebrows, she wasn't hairy at all.

The girl's head was large in comparison to people of the last few millenniums, extended more at the back. Her nose was high up and flat on her face, and she had really big eyes. Leaf thought her long red hair was beautiful, as it caught the sun it looked like fire.

Grammy gave the girl a piece of her homemade sponge cake. The girl grabbed it and shoved it in her mouth. She seemed pleased and very hungry. The girl pointed back down to the beach. With crumbs flying she said, "Tunna aba ply, Tunna tembarr guna. Tunna aba ply."

She pulled on Grammy's hand as if she wanted them to come with her.

"Urr ply."

"I think she wants us to go to the beach with her," Leaf said to Grammy.

"Ply?" Grammy asked her if that meant beach by pointing towards the beach.

"Urr ply." The girl nodded and beckoned them to follow. "Urr!"

"Urr must mean come," Leaf said, writing down urr for come and ply for beach in her Quikid World notebook. They followed the red haired girl to the beach. It was so much colder than before. Grammy got their coats out of her bag and they put them on. The girl stared at them and touched their coats with wonder. Both their jackets had fur line hoods which the girl ignored. It was the puffy synthetic material that the girl was in awe of.

The rocks on the beach were few but bigger than before. The

145

beach was much longer now, stretches of sand covered with seals.

"Tunna, tembarr guna. Inkana um!" she said, pointing towards a boy with long dark hair, skin darker than her own, a big forehead and extended skull. He was driving a spear into one of the seals. Leaf cried out horrified that he was murdering a seal and the boy looked up. He raised his bloody spear and started running towards them, screaming.

"NI! BANA! NI!" The girl jumped in front, protecting them, and the boy stopped.

"MENA! Dana inkana. Aba como. Aba cana," the boy shouted at her. She waved her hands about in protest.

"Ni bana! Ni bana! Show inkana," insisted the girl and gave him what was left of her cake. The boy lowered the spear and ate the cake. Grammy got out some more for them.

"Don't say anything about the seal, Leaf. It is how they survive. They need to eat," whispered Grammy in warning. Leaf tried not to look at the bloody seal.

The red haired girl placed her right hand on Leaf's forehead and then she banged on her chest with her left hand saying "Onga" over and over. Leaf realized her name must be Onga. Leaf put her left hand on the girl's forehead. The girl took Leaf's left hand down and replaced it with the right hand and showed Leaf to bang her chest with the left hand.

"Leaf" Leaf said, loud and proud, introducing herself.

"Lif'" they repeated. The girl placed her right hand on the boy's forehead and banged on his chest with her left hand, "Tunna"

"AHHH, Tunna. Right, Tunna is his name," said Grammy, pleased at having understood.

"And my name is Grammy," Grammy said, thumping herself on the chest.

146

"AndmynameisGrrammmy," the children repeated.

"No! No! Grammy."

"Nonogrammy."

"Grammy!"

"Grammy!" they repeated, nodding.

"Tunna, tembarr guna aba um," Onga demonstrated with lots of hand actions.

"Guna," she repeated, pointing at the seals. Leaf wrote it down. The girl watched her intently and then grabbed the pencil, looked at the paper and the writing. She drew a line, looked at the pencil and gave it back.

"Um," Onga said, pretending to eat. Leaf realised that Um meant eat and Guna meant seal. She wrote it down and again the girl watched close up as the lead in the pencil formed the words on the page.

"Te," Tunna showed them his spear. He was more interested in showing them all his prize possessions and had not taken any notice of Leaf's word forming trick with a magic stick on weird white stuff.

"Cor Te," and he showed them a short homemade knife he carried on a leather band around his waist.

"Inkana," Onga said several times, pointing to all of them. "I think Inkana means people," Grammy declared, delighted. Onga pulled on Leaf's arm and beckoned.

"Urr, urr aba como, urr inkana." Onga repeated three times. "I think she wants us to go with her to meet her people," Leaf informed Grammy by looking at the new words in her notebook.

"Oh why not be sociable," Grammy said smiling, obviously taken with these two and it was a bit late now, they had been seen. So they followed Onga, Tunna and the bloody seal back up the track. Their homemade door had disappeared. There was just an animal skin over a hollow tree. There were no hippies and no ruins, just green pastures and hills and huge rocks.

They trekked a long way, climbed a green hill up to the area where the restaurant, souvenir shop and ticket office had been that morning. Now it was levels of strange looking leafy vegetables and rocky cliff. Half way up Grammy considered the dangers that awaited them and the adults they would encounter. She was about to take Leaf and turn back when Tunna and Onga, followed by Leaf, climbed into a hole hidden between the rocks.

"Urr" Onga's head popped back out and she beckoned to Grammy. So Grammy followed down into the hole. There were steps made from dry mud and they climbed down into the central caverns. There was another world going on down there. About thirty Neanderthal families were living inside the caves but they all looked busy packing up. The few that noticed them stopped and stared, completely bewildered by their presence.

"ONGA!" A deep, angry man's voice shouted. Everyone looked up and stared at them.

"Pun. Onga pun, Tunna pun. Tunna bana Onga," Onga was trying to explain that the angry man was her father. Tunna was her brother.

Her father was not any taller than Grammy but he was huge in body, looked immensely strong and very scary.

"ONGA! Onga aba coma hanga dana inkana?" her father shouted at her for bringing strangers into their home. In curiosity he began touching their clothes and pulling at their bags. They smiled politely and moved away from him.

"Ni show inkana aba ply. Opo guna!" Onga told her father, snatching the seal from her brother and dumping the bloody seal into Leaf's arms, implying to her father that Leaf had helped them catch it. Leaf wanted to scream and throw it away from her but paranoia told her that if she did, this man might eat her.

148

"Como inkana aba. Tod urr! Caringa aba. Guna aba! Inkana aba." Their father was very cross and told them to get to work packing up. He snatched the seal and stomped off. Tunna followed his father, sulking now his father thought a girl had helped him spear the seal. He shot his sister a cold look.

"Errrr! Yuck! That was so gross!" Leaf protested, looking in dismay at a few spots of blood on her clothes.

"It's not much. You can hardly see it," Grammy assured her. Leaf rolled her eyes.

"I stink like fish," Leaf protested.

"Urr," Onga beckoned Leaf and Grammy to follow her. She took them to where a woman, who also had long red hair, was packing up sticks and leafy vegetables into clean animal skins and binding the packages with long thin strips of leather. Onga put her right hand on the surprised woman's enlarged forehead and banged on her mother's chest with her left hand.

"Munna!" Onga introduced her. The woman looked shocked to see them but Grammy smiled and put her right hand on her own forehead and banged her chest introducing herself with a big smile. Then she introduced Leaf. The woman just stared at them. Grammy reached into her bag and gave the woman two of the tomatoes, two of the avocados and two oranges. The woman half smiled and then laid fresh skins on the floor and showed Grammy how to place the sticks on them.

"No custom of tea and biscuits around here then," Grammy joked, and got to work.

"Onga, Leaf, aba taga aka, Ennunna, Punnunna barr" the mother instructed Onga and Leaf. Leaf just followed Onga through the caves and back outside, where Onga started to gather flowers. So Leaf collected flowers too.

When they had their arms full, they took them up the hill to a patch of high ground where two Neanderthal men, using crude

149

knives and clay bowls, were digging a hole in the ground two metres long, about a meter wide and a meter deep.

Onga placed her flowers in a pile on a patch of grass beside the men in the hole. She indicated for Leaf to put her flowers there too. The men stared up at Leaf. They shouted something at Onga and she shouted something back and walked away.

Onga took Leaf to a small cavern at the back of the caves where two bodies were lying on the floor, their lower halves covered by animal skins. Leaf realized that they were dead. She was really scared as she had never seen a dead person before. Onga was acting all calm about it, but she seemed sad.

"Enmunna Onga," Onga told her and pointed to the dead woman. Then she pointed to the dead man by the woman's side and said, "Punnunna Onga."

"Grammy enmunna Leaf?" Olga asked and Leaf realised Enmunna meant grandmother, so Punnunna probably meant grandfather.

"Yes, Grammy enmunna," Leaf replied, very sad that Onga's grandparents were both dead. Onga's mother and three other women came to wrap the bodies completely in animal skins. The two men Leaf had seen digging on the hill came in with four other men. They picked up the bodies and carried them through the caves.

Onga and Leaf followed them out with all the other families who emerged into the light.

They followed in a funeral procession up the hill to the dugout grave. Grammy came with Onga's mother. The wrapped bodies were placed beside each other in the freshly dug hole.

Onga's mother placed a shell on each of the bodies and then other people picked up flowers from the pile and threw them on the two corpses.

150

No one cried, except three women who were jumping and shrieking and splashing water over everyone. The bodies were covered in leaves cast by everyone present. Finally, the earth was thrown on top, handful by handful. Even Grammy and Leaf threw fistfuls of dirt into the grave. Everyone worked together to bury them. Leaf and Grammy felt honoured to be included in this very personal ceremony. Then everyone picked up a stone and placed it in a figure eight covering the grave.

"Untoe eta! Ennunna, Punnunna, barr, aba untoe eta d pi," Onga told Leaf, drawing the figure eight in the dirt with her toe. Leaf somehow understood that although her grandparents were dead (Barr) they would be joined together (Untoe) forever (Eta) by the stones (Pi). Onga had been teaching her the names of things as they went along and the rest Leaf was able to work out using common sense.

Everyone stared at Grammy and Leaf but no one said anything because they were standing next to Onga's father who seemed to be a very important person. The others seemed a little afraid of him or maybe it was out of respect for his parent's funeral. After a good long stare at Leaf and Grammy, the people went back into the caves and continued packing up.

"Como Ikana aba," Onga explained. Leaf looked in her notebook. Como –village. Ikana-people. Aba – to go.

"Aba? Go where?" Leaf asked.

"Inkana aba ingada puna." Onga demonstrated rowing in a canoe.

"Soh tod, cartinga ingada. Aba car." Leaf did not really know what she was saying but by her hand actions she understood something about the sun being hot and them having to go somewhere colder.

"Why are they leaving Grammy?" Leaf whispered sadly to

Grammy.

"I read that they needed cold climates to survive so they probably came here for the winter but they are finding it too hot this year. Plus the deaths of two of their elders must seem like bad luck to them, so they are moving on," Grammy replied.

When all the possessions where packed up, the village people left the cave and started a journey down to the beaches where they had canoes hidden in the rocks. Grammy and Leaf followed along.

The men started yelling from the cliff.

"TENEH! TEMBARR." They waved their spears because a mammoth had been spotted. Leaf and Grammy were very afraid of the huge hairy elephant. The men and their spears charged down the hill. They speared the beast multiple times in the throat, and with ropes bought it crashing down. The ground shuddered under its weight. The tribe cheered.

The men cut large strips of flesh from the fallen beast and the women laid clean skins on the ground to wrap the meat in. Each family was given a huge package of meat. Leaf was trying not to cry for the poor hairy mammoth. She could not look and hid behind a rock until they were all ready to move on. Within fifteen minutes, the whole beast had been stripped by twelve expert butchers. All the men carried the meat packages on sticks and the swarm of people continued on towards the beach.

At the water's edge, Onga's father slapped a big wet fish into Grammy's arms. He'd caught it that morning but now he had so much meat he could give it away.

"Um dow, Grammy,'" which meant "Eat fish, Grammy."

The families got into their canoes and started to drift away.

"Abapuna, Lif. Abapuna, Grammy. Abapuna, imi sapi show inkana," Onga and her mother called out, which meant "Goodbye, Leaf. Goodbye, Grammy. Goodbye, small headed love people."

"Abapuna," Leaf and Grammy yelled, waving back to them.

When the boats had disappeared from sight Grammy suggested they light a fire and cook the big fish, and then get back to the twenty-first century Nerja, find some late afternoon sun and a hostel to sleep in for the night.

They collected large rocks and made a circle in which they placed twigs, dry leaves and some wood. Grammy lit a fire with her lighter which she always carried for times like these. They washed the fish in the sea to give it a salty taste and cooked it on the fire. Grammy added thyme and wild garlic which grew on the cliffs. She picked a lemon from a nearby tree and squeezed its fresh juice over the fish. Delicious! They ate it with tomato, avocado, oranges, and complete satisfaction. Then they washed their hands in lemon juice and again in the sea to rid their fingers of the greasy fishy smell.

"Did you know that six million years ago the Mediterranean Sea was a desert? It dried up more than thirty times. Then when the sea levels got really high, the Atlantic Ocean flooded over the mountains of Gibraltar flowing down the mountainsides to the Mediterranean."

"Weird to think there were times when it could be walked on," Leaf replied.

"That is how people used to travel here," Grammy told her.

"Grammy, we have to make the door!" Leaf shrieked in sudden panic.

"We had better get on with it before it gets darker."

153

THE WHITEASH KEY

They collected reads and grass and wove them together into the shape of a door as best they could. It took an hour and it was not a good looking door. It certainly wouldn't keep the wind out.

It was getting really dark. They secured the make-shift door between two trees, hung Grammy's padlock on it and put the Key in the lock.

"Maro, Malaga, Costa del Sol, 3 p.m. on Saturday the 29th of November, 2014!"

Grammy pulled the door open and on the other side the sky was bright blue and they were warmed by the heat of the day. They decided to walk back to Nerja which took about forty-five minutes along the coastal road. The view was so beautiful.

When they reached the town they took several left turns through the buildings and down white cobbled lanes looking for the Balcon de Europa in the centre of town with its long L-shaped plaza, cafés, and a little white church.

The actual Balcon extended off the plaza with the church, a long promenade lined with palm trees that jutted out over the sea, amazing views of beaches and a backdrop of mountains and white houses.

"Let's have a drink at that café in the sun," said Grammy, taking off her coat and putting her dark glasses and big floppy straw hat back on. Leaf ordered lemonade and Grammy had a café con leche (coffee with milk).

Grammy closed her eyes and threw her head back into the warm sunlight. Leaf chewed on her straw and watched all the people going by. They would never believe where she and Grammy had been that day.

After they finished their drinks, they went down pretty

cobbled lanes in search of a hostel for that night. They passed modern boutiques and old houses selling fruit, vegetables and nuts in the doorways.

"That is cactus fruit." Grammy pointed to a green crate on the doorstep of a tiny one-story paint-peeling house. Inside the crate were lots of small fruit, the purple and yellow skin covered in needles.

"They are difficult to peel without getting a handful of painful needles but they are juicy and delicious!" Grammy informed her.

An old man in a cap with a face wrinkled like a prune came to the dark doorway and smiled a toothless grin. He picked up a knife and a cactus fruit and professionally peeled it for Leaf to try. It was delicious.

The old man gave a hand gesture for them to wait and he shuffled off to his kitchen. He returned with a bowl of peeled cactus fruit that had been chilling in the fridge.

"Un euro por medio kilo. Son muy buenas." Unable to resist his gummy grin, Grammy got out a purse and the old man tipped the fruit into a recycled plastic bag.

"Vais con Dios," the old man said, "Go with God!"

"Adios," they replied with their hands and lips covered in cactus juice.

They left their things in a fairly priced room. Taking only towels and suntan lotion, they went back to the Balcon and down to a lovely little beach they had seen to the left of it which had a restaurant/bar called Papagyos playing chill-out music. They spent the day playing in the sand, building castles and eating ice creams.

Early that evening, they walked barefoot along all the beach coves, through the rocks, up hidden stone stairs, climbed over walls and trekked through beautiful greenery until they reached the main stretch of Burriana Beach. They ate Paella (a dish of shellfish, meat and saffron rice) in a long outdoor Spanish restaurant at the end of the main Burriana beach called Ayo's, named after the owner.

Ayo was a semi-famous character in these parts, an old man seen every day with his legs clad in cardboard, stirring his enormous paella. Ayo was the friend in the famous photographs taken when the caves were discovered and became international headlines.

When he grew up he started several businesses including his restaurant that had regularly featured in a popular Spanish television series called 'Verano Azul' which meant Blue Summer.

Down a cobbled alley, where the stars were replaced by a plenitude of flower-filled plant pots overhead, they came across a traditional Flamenco bar in a disused olive mill. A dark haired man named Fernando sang beautifully, increasing in tempo with his quick and professional fingers that moved impressively over the guitar strings. The atmosphere heightened by the quickened steps of the girls who were dancing Flamenco.

Grammy asked for "un vino tinto" and Leaf ordered a bottle of agua con gas (fizzy water). They claimed a small wooden table to put the glasses and the bottle on. Leaf sat on one of the child size stools and looked around at the antique farming tools hanging on the walls. Grammy joined in the flamenco dancing and had a great time. Grammy had a natural talent in most forms of dance. Leaf watched her in awe. She was so confident and beautiful.

The next day they walked around town and had lunch on the small balcony of a café next to the Balcon, overlooking the beach they went to the day before. Grammy had spinach quiche and Leaf had the most delicious chicken and garlic mayonnaise sandwich. They washed the food down with iced organic fruit smoothies. They could choose up to two fruits off the smoothie menu which explained what each fruit was good for and its vitamin content. Grammy chose strawberry and watermelon. Leaf had tangerine and guava. Both were delicious!

After the bill was paid at the front desk on the way out, they followed the pretty cobbled stairs down to the beach to soak up the Mediterranean sun for a couple of hours. Grammy laid their towels out on the sand close to the water's edge by a large rock in front of a quaint house cut into the cliff, actually it was just a store room of a fishing family but it was freshly painted white and had a bright blue front door and blue poles for a porch. The white walls were adorned with colourful potted flowers.

Grammy stripped down to her flowered bikini that she had bought on the way back to the hostel the night before. The six other pasty English sunbathers also wore swimwear. The two Spanish women on the beach went topless. Leaf tried not to stare and just took off her shoes and socks and sat in her rolled up jeans and T-shirt.

"I could live here forever!" exclaimed Grammy.

"Me too, but I have to go home soon because I have school tomorrow and I have to write up my report," Leaf sighed. She turned to face her grandmother.

"GRAMMY! Cover yourself up," Leaf insisted, completely shocked to see her grandmother topless.

"Oh chill out, Leaf, we are in Spain." Grammy gave a contented sigh, rolled over on her tummy and nodded off for a cat nap.

They sunbathed for an hour and then fully dressed they went

157

for a last walk along the beaches. There were no seals as people had wiped them out by the twentieth century. As it was November, there were no locals and not many tourists on the beach either but most the days were warm enough for the people from England to enjoy sunbathing.

"I suppose we ought to think about getting home then," Grammy said, sounding very disappointed.

They walked back through the rocky coves to the little white hut with the blue door on the beach by the Balcon. Grammy put her sun hat and her sunglasses into her big beach bag. She placed Leaf's Key into the lock of the little blue front door.

"In the kitchen at my house at five p.m. on Sunday the 30th of November, 2014" Grammy said and suddenly they were at her house and it was back to doing boring old homework. Except Leaf could not wait to hand her project in on Monday morning. She knew she was going to get an A+. For someone who had presumably spent a whole rainy November weekend indoors surfing the internet, Leaf had a rather lovely and inexplicable suntan.

Chapter Eleven

PUPPY LOVE

Leaf was really enjoying the gift of the Key but it was lonely having no one but her grandmother to share all her news with. Grammy was great but she was too old to go to most the places that Leaf wanted to go. Not that Grammy would have thought that. Leaf wished she could share the secret with a friend. She wanted someone younger than Grammy who she could take with her on her adventures. Leaf knew the rules. She knew she could not tell anyone about the Key but no one said she couldn't take a dog on her adventures. Christmas was approaching and maybe this year Mum would let her get one.

Leaf looked at Snuffles lying on her bed, the white teddy dog she had since she was four, and wished he was real.

"Please, Mum, I'm old enough now. I am responsible and I will look after it, walk it and feed it, I promise. I'll even pay for his flea stuff every month out of my pocket money. Please Mum?" Leaf pleaded the next morning over breakfast.

"Leaf, you know I do not believe in buying animals, but I did say you could have a dog when you are old enough to take care of it and you are quite responsible. If you can find a homeless one that is suitable then you can keep it. I will pay for its vaccinations and everything else that it needs as your Christmas present," Mum compromised. Leaf hugged her mother. She loved her mum so much.

Leaf scanned the streets for homeless dogs and all day at school she was thinking about where to find one. She went to

159

the school library during lunchtime and used a computer to search for DOGS NEEDING HOMES. A website came up for Battersea Dogs Home. That will do, Leaf thought.

"Grammy, could you come to the school with the Key? There is somewhere I would really like to go." Leaf said into her mobile phone. She was hiding in the cloakroom because students were not allowed to use mobile phones at school.

"Okay, I was just coming back from the post office so I am only about ten minutes away. Where do you want to go?"

"I'll tell you when you get here. I'll meet you in the entrance hall in ten minutes." Leaf told her.

"Well?" Grammy asked when she arrived twelve minutes later. Being inside the school was giving her a nervous twitch. Her pink T-shirt had a quote on it by Oscar Wilde:

I HAVE NOTHING TO DECLARE EXCEPT MY GENIUS

"Grammy, close your coat, you are such a protagonist," Leaf scolded, using a word she had heard her mum say.

"OOOH! Such big words! Oscar Wilde wrote this. Your headmaster would probably love it!" was Grammy's response.

"You really need to stop using that monatomic gold facemask because you are starting to look like you have had major plastic surgery and your face looks almost stuck," Leaf told her.

"It does feel a bit tight these days," agreed Grammy, she could hardly blink her face felt so stretched.

"Anyway, Mum said I could have a dog if I can find a homeless one. There is a place called Battersea Dogs Home. I want to go there and get a homeless dog."

"I know the place. Why don't I just drive you there after

Puppy Love

school? Are you sure your mum said you could have one?" Grammy asked.

"She did! I promise. But I'm supposed to find one, not go somewhere to get one. Let's just go now Grammy with the Key. I won't miss any school and Mum won't know we went to the dog's home. Please, Grammy. Please. Please. Please," Leaf pleaded.

"Oh all right," Grammy resigned, never able to resist her granddaughter's pleading. Grammy handed her the Key. There was a lock on the outside of the toilet door. Leaf put her Key in it.

"Inside Battersea Dogs Home, today at six in the morning. Not in a cage! We want to be where people view the dogs." She turned the Key three times to the left, operating the lock's mechanism in reverse and went through the open door, pulling Grammy behind her.

They walked out onto a cement corridor with a sour smell. There were large cages on either side with one to four dogs in each. Leaf walked along looking at the dogs.

There was a beautiful black Great Dane. The card on his cage said his name was Duke and that he was a Black Boston Great Dane aged eight months old. He watched Leaf, and then he stood up and came over to say hello. He was huge, like a small horse. Mum would freak out if Leaf took him home. Leaf laughed at the thought of Mum's face.

"NO WAY!" cried Grammy.

In the next cage there was an Alsatian puppy that Leaf liked but he was playing happily with two smaller mixed-breed dogs and Grammy said it would be a shame to separate them as they all seemed to be friends. In the cage beside them was a tall Afghan hound with very long hair.

"Too much grooming," Grammy told her. Next there were three Jack Russell's that constantly barked.

"Too noisy!"

Further along was a sweet-faced middle-sized short-haired female dog that seemed to be smiling at Leaf.

"Hello there!" Leaf said. The dog wagged its tail and licked her hand through the bars.

"What is your name then?" The card on the cage read: My name is Bubba. I am a very loving American Staffordshire Bull Terrier in need of a home. I am only one year old and I need lots of cuddles. I like children and playing with other dogs. Leaf thought Bubba was perfect.

"Bubba, would you like to go home to live with Mum and me? We would love you and take care of you. What do you say?" Bubba jumped for joy and wagged her tail.

"Isn't that one of those dangerous dogs?" Grammy asked.

"Does she look dangerous to you, Grammy?" Leaf replied sarcastically, as Bubba stuck her tongue through the bars and slobbered her to death with affectionate licks.

"I suppose not. She does look sweet. I love the way she has a big grin." Grammy nodded her approval. Leaf put the Key in the lock of Bubba's cage.

"Open this cage." Leaf turned the Key three times to the left and went inside the cage.

"WAIT, LEAF! Put your hand out and let her come to you," Grammy warned. All the other dogs started barking and making lots of noise. She bent down and Bubba rushed to lick and hug her. She was sturdy and strong and almost knocked Leaf over.

"Come, Bubba, we need to get out of here before someone comes." Leaf tried to pick Bubba up but she was solid muscle, too heavy and awkward to carry. Leaf took off her belt and tied it

162

to Bubba's collar.

"We ought to leave a note," Grammy said and dug in her handbag for a pen and a piece of paper.

To whom it may concern,

Please do not fret as Bubba has been adopted by a wonderful family and shall be loved and very well taken care of. Here is a £20 donation.

Grammy left the note and money on the floor of the cage and held the door open for her granddaughter and her new dog.

"Come, Bubba. Let's go home." Leaf led her out of the cage. Bubba happily followed prancing like a proud show pony. All the other dogs were going mad and barking like crazy.

Leading Bubba up the cement corridor, they took a left and more dogs in cages started barking. They went through a door and entered a small room of cages for homeless cats. Bubba just waved her tail saying goodbye to them all and followed Leaf and Grammy to a toilet door marked W.C. (water closet). Leaf put her Key in the lock.

"Outside my school, Joan of Arc Elementary, at one-thirty in the afternoon, today!" She turned the Key three times to the left and opened the door.

"You realise by taking that dog at six o'clock this morning you changed the past," Grammy scolded as they came out of the front door of the school.

"Seriously, Grammy, what were the chances of Bubba getting adopted before lunchtime?"

"Low I suppose. What are you planning to do with the dog between now and home time?" Grammy asked.

163

"Well I was hoping you would take her and bring her over to my house later saying you had found her. Pleeeease, Grammy. I have to go now before I get caught outside the school." She handed over Bubba who still attached to her belt.

"Leaf, the things you get me into, honestly!" Grammy despaired and walked away to her car with Bubba in tow.

"HI, IT'S ME! AND I BROUGHT A FRIEND," Grammy called out, as she unlocked the back door with her key. She had often teased Mum by saying that only having the key to the back door was like only being allowed to enter by the servant's entrance, and how dare she regard her mother only for servitude. Mum always managed a quick and funny response, like, "While you are here could you help me by carrying the washing machine upstairs?"

Leaf and Mum came out of the living room where they had been cuddled up on the sofa before bedtime wearing pyjamas, eating popcorn and watching the Gilmore Girls on DVD.

In the hallway, they encountered Grammy wearing a mischievous grin with a muscular Bubba who was proudly wearing a brand new pink collar, a pink harness, a pink lead and her own heart-winning Staffy grin.

"Oh isn't she lovely!" Mum exclaimed, bending down to pet her. Bubba wagged her tail and licked Mum's nose.

"Where did you find her?" Mum asked Grammy

"By the bins," Grammy replied. She had seen a couple of bins near Bubba's cage so she wasn't lying in her mind.

"Was she wearing a collar? Does she have a microchip? Have you had her checked?" Mum asked.

"No collar. No microchip. I bought this and a few other things for her this afternoon. Her name is Bubba," Grammy told her without thinking.

"How do you know? She is supposed to be homeless," Mum was suspicious. Grammy could not think of a good excuse for knowing a homeless dog's name.

"She told me," was the best she could come up with.

"Well Bubba it is then!" said Mum, conspiring in her mother's craziness.

"She also told me that she needs a home and she likes all-women families. I thought you and Leaf could have her, if that is okay with you?" Grammy asked Mum, milking the madness by this point.

"We can keep her, can't we?" Leaf pleaded. Mum smiled and nodded. Leaf leapt for joy. Bubba gave Mum a big lick.

"What's the matter with your face?" Mum asked Grammy.

"Oh nothing, very expensive face cream and a little tuck here and there, but I might be overdoing it," Grammy told her and coughed in what Leaf could tell was discomfort at not wanting to talk about it.

"I'd say!" scoffed Mum.

"I took Bubba to the vet to check for the microchip and while I was there I got them to put anti-flea stuff on her. She does not seem to have any fleas but just in case. She smells quite nice and looks very clean. Right, I must go as it is late and Leaf has to get to bed." Grammy gave Mum and Leaf hugs and kisses and went on her way.

"Thanks so much, Grammy" Leaf called after her from the doorway. Grammy gave her a wave as she climbed into her Mini. She honked her horn and sped off with Janice **Joplin's Lord won't you buy me a Mercedes Benz** blaring out the window.

165

After cleaning her teeth, Leaf jumped into bed with Bubba and settled down in a cuddle for the night. Bubba was like a hot water bottle snuggled up against Leaf's tummy. Grammy was right she did smell nice, like warm biscuits. The instant love between them was obvious. Leaf and Bubba were the happiest they had ever been.

.

Chapter Twelve

JOULUPUKKI

It was the 12th of December and Leaf was helping her mum to decorate their Christmas tree. Mum had retrieved the dust covered box of decorations and the wrapped fake fir tree from their small jammed-packed loft.

They tenderly unfolded each of its branches and extended it to its full one meter-high glory. It was like seeing an old faithful friend again. They had named him Charlie and had a traditional song for him. Mum perched him on the sideboard next to the television in the living room.

First, they wrapped the string of lights around him, and then they draped the coloured chains of beads, red, blue and gold. Hanging the decorations was Leaf's favourite part. Mum always bought one new decoration each year and each one held its own special Christmas memories. Leaf pulled a blue glass angel out of the box which was from the Christmas they had the sushi feast. Leaf hung the angel on the tree, hungry now for sushi. Pulling a reindeer decoration out of the box, she was reminded of the Indian Christmas when Mum, Leaf and Grammy had all worn pretty saris and eaten Indian take-away.

They all agreed that traditional Christmas lunch was boring and as they were not a religious family they made up their own traditions. There was a sparkly Cinderella shoe to hang next from the Cluedo Christmas. Mum had arranged a murder mystery suspense dinner and invited a few of her friends, including Mum's best friend Harriet and her daughter, chatty Scarlet. They all had to come dressed up as a character from the game of Cluedo and someone got murdered during the after-dinner mints and the other guests had to work out who did it. Leaf got to dress up as Miss Scarlet, the glamorous film star. She wore Grammy's fake fur coat, Mum's big sunglasses, red lipstick and Mum had curled her hair. There was lots of laughter until two in the morning. There were so many fun memories for Leaf to hang on the tree.

"Okay, let's light Charlie up then," Mum said, plugging in the tree lights. Leaf turned off the main living room light. The room twinkled and glowed in flashes of colour. Leaf thought it was the most beautiful Christmas tree ever. They held hands as they admired their team effort and sang.

♫Oh Charlie Tree, oh Charlie Tree, how lovely are your branches♫

Leaf hung their stockings and one for Bubba from a shelf in the living room because they did not have a fireplace. Grammy also hung stockings every year for them on her huge stone fireplace. Leaf wondered if Santa thought they were cheeky for hanging two stockings each. Mum said that is why he did not leave much in their home stockings, because he left the main stocking gifts at Grammy's.

"Mum, does Santa really exist?" Leaf asked as Mum came into the living room with two mugs of sweet tea.

"I would rather you think that through for yourself, Leaf, because maybe he only exits if you believe he does," said Mum, handing her a mug.

"How old do you think he is?" Leaf asked, sitting down with Mum on the sofa.

"Well now, I think he started delivering gifts around AD 320 so I guess he was born about AD 300. He was born in an area of

168

Greece that is now Southern Turkey," Mum told her.

"Is that why other people have greasy turkey for Christmas dinner?" Leaf joked. Mum laughed but said she didn't think so.

"AD means Ano Domini, in the year of our Lord in Latin, and it means any year after Jesus was born and BC was prior to Christ being born," Mum stated, hoping she had remembered that correctly.

"It is easier to remember if you think of it as AD after delivery and BC before Christ."

"Santa would be well old by now. How could he stay alive and be fit enough to go around the world squeezing himself down people's chimneys?" Leaf was puzzled.

"Exactly! How old would he be?" Mum liked to test her at maths, "If it is now 2014?"

"Errrrmm ... He would be 1714 years old?" Leaf answered proud to be good at maths.

"Well done!" Mum replied, hoping it was right as she had not bothered to work it out as she wasn't very good at maths herself, but it sounded about right.

"Now do you think someone who is that old is still going around squeezing himself down chimneys? He must be so old and decrepit his limbs must be falling off. I'm surprised we don't find bits of him decaying on Grammy's roof," Mum said, sarcastically.

"MUM!" Leaf did not approve of her mother's sick sense of humour.

"Maybe he is like a vampire and can never die," Leaf suggested.

"And how did he get that way? Was he bitten by a rabid Easter bunny?" Mum teased.

"MUM! That's not funny!"

169

THE WHITEASH KEY

Leaf wasn't getting any straight answers out of her mum on this one. So she decided she would just have to ask Grammy or investigate for herself. She went to her bedroom and called Grammy with the last of her weekly mobile phone credit.

"I really do not know what I should tell you, Leaf, but I do know of a place where you can find the answers. I'll tell you what, I'll come over tonight when your mum is asleep and we can use the Key to find out the truth and go on a quick Christmas outing. I'll come just before midnight, listen out for me and open the door," Grammy instructed.

When her mum went to sleep that night Leaf crept out of bed and put on jeans, her warmest jumper, a woolly hat, gloves, scarf and a big bulky coat. She presumed that Grammy would be taking her to the North Pole. She knew it was freezing there because on cards Santa was always overdressed even indoors.

She put her front door keys, phone and her Quikid World notebook in her coat pocket. Bubba jumped off the bed wagging her tail wanting to go out too. She put Bubba into a little pink fluffy cardigan from one of her teddies. It actually used to belong to Leaf when she was five. Bubba loved to get dressed up. Silly dog! Leaf arranged Bubba's pink harness over the cardigan, attached the lead and guided Bubba quietly down the stairs to the front door.

Luckily, Mum always left the light on in the stairwell otherwise they probably would have fallen and broken their necks. They crept out the front door.

It was almost midnight. Leaf could see her breath. She waited in the cold dark night for Grammy but with Bubba by her side Leaf felt less fear. She was however glad to see Grammy who was wearing a warm scarf, her fake fur coat and expensive faux leather gloves. Grammy gave Leaf a hello kiss, put her fingers to her lips telling her to keep quiet, and pulling the magic Key out of her coat pocket Grammy slipped it in the lock of the front door and turned it three times to the left on the stroke of midnight.

"Santa's village on December 20th, 2014, at five in the evening." Grammy presumed Santa should be at home on that day around that time. Grammy opened the front door and holding Leaf's hand, which was holding Bubba's lead, the three of them stepped into Lapland.

Bubba was not used to time travel and vomited on the white snow. Leaf scooped it up in a plastic bag from the small bag dispenser hanging on Bubba's lead, made a knot in the bag and deposited it in the nearest rubbish bin.

There was a bin on each side of the cul-de-sac. Even the bins were pretty, dark green decorated with wreaths of holly, white fairy lights and red ribbons. When Leaf dropped the bag of dog sick in it, it felt so wrong.

They were in a small snow covered village strung with colourful lights and decorated Christmas trees on every corner. There was a man wearing a red woolly hat and green gloves, up a ladder trimming a Christmas tree. Leaf plucked up the courage to ask him where they were exactly.

"Why, you are in Joulupukki's very own village, near the town of Rovaniemi," he told her. Leaf looked confused and wondered how they had ended up here.

"We were trying to get to Santa's house," Grammy told him.

"It is the tall house you see over there, the one with the roof that looks like a kitchen extractor fan. Around here Santa is called Joulupukki and this is his village, the happiest village in

Finland. Here it is Christmas all year round. Of course we have to make the snow in the summer with big snow cannons. Shame I think, just when the Saxifrage starts to bloom and cover the ground with tiny purple flowers. The snow completely kills off the pretty Dryas too. They are little yellow flowers that track the sun. Can't track the sun under a pile of snow now can they?"

"Such a shame," Grammy agreed.

"Joulupukki says we must have snow all year for the visitors to feel like it is Christmas. I was a landscape gardener by trade but now I just get to prune the evergreens and Holly. Even the fir trees you see are imported because the roots of trees cannot penetrate the frozen ground. Still, the snow keeps away the swarms of black flies and mosquitoes that send the reindeer and everyone else mad in the summer," he told them, cutting a distended twig off the tree.

"Do the reindeer get cold in the snow?" Leaf asked.

"They usually move south for the winter, mostly to calve and find new food sources but actually reindeer do not feel the cold because they have hollow hairs which trap the heat. We keep twelve reindeer in the village. We feed them fresh hay and oats but they spend most of their time scrapping back the snow in search of cotton grass, mosses and lichens," he informed her.

"It is very dark. Is it only five o'clock here? Can you see enough to be cutting those trees?" Leaf asked, worried he might chop his fingers off.

"I'm used to it. There is no daylight here during the winter and in the summer there is no night time." No daylight and then no night time, what a strange place, Leaf thought.

"You might get to see the Northern Lights later, if you are lucky and the sky is clear."

"Northern Lights? What are they?" Leaf asked with curiosity.

172

Joulupukki

"It is officially called Aurora Borealis. It is when high energy protons and electrons from sun spots are brought in by solar winds and trapped in the earth's magnetic field. It creates very pretty colours across the sky," he replied. "What a sweet dog you have, very well behaved." He climbed down his ladder to pet Bubba. Bubba licked his hand and wagged her tail.

"Anyway, if you are looking for Santa he'll be at home now. It is the house down there on the right, the one with the snowmen outside," he told them, pointing the way.

"Nice to meet you," Grammy said as they walked away. The man waved goodbye.

They found the house easily and Bubba did a pee next to one of the snowmen. Leaf quickly kicked more snow over the patch of yellow. Grammy knocked on the door. Fresh snowfall covered the roof and warm lights emanated from the windows. The door was opened by a girl of about twelve years of age. She wore her curly blonde hair in plaits and had a round friendly face.

"Hello. Come in." She greeted them with a warm smile.

"We've come to see Santa. Is he your dad?" Leaf asked.

"Oh no, I just help around here. My name is Tessy. Come this way. Santa is in the living room. It's okay, your dog can come too."

They followed Tessy to the living room. The whole house smelt of cinnamon and oranges. Tessy knocked and then pushed open the big oak door. The room was warmly lit by a big fire roaring in the hearth. The furniture was of brown leather and the walls were papered in red velvet.

"People to see you, Joulupukki" Tessy announced. Father Christmas was sat in his favourite leather armchair, reading a book and drinking a mug of hot chocolate. He had a long white beard but his clothes consisted of a knitted red jumper, a pair of red and yellow tartan trousers and an old pair of slippers. He was dressed more like Rupert the Bear than Santa. He looked up, lowered his glasses to the tip of his nose and smiled as he stood to greet them.

"Hello there. Take off your coats. Throw them on that chair over there. Please, have a seat on the sofa. Would you like a cup of hot chocolate? It is delicious! Mrs. Santa Claus makes the best! Come, bring your little doggie in and warm yourselves by the fire."

"Please, Tessy, would you bring mugs of hot chocolate for our guests." Leaf was glad he didn't wait for her to answer as she did want some of that divine smelling chocolate but had felt embarrassed to accept. She had this weird thing where she felt it was somehow rude to accept the things she wanted without making a fuss and usually said no thanks I'm okay, refusing a second time and shyly accepting on the third. This had become such a habit that she hoped people would not give up before the third try of wearing her politeness thin because she often desperately wanted a drink or whatever it was. She wished she could just be direct without seeming rude. She wished she could just say thank you in that charming and confident way that her best friend Sarah did. Sarah would say, "Thank you that would be lovely" in a grown-up way that adults found adorable.

Grammy took off her coat and put it on the chair.

"Only jumper that was clean this morning. What are the odds?" Grammy joked. BAH HUMBUG spelt out in large silver letters was festively decorated with knitted sprigs of holly across the front of Grammy's jumper. Santa chuckled. Leaf raised her eyebrows and shook her head. Grammy and Leaf sat down on the sofa and Tessy went to get the hot chocolate.

"My name is Bernadette Latoure. This is my granddaughter,

Leaf, and this is Bubba," Grammy introduced them, as Bubba settled on the floor by her feet in front of the fire. Leaf was dying to touch the wallpaper to see if it was soft and velvety.

"I am Nicholas Johann Claus, but you can call me Nick or Joulupukki or Santa, whichever you prefer."

"Nice to meet you, Santa. Bubba and I came here to see if you really existed. I feel a bit silly now that I am here sitting in the same room as you. Are you really 1714 years old?" Leaf just blurted out suddenly. Then she felt rude having asked his age as you weren't supposed to do that with adults.

"Ho ho ho! No, I'm sixty-eight if you must know," Santa chuckled, "Many children come here seeking the truth about Father Christmas so I will tell you. Ahhh here's Tessy with the hot chocolate."

"Thank you very much," Leaf said to Tessy. It smelt so good! Tessy smiled, handed a cup to each of them from the plastic Christmas tray she was carrying and went off to help Mrs. Santa Claus with something.

"Well, Leaf, you were right about the original Saint Nicholas being born in the third century. He was born in the Village of Patara which was at that time was part of Greece. His parents died when he was quite young. They had been rich and left him a nice sum of money. Having been raised to be a good Christian, Nicholas used all his inheritance money to follow the words of Jesus, "Sell what you own and give the money to the poor." He sold everything and gave away all his money," Santa told them.

"There are people who believe that before Jesus began his ministry he travelled to India and studied Buddhism. It is said that later he returned to Palestine and spent time living with a strict sect of Essene Jews from whom Jesus learnt to be humble and live without possessions. Jesus' brother James was

175

extremely humble and Jesus admired his example."

"Later Jesus moved away from this sect because they were fanatically religious and believed in fighting to the death against the Romans. This was against Jesus' nature. He preferred to follow the principles he had learnt from Buddhism to love thy neighbour and thy enemy. Jesus had also learnt some good things from the Essene Jews and continued to believe in living without materialism and helping those less fortunate. Nicholas, following the example of Jesus, gave all his money away to the poor, the sick and those in need."

"Nicholas was made a bishop at an early age because he had dedicated his life to God. He was later exiled and imprisoned by the Roman Emperor Diocletian who persecuted Christians. Nicholas died on the sixth of December AD 343 and in Europe this day became an occasion to celebrate him, although the Dutch celebrate the evening before, on the fifth."

"In the Netherlands and Belgium there are accounts that Saint Nicholas arrived on a steam ship from Spain and rode around Holland on a white horse distributing gifts to poor children. All over Europe there were tales of Saint Nicholas making him the patron and protector of children, poor people, travellers, the wrongly accused, prisoners, thieves, murderers and of all in need or in trouble. There are churches named after him all over Belgium, Rome, Holland and England," Santa said and took a swig of his hot chocolate.

"In 1087, his remains were taken to Bari in South East Italy. He became known as the Saint of Bari and to this day people still visit the Basilica di San Nicola which is the church built over his crypt."

"I've been there," stated Grammy. Santa raised his bushy eyebrows to show he was impressed.

"One of the popular stories of Nicolas tells of a poor man

176

with no money to give as dowries so that his three daughters could marry, which would mean they would be sold into slavery. Mysteriously, bags of gold were tossed through the man's window, enough for his daughters to wed. When the gold was thrown through the window, presumably by good old Nicholas, some of the coins landed in shoes and stockings that had been drying by the fire. This is why at Christmas it became tradition to hang stockings and why the Dutch and Germans lay out shoes or boots hoping for them to be filled with gifts from Saint Nicholas," Santa told them.

"At my dad's house we put out rain boots on the 6th of December and they get filled up with sweets," Leaf told him, "My dad is half German."

"How is Christmas connected to the birth of Jesus then? Is the 25th of December even his real date of birth?" Grammy inquired, always one with a conspiracy theory. Santa smiled.

"The Bible gives no specific date for the birth of Jesus, but it left us clues. The basis for Judeo and Christian theology dates back to ancient Egypt, including festivals such as Easter, Passover and Christmas. Christ was the name given to all messiahs. Many Messiahs were bestowed the same birthday of the 25th of December because on the 24th the brightest star Sirius, which is the star of the east, aligns with the three brightest stars in Orion's belt which were called The Three Kings. The three king stars follow the star of the east to point to the exact location of where the sun will rise on the morning of the 25th of December, the birth of God's sun on the Winter Solstice."

"Pagans celebrated the Winter Solstice in December and when the Roman Emperor Constantine ordered the people to convert from Paganism to Christianity it was an easier transition for the people to keep their festive dates. That is why Christians go to church on Sundays because this was the day that Pagans worshipped the sun. Stories also spread that Jesus rose from the dead on a Sunday."

"We know from the Bible (Luke 2:8-20) that Jesus was born in the lambing season because the shepherds were watching their flocks at night and they only did this when the lambs were being born. Lambs are born in the spring. Jesus was born in the town of David, where lambs were sacrificed for the temple, and he was born at the same time as the sacrificial lambs. In the Bible, an angel told the shepherds that on that day in the town of David a saviour had been born, and that they would find him wrapped in cloths in a manger."

"We now know the exact date of the birth of Jesus from many sources such as the Dead Sea Scrolls, the Tabernacle, and information hidden in the vaults of the Vatican, and from the writings of John. Jesus was born during Nissan1, which was the true New Year's Day for Jews. When Jesus was born Nissan 1 occurred in March. The Dead Sea Scrolls tell us that a star from the east shone in the centre of the sky from morning until evening on the first month of the Jewish year." Santa paused for a sip of coco.

"The Magi (The Wise Men) were not actually at the birth of Jesus. They came two years later. They were astrologers and known as the wise men of Persia. Daniel, who became the head of the Magi, saw Jupiter the king star in the sky on the night of the birth, and claimed a king had been born in Judah. Judah was related to the constellation of Aries, and at that time there was a convergence of Venus, Mars, Saturn and Jupiter as Isaiah had predicted."

"Therefore, knowing about the lambs being born and the position of the stars we can work out that Jesus was born on the 20th of March, 6 BC in the town of David in Judah. March falls under the constellation of Pisces, the symbol of the fish and so

Jesus became the fisherman. My wife read in a book that for the last two thousand years we were living in the age of Pisces, and now we are embarking on the age of Aquarius. Anyway, on the 20th of March, 6 BC the calendar changed from BC (Before Christ) to AD (In the year of our lord)."

"It was actually Pope Julius who declared the 25th of December to be the day to celebrate the birth of Jesus Christ as that was the official birthday given to all messiahs, such as Horus, Buddha, Krishna, Dionysus and many more. When Jesus was alive the Pagan God Mithra, known as the Light of Creation, the Good Shepherd, who was born of a virgin mother, had his birthday on the 25th of December. Mithra rose from the dead after three days. Most of the messiahs have the same story. Yet way before Jesus, began our Christmas traditions. The Vikings sacrificed a wild boar to Frey the God of fertility and farming on the midwinter solstice. This meat was then cooked and eaten and so began the tradition of the Christmas ham," Santa said and then he chuckled, "I do like a bit of Christmas ham." He rubbed his belly. Grammy and Leaf laughed. Bubba snored.

"We hang Mistletoe because the Vikings believed it resurrected the dead. The Yule Log was a large yellow log decorated with sprigs of fir, holly or yew. The Vikings carved runes symbols on it asking the gods to protect them from misfortune. From this tradition we now have the yummy Yule log cake. Mrs Santa makes the best Yule log cake every day." Santa smiled from ear to ear. He knew he was a lucky man to have the world's best wife. Then he remembered to finish what he had been saying.

"Vikings also decorated evergreen trees with food, clothes, and small statues of the gods to entice the tree spirits to return in spring and that is why today we decorate Christmas trees. Christians have continued the pagan associations with holly for hundreds of years after the druids stopped practising their art. It was believed that if girls tied holly to their beds at Christmas that they would not turn into witches the next year." Santa chuckled. Christmas was his favourite subject.

"In the Scandinavian legend, Thor the god of thunder rode the skies in a wagon pulled by two goats, later replaced by Jultomten (Santa Claus) and his reindeer. It was the Coca-Cola company that gave Santa his red suited image. Our pre-Christian ancestors used to dress up someone from the village as Old Man Winter in a hooded fur coat and he would travel around on a white horse being welcomed into homes to join the winter solstice festivities. This may also have been to celebrate the god Odin who had a long white beard and rode a white horse called Sleipnir."

"When Britain was invaded in the eighth and ninth century, Odin became known there and evolved into Father Christmas. The first pictures of Father Christmas were of him wearing a bishop's outfit with a mitre and crook," Santa stated, proud to know so much about the origins of his heritage.

"So we presume Saint Nicholas was the original Santa Claus, but how in the end it came to be me is another story, but would you like another cup of hot chocolate first?" the old man asked them.

"Oh yes please. It is the most delicious hot chocolate ever!" Leaf declared, suddenly not shy at all. To Leaf the atmosphere was like that of being at her grandparent's house when she was a small child and her grandfather had still been alive. She hardly remembered but the feeling remained and was triggered by being in Santa's company.

"Did I not tell you that Mrs. Claus makes the best!" he exclaimed, grinning proudly.

"Hang on a minute and I'll just pop into the kitchen and see if I can scrounge some more."

Joulupukki

When he had left the room, Leaf took the opportunity to jump up and touch the wall. It really was soft and velvety. Bubba jumped up too from where she had been quietly lying on the floor. She sniffed at the wall and then lay back down in front of the fire, obviously not impressed.

"Sit down, Leaf! He'll come back and find you poking about," Grammy warned her. Leaf sat back down on the sofa and looked at the photos of Mr. and Mrs. Claus on the mantelpiece above the fireplace. Mrs. Claus looked kind like her husband.

"There you go," Santa said, returning to the room with two full mugs.

"Thank you," Leaf replied politely, as he handed her one.

"Most kind!" Grammy smiled, taking the other from him. "Now where was I? Oh yes, how I got to be Santa. Well, my great, great grandfather was made Santa over three hundred years ago. He had the first toy workshop hidden away in a secret location somewhere on the mountain Korvatunturi. His toys were sent to poor children all over the world. His son became the next Santa and his son after him and so it went and on for generations."

Leaf was pondering on what would have happened if one of them had chosen not to become a Santa. What would have happened if she had not wanted to be the next Key Guardian? Leaf wondered what Prince William would think about this. She decided that sometimes you just had to accept your destiny and hope for the best and so far it all seemed to be going jolly well.

"When my grandfather inherited the role of Santa, he decided that people should be able to visit Father Christmas and his workshop, and that all this work was much too much for just one old man. So he moved down from the mountain and asked the people of the lovely town of Rovaniemi to help him build a Christmas village where children and adults from around the world could visit all year, a place to where the letters from the needy and good children could be easily delivered to Santa. Hence this village was born, and then fifty years later so was I. Ho, ho, ho."

"When my father, Nicholas Michael Claus died, I became Santa and when I die my son Nicholas Jacob Claus will become the new Santa. And so Santa lives on. So you see, Leaf, Father Christmas does exist. But no, I am not 1714 years old." Santa told her with a chuckle.

"Well do you put presents in my stockings or do my mum and my Grammy do that?" Leaf asked, determined to get to the bottom of this great mystery. Santa looked at Grammy and smiled.

"I'm afraid I'm not allowed to tell you that, Leaf. You need to work that one out for yourself. How about we go to the kitchen and you can meet Mrs. Claus. You can help her decorate some Christmas cookies if you like?" Leaf got up, as did Bubba and Grammy. They followed Santa to a huge kitchen.

"Hello, I'm Mrs. Claus," a happy robust woman introduced herself, wiping her hands before shaking theirs.

"Would you like to decorate some Christmas cookies to take home?" she asked Leaf.

"Yes please! And thank you for the hot chocolate was totally yummy. My name is Leaf and this is my grandmother and my dog Bubba." Leaf did not feel at all shy with this woman who looked like an adorable granny or a giant lovable gnome. Under a floppy red mop cap that matched the colour of her dress, she had lots of grey curls, button blue eyes, big rosy cheeks, a

182

little round nose, and the most welcoming smile. She wore a green flour dusted apron and had robust arms meant to hug at least half a dozen grandchildren.

"You are most welcome, Leaf. What nice manners you have. Come over here then. These cookies are cool enough to decorate, so just help yourself to anything in the bowls. Would it be okay if I give Bubba a few bits of boneless chicken left over from lunch?" Santa's wife asked.

"Oh yes, she would love that. Would you mind if she had a bowl of water too?"

"Of course, my dear," Mrs. Claus got Bubba a bowl of water and a plate of food. Bubba woofed her chicken down and lapped up the water.

"Would you like a cup of tea?" Mrs. Claus asked Grammy. "Take a seat at the table, dear."

"That would be lovely, if it is not too much trouble," Grammy replied.

"No trouble at all. I was about to have one myself. Milk? Sugar?" Grammy nodded and took a seat at the scrubbed wooden table.

"What a lovely kitchen you have!"

"Thank you! We certainly do a lot of cooking in it." Mrs. Claus chuckled to herself at the understatement. She brought a plate of star shaped cinnamon biscuits to the table for Grammy to nibble on while she prepared the tea.

Mrs. Claus started a conversation about food and in two minutes they were swapping recipes. Santa busied himself by putting chopped logs into the hot stove, and then joined the ladies for a biscuit or two.

Leaf looked at the long kitchen table covered with bowls of colourful ingredients for decorating cookies. Mrs. Claus had

183

given her five large cookies to decorate in different shapes: a Christmas tree, a snowman, a Santa cookie, an angel and lastly a big old boot. Leaf got to work. She decorated the tree cookie with little pieces of different coloured jelly sweets and ripped up rainbow strips. The snowman got black liquorice eyes, an orange jelly tot nose, a rainbow strip scarf and three chocolate buttons. The Santa biscuit got a glacier cherry nose and blue eyes made with little bits of blueberry bubblegum.

She dipped the angel's dress in pink sherbet, squeezed out vanilla icing hair from a small nozzle, the mouth was a little sweet of red lips, one pink rainbow drop for her nose and eyes of tiny pieces of blue bubblegum. Lastly, she tied a black liquorice lace into a bow and stuck it on the boot. Done!

"That was quick! They look lovely, Leaf. Very artistic," remarked Mrs. Claus, getting up to have a look. Grammy got up to look too.

"I'm going to give them to my mum for Christmas," Leaf told her. The two old ladies smiled.

"Then I have a special Christmas cookie box you can put them in, to make them look more like a present," Santa's wife offered kindly. She carefully placed the cookies inside and tied the golden box with a green and red Christmas ribbon.

"Thank you so much, that looks great!" Leaf gave her a hug of appreciation.

"I am having such a nice time! I am sorry I ever doubted your existence," Leaf said to Santa who was scratching Bubba behind the ears, and Leaf gave him a hug too.

"Would you like to come outside and see the reindeer and meet my son who is feeding them right now? We have five reindeer to pull the sleigh. They are all female of course, as male reindeers lose their antlers in the winter. Would you like to meet them?" asked Santa, pouring himself another cup of chocolate.

"We ought to be getting home in case my daughter wakes up and finds her daughter and dog gone," Grammy insisted.

"She doesn't know you are here?" Mrs. Claus looked at Leaf concerned, and wondering why Leaf's mother was asleep at only six in the evening. She hoped she wasn't sick.

"She was taking a nap, so we had better go," Grammy gave as explanation.

"Can we come another day?" Leaf asked.

"Of course, any day of the year, we are always here. Next time I will show you my workshop. Do you have far to go to get home? We do not want you wandering about alone in the dark, it is slippery out there," Santa said, also seeming concerned now.

"We will be home in a flash. We are staying close by," Grammy assured them. Leaf looked at her. Leaf really hated all this lying that went with being a Key Guardian. She made a mental note to have words with Grammy about it in private.

"Well then, we look forward to your next visit. Here are your coats, hats and scarves." Santa helped Leaf and Grammy into their things and Mrs. Santa gave Leaf the cookie box for her mum.

"Thank you both for your kindness. Come on, Bubba." Grammy said, giving Mrs. Santa a hug. Bubba got up from where she had happily collapsed on the warm floor. Leaf took Bubba's pink lead out of her coat pocket and attached it to Bubba's harness that she was still wearing on top of the little pink cardigan.

"Goodbye. Get home safely." They both said, hugging Leaf and Grammy.

"I'll see you to the door," said Santa.

"Bye, Tessy," Leaf said to the girl who was entering the

kitchen just as they were leaving.

"Merry Christmas," Tessy replied, cheerfully.

"One of my elves" Santa half joked, referring to Tessy who had now disappeared into the kitchen. Leaf laughed.

"Well Goodbye, Santa. Merry Christmas!"

"Ho, ho, ho," Santa chuckled as he opened the door for them.

Grammy, Bubba and Leaf walked off down the snowy path. They looked up and saw a strange green glow spread across the clear night sky with waves of red, violet and blue. It was breathtaking.

"Those are the Northern Lights, Aurora Borealis." Grammy sighed, peacefully. Leaf had never seen anything so magical. After five minutes of staring up at the mystical heavens, their necks hurt so Leaf hurried Grammy along the street.

Once they were out of sight of Santa's house, Grammy walked them up to the front door of another house. She put the Whiteash Key in the lock and said, "Leaf's house at midnight on December 20th 2014," and she turned the Key three times to the left.

They found themselves walking into the living room. Mum had forgotten to unplug the tree lights and they twinkled and glowed festively. Leaf put the box for Mum under the tree and unplugged the lights. Grammy gave Leaf a kiss goodnight, crept out the front door and went home to her house.

"Come on, Bubba, let's go to bed," Leaf said quietly, taking off Bubba's pink lead, harness and cardigan.

They went upstairs and crept into the bathroom so Leaf could pee and brush her teeth. She and Bubba snuggled up together in Leaf's bed.

"Merry Christmas, Bubba!"

Joulupukki

Bubba farted a chicken smell and started snoring.

Chapter Thirteen

THE SINGING MERMAID

The door was open and Leaf was dancing about her bedroom pretending that her hairbrush was a microphone. Eartha Kitt's **C'est si bon** was blaring out loud on her CD player.

Leaf could hear her mum singing the song badly as she walked down the hall with a basket of washing. Leaf was talented and she loved to sing more than anything. Her mum was paying for singing lessons three times a week after school, but as much as Leaf loved singing, she was not enjoying the classes as much as she thought she would. Her fifty-year-old teacher had bad breath because he smoked and his mother always made him cups of coffee and tuna fish sandwiches.

He made Leaf sing scales, church hymns and classical songs. Leaf always let it rip when she sang Hallelujah. Leaf wanted to sing like Anastasia or Christina Aguilera. She had a deep toned voice which really suited the powerful soul songs. She loved singing along with her mum's Tina Turner CD or to Grammy's old tapes of Aretha Franklin and Gloria Gaynor.

When Leaf was little, she used to sing in the bath as her mum washed her hair. Her mum used to tell her that she must be a mermaid because mermaids had such wonderful singing voices that the sailors would fall into love trances and crash their ships on the rocks. Leaf wondered about their amazing voices. If mermaids really existed maybe she could ask them to teach her some singing tricks, or some really amazing scales with which she could improve her own singing and she could become famous. So she phoned Grammy.

That weekend Leaf was at her dad's. Technically it was his girlfriend's flat which always made Leaf feel uncomfortable. It was like she was a guest, except she was not treated like a guest. They were always telling her to clean her room and eat up food she did not like.

Dana, her Dad's girlfriend, was from Russia. She was okay, but Leaf resented that her dad had left her mum for another woman and then left that woman for Dana. Mum seemed fine about it, she liked Dana. Mum always said she was not the jailer of Dad's heart.

"People fall in and out of love, what can you do? At least he was honest about it and always pays his part of the maintenance for you on time," was Mum's opinion. As long as Mum could raise Leaf in a friendly environment and they had enough money to eat and pay bills, Mum was able to let it go.

Mum said Dad had always made sure that the quality of their lifestyle had not changed due to his choices. He still helped out, came round to fix the boiler whenever it broke, he bought Mum a new washing machine when that broke and a new fridge. He had promised to get internet installed in their house when he could afford it. He and mum were still good friends. He even came round to have a cup of tea with Mum when he needed relationship advice. Leaf on the other hand found it harder to let go.

After dinner at Dana and Dad's flat, where Leaf had to eat broccoli (yuck!), Leaf said she had some homework to finish and went up to her room. She put her swimsuit on under her clothes, packed a towel, a pair of goggles, flippers that she had never had the chance to use before, and a bottle of factor fifty

189

suntan lotion, so she didn't end up with a suntan she could not explain like the last time she and Grammy got back from Spain.

At midnight, when Dad and Dana were asleep, Leaf crept down the corridor and opened the front door for Grammy.

"Ready?" Grammy whispered.

"Hang on, I just have to grab my bag," Leaf whispered, seeing Grammy's beach bag had reminded her. She ran back to her room, grabbed the bag, and was about to return when she saw Grammy press herself against the wall behind a tall potted plant. Leaf slipped back into her room as her dad padded half asleep into the bathroom. They heard him urinate loudly, fart and return to bed without flushing or washing his hands. Leaf heard him shut his bedroom door and she quietly ran back to Grammy at the front door.

"Ready!" Leaf whispered, "Do you know where to go?" Grammy nodded and put the Whiteash Key in the lock.

"A front door near the beach in the village of Oia, Santorini, where the mermaids live in the underwater caves, any lunchtime during the summer of 2009," Grammy said, turning the Key. She had spent the last two hours researching sightings of mermaids on the internet and the latest sighting had been in 2009 near the volcanic Greek Island called Santorini, and some people believed that the mermaids might live in the sea caves there.

Grammy opened the door and hand in hand they stepped out into a scorching hot day near the dock of Ammoudi in Oia, Greece. They were on high red cliffs topped by grey rock, and white houses were sunk deep into the volcanic soil. Leaf and Grammy followed the steep zigzag path down to the Ammoudi bay. The whitewashed village with blue domed roofs cut into the lower part of the cliff, all the way down to the cobalt blue and turquoise sea with restaurants right on the waterfront.

As it was lunchtime everyone was busy eating, so no one took much notice of them passing by. They followed a dirt path on the left, climbed the rocks, and came to a lovely little cove with no one else around.

Leaf took off her street clothes and pulled the wedgie her swimsuit was causing out from between her bum cheeks. She attached the snorkel to her goggles and flippers in hand, she climbed the huge rocks.

"Have a swim about and see if you can spot anything that resembles a mermaid. I'll just wait for you right here until you get back. Don't go too far or for too long, okay," Grammy said, nervously. She was starting to regret this trip. She was not a good swimmer, afraid of the water and probably would not be able to save Leaf if anything happened.

"Please be careful, Leaf, if you go into the caves. Don't go far on your own, it could be very dangerous. I am really not sure about this now," Grammy stated, feeling slightly panicked.

"Don't worry, Grammy, I will be fine. Back soon. Don't go anywhere," Leaf, who was a strong swimmer, told her confidently. She put her flippers and goggles on and waddled to the edge of the rock.

"ONE. TWO. THREE." Leaf jumped. The transparent water splashed up around her. She surfaced, and blew the water out of her snorkel before putting her head back under and kicking out with her flippers. She could see some caves below but needed to go deeper. Leaf surfaced, removed the snorkel from her mouth, took a big gulp of air and dived down.

There was colourful coral, mostly red, yellow and black. Lots of small Parrot fish, sea sponges and clams around the rocks. She swam into a cave. The light from the sun above gave the

191

water a beautiful turquoise glow. Leaf kicked hard with her flippers and swam deeper into the cave. She swam through a tunnel into another cave, and seeing light above, she surfaced, finding herself in a large cave only half filled with water. She gulped in the air above the surface.

There was a small sandy beach inside the cave. Three girls in jewelled bikini tops were sitting on the sand talking and laughing. Leaf was shocked when she saw that all three had a different coloured fish tail. She had not really believed mermaids existed. When they noticed her two of them dived into the sea and swam away in fright. The third was about to make her escape but froze when Leaf spoke.

"Please don't go. I won't tell anyone you are here. I came to ask you something, please don't go." The mermaid relaxed. She had long brown hair and a bikini top to match her pink tail. Leaf swam up to the beach and removed her goggles and snorkel. The mermaid was obviously a curious creature and waited for Leaf to come out of the water onto the beach. The mermaid stared at her legs.

"What did you want to ask?" she questioned.

"I heard that mermaids are wonderful singers and well I hope to be a famous singer one day, so I was hoping you might give me a few tips," Leaf told her. The mermaid laughed.

"Oh you silly humans get everything so confused. It is not the mermaids who can sing. You confuse us with the Sirens who were half bird, half woman. The Sirens were evil creatures, not that they had much choice in the matter poor things. They would cause sailors to crash onto the rocks and then the Sirens drowned them," the mermaid told her.

"Oh, I have never heard of Sirens," Leaf said, looking apologetic.

"There were only three Sirens. They started out as mortal

human women who were the handmaidens of Persephone. Persephone was kidnapped by Hades the God of the Underworld when she was in Sicily gathering flowers because he wanted to steal her virginity and make her the underworld goddess.

Her mother Demeter, who was the goddess of agriculture and fertility, searched every corner of the earth for her daughter. For nine days and nights she searched without stopping to eat, drink or sleep. In fury she destroyed land and crops in her wake."

"She gave Persephone's handmaidens the bodies of birds so that they could fly around helping her search for Persephone. They searched and searched for years, but Persephone was never found and eventually the winged handmaidens gave up. Demeter was so angry that she cursed the girls to remain half bird forever, and that if any mortal man should be able to resist them, the Sirens would die."

"Odysseus knew about the Sirens and when the beautiful winged maidens sang their enchanting song seductively around the masts, Odysseus ordered his crew to cover their ears and not to look at the Sirens. Like this, they were able to resist the three maidens and sail safely away. So the Sirens hurled themselves into the sea and died."

"How very sad," Leaf replied, "But I don't understand why they killed themselves in the end?"

"I don't know. Maybe they thought it was better than whatever Demeter was going to do to them. Anyway, it sucked to be a Siren. Mermaids try to help people as much as they can without being seen. We try to warn sailors of bad weather approaching and save them when they are drowning, but we sing no better than ordinary people. There are two or three of us that can sing, but Eponina is by far the best."

"Eponina? Who is she? Do you think she would help me?"

Leaf inquired.

"Eponina was taught to sing by her grandmother who once swam to a Cornish village in England. She heard the singing of a chorister named Matthew Trewhella. Eventually they met and fell in love. Matthew taught Eponina's grandmother to sing, and she taught Eponina. What a gift that girl has, enchanting really. She has perfected an unearthly style. Now she teaches a singing class to the little ones."

"Do you think she would teach me?" Leaf asked.

"Quite frankly, I don't think anyone is going to be too happy that you are here, but now you are we may as well ask. First we should take you to see Medine and get that knee seen to." Leaf looked down to see blood dripping from a cut on her knee.

"Oh, I must have cut it on a rock" said Leaf, starting to cry. She realised that she had left her healing fairy dust necklace at home.

"What are you crying for? It is only a bit of blood! It can't hurt much as you did not notice until I told you. Surely a brave girl like you isn't scared of a little blood. What is your name brave adventurer?"

"My name is Leaf and yours?" Leaf asked, pulling herself together and wiping away her tears.

"Zenna is my name. Come Leaf, let us go find Medine and she will make that knee as good as new." Leaf limped to the edge of the sand. Zenna gave her a big spiralled shell and told her to use it to breathe underwater.

"It is a magic shell. We use them to save drowning sailors. Come, follow me, I will swim slowly." Zenna flapped her tail and jumped into the water. Leaf put her goggles back on but left the snorkel dangling, and used the shell to breathe as she followed Zenna through a series of underwater caves and tunnels. Zenna pointed upwards indicating for them to surface. They were in another cave only half filled with water. Leaf breathed in the air.

"Wait here." Zenna told her and dived down again. Leaf climbed out of the water onto a rock to sit and wait. About ten minutes later Zenna returned with another mermaid and a merman.

"This is Medine and her husband Loki, they will help you while I go to find Eponina." Zenna told her and swam away. The mermaid and the merman stayed in the water, swimming around the rock she was sitting on.

"Let me look at your knee then. Oh it is only a scratch. It will be healed in a second. Close your eyes," Medine instructed her. Leaf closed her eyes. She felt Medine put her hands around her knee, which got very hot.

"There you go. All better," Medine said and Leaf opened her eyes to see her knee was completely healed.

"Thank you. Did you heal it with magic?" Leaf asked.

"We healed it with love," Medine told her. Her Greek accent was thicker than Zenna's.

Zenna returned and told Leaf that Eponina would see her. She was to follow and they would take her to Eponina.

The mermaids and the merman dove down and Leaf followed using the shell to breathe underwater. They swam down passageways and between big rocks.

At the mouth of a huge tunnel, Medina and her husband waved goodbye and Leaf continued to follow Zenna down a smaller tunnel on the right. They surfaced in a huge cave with stalactites hanging from the ceiling. A plump big breasted mermaid in a blue jewelled bikini top with a turquoise blue tail was waiting for them there. They all pulled themselves up onto the sand and Eponina and Leaf introduced themselves to each other.

The Singing Mermaid

"I have never taught a human to sing before, but as a human taught my grandmother, who taught me, I think it only right to return the favour but it is not something I can teach you in five minutes. You can spend the rest of the day with me and Zenna will come back to collect you before sundown," Eponina told her. Leaf had forgotten all about Grammy waiting for her. Leaf spent hours with Eponina in the cave which had wonderful acoustics. Eponina taught her to sing high notes she could never reach before and a magical melodic quiver she had never heard anyone ever sing. By the end of the day Leaf's throat was very sore but it had been worth it.

During the ten minute break, Leaf asked Eponina if she was born a mermaid.

"Of course I was born a mermaid!"

"But how did mermaids come to be?" Leaf persisted.

"Well our first ancestor was the goddess Atargatis in 1000 BC who loved a mortal shepherd. She killed him by accident, I'm not sure how, probably just with her presence, you know how overbearing gods can be," – actually Leaf didn't, but anyway – "She was so upset that she jumped into the lake and took the form of a fish. Over time she became a mermaid. She had children that became the first of our kind but there are humans on land that also come from this magical blood line, when mermaids mated with humans. They look mostly human but a few of them were born with the mermaid syndrome, born with their legs fused together. This seems to cause them bladder and kidney complications and they usually die a few days after birth."

"That is very sad." Leaf sighed.

"I believe only about four special cases have ever survived on land, my bloodline seems to have been the luckiest as my mother was born in the sea."

"Shall we continue with the singing now?" Eponina asked, not wanting to talk about it anymore.

Before the sun set Zenna returned.

"We need to go now, Leaf, before anyone else finds out you are here and the sun will soon go down," Zenna urged her. Leaf thanked Eponina and kissed her on her cheek. Then she had a sudden panic attack remembering Grammy and dove back into the water.

Following Zenna back through the underwater passages and out into the open sea, Leaf saw the shipwreck of the Sea Diamond cruise ship, a big octopus, barracudas and several red snapper fish.

Zenna indicated for them to go up. They surfaced and Zenna told her that she could go no further without fear of being seen.

"That is Oia over there. Can you find your way back from here?" Zenna asked, pulling herself up onto a rock and pointing to the shore.

"Yes, thank you so much. I will never forget any of you," Leaf replied.

"You must never tell anyone about us or my people would be in grave danger."

"I promise. I will only tell my grandmother but she won't ever tell," Leaf assured her.

A dolphin jumped out of the water and whistled. Zenna waved to her aquatic mammal friend. It rose out of the water again, made a clicking noise and disappeared into a wave.

"Well goodbye, Leaf. It was lovely to meet you. And don't cry over little cuts. Remember that you are a brave explorer. Maybe the bravest human I ever met."

"Goodbye, Zenna" Leaf called as Zenna dived into the water. Leaf realised she still had the shell and hoped Zenna would not mind if she kept it. She used it to get to shore. Remembering Grammy she kicked faster. She swam to the cove where she had left Grammy and her bag of clothes hidden in the rocks.

Grammy was sobbing on a rock. Standing beside her was a stern looking Rivertos who was frowning at Leaf most disapprovingly as she climbed up the rock. When Grammy saw Leaf she got hysterical.

"Where the hell have you been, Leaf?" the old woman screamed at her. She was frantic. It had been hours and Grammy had thought Leaf had surely drowned.

"I was so worried. Eventually I had to throw a note into the sea for Rivertos to come and save you because I was so scared. He just arrived. I am so sorry for the hassle, Rivertos."

"Well at least she is okay, no harm done. I'll be off then as you don't seem to need me," said the wizard, and with a pop he was gone.

"I was so scared. Never do that to me again!" Grammy said furiously, wrapping Leaf in a towel and hugging her close.

"I thought my heart was going to give out. How would I explain to your mother that I lost you in Greece looking for mermaids? I did not know what to do. I thought you were dead, Leaf. Do you know what that felt like? This has been the worst day of my life!"

"I'm really sorry Grammy, but I met them. I met the mermaids, Grammy, and one of them taught me to sing, listen to this..." Leaf sang the scales she had been taught. Grammy was astounded. She had never heard such mellifluous sounds.

"Beautiful, Leaf, but can we go home now before I have a heart attack. Really I am so angry with you."

"I am so sorry, Grammy. Promise you will never tell anyone else about the mermaids, Grammy. They swore me to secrecy."

"I promise. Now let's go!"

Leaf dried herself with the towel and got dressed. Then they climbed back over the hot rocks and followed the dirt track back to the dock. From there they watched one of the most beautiful sunsets.

Grammy and Leaf climbed some steps up to an old cottage, passing a man with three donkeys on the way. Grammy smiled and the toothless man winked. When he had passed, Grammy looked around and seeing no one was about, she went up to a blue cottage with a hemispherical roof and stuck the Key in the lock of the front door.

"On the pavement outside Leaf's dad's flat, 31 Brompton Road in Finchley, North London at five past midnight," said a very tired Grammy, turning the Key three times to the left.

Leaf placed the large spiral shell on the shelf in her room at her dad and Dana's flat, and treasured it forever.

Chapter Fourteen

WILBUR WIGGINS

Leaf's dad didn't trust Bubba because of her breed. In Germany, where his mother came from and where he had been raised, it was illegal to have Staffies and Stanfords and some other types of pit bulls. They were killing them in Germany and several other countries. Leaf cried her heart out when she heard that. Bubba was the sweetest, most loving dog anyone could ever meet. It was very unfair for dogs to be judged like that.

On Hampstead Heath, Leaf had met other owners of American Staffordshire Bull Terriers and they all agreed that their dogs were great with kids, other dogs and were very sociable and loving. Lots of little dogs had tried to attack Bubba but Bubba just walked away to find someone else to play with.

It was great when there were big dogs on the heath wanting to play because although Bubba was only a medium sized dog, she was all muscle and did not realise her own strength. She always ran over to play at full speed. She liked to jump and play rough.

A man with a Jack Russell had yelled at Leaf once for having Bubba off the lead but Bubba had not done anything, his Jack Russell was the one being nasty. Mum said the bigger the dog the nobler they are and that little dogs often had size complexes like some little men and they often liked to fight to prove themselves.

Leaf had taken Bubba to her dad's on the weekends she spent with him but now Dana was pregnant Dad seemed to be turning against Bubba. It wasn't fair! Leaf wasn't sure what she felt about Dad having another child, so she tried not to think about it. Leaf agreed to take Bubba to dog school to get her trained.

Mum could not afford it so Dad said he would pay for dog school and signed Bubba up for six months training. So Leaf and Bubba had to go every Saturday morning for two hours to the class held in the trainer's big back yard. Mum would drive them there and pick them up afterwards.

There were eight dogs and their owners in the class. Bubba loved all the attention she got, the belly rubs and stroking from the other owners and she had made friends with almost all the dogs, except a yappy Chihuahua that always bared her teeth at Bubba and everyone else.

At first Bubba actually seemed to like being told what to do and Leaf learnt a lot about dogs and how they interpreted the world around them.

In the first class Bubba and Leaf learnt the hand sign for sit. Palm up, then raise the fingers so that the hand is bent with the fingers pointing up, while saying, "SIT!" in a calm but commanding voice. They also learnt "WAIT!" by showing the dog the palm of the hand as if telling someone to stop. These became Bubba's favourite words. Bubba loved to show Leaf she understood her. When they went to the shops and Bubba had to be tied up outside, Leaf would tell her to sit and to wait, using her voice and hand actions. This seemed to tell Bubba that Leaf was in control, would be fine on her own without protection, and reassured her that Leaf would be back to get her soon. Bubba would wait quite happily outside the shop knowing Leaf would be back any minute.

When Leaf went home to her mum's on Sunday evening, she

proudly showed Mum what Bubba could do. Mum was very impressed and told Bubba she was a good dog. Bubba grinned and wagged her tail happily.

When Bubba had first come to live with them, Mum had to apply for special paperwork and licences and insurance because of Bubba's breed, but she was worth it because Bubba had brought even more love and affection into their lives, and now they could not imagine life without her.

In April of 2015, Leaf's whole class were going on a school excursion. They were taking a coach to the countryside to spend a day working on a farm. Leaf adored animals and was really looking forward to it. Mum took Leaf to school at the usual time but they did not go in. Mum waited outside with her for the rest of her classmates, the teacher and the coach to arrive. Then Mum handed over a packed lunch and Leaf's rucksack and waved her off. Leaf sat on her own, next to the window, and waved at Mum.

Duncan also sat on his own a few rows up the bus but Leaf did not dare to sit next to him or the others would have teased them both.

Most of the class sang songs on the way. Leaf joined in when she knew some of the words but then everyone else would stop singing to listen to her. One kid called her a show off and other children started saying that she thought she was so special. So Leaf took pleasure in looking out the window at the passing scenery. She thrived in nature and loved the big open spaces, colours and smells of the countryside. She felt so at peace as she stepped off the bus, no longer bothered about being called a self-loving-show-off.

202

THE WHITEASH KEY

Leaf was glad she had brought her hoodie because even though it was a dry day, there was still a chill in the air. The grass smelt of fresh dew. Yesterday's ploughed field scented the air with moist soil and manure. The farmhouse walls emanated the aroma of damp and stored apples. There was a faint stench of chickens too. Leaf took in each and every smell as they traipsed across the farmyard. Other children complained about the pong but Leaf liked the smell of the countryside.

The farmer appeared from the stable, introduced himself as Farmer Wiggins and welcomed them to Wiggins Farm. A short fat ruddy woman with a big grin and huge boobs appeared from the farmhouse with five children, aged six to seventeen. Farmer Wiggins introduced them as Mrs. Wiggins and their five little Wiggies: Ben, Lucy, George, Harold and Martha.

"Ben is seventeen and today will be showing you how to milk the cows and clean the pigs. Lucy is almost sixteen. She will be giving each of you a quick basic lesson on how to ride a horse, also how to groom horses and clean their stables. We only have three horses on the farm. One is a big Shire workhorse. The other is a show jumper, Lucy's pride and joy. They have won lots of medals in show jumping together. The third horse is an old Shetland pony which is very sweet."

"She's mine!" little Martha bust out proudly and everyone laughed. Farmer Wiggins continued, "Harold and George are terrible twins. They are eleven. They will show you how to herd sheep. And Martha will be in charge of feeding the chickens and ducks and collecting eggs."

"I'M SIX," Martha yelled out, proudly. Everyone laughed again. Farmer Wiggins continued, "I'll be showing you how to plough a field. Mrs. Wiggins will be in charge of tea and scones. We are going to split up into six groups and each group will go with a different Wiggy. Every half hour we'll swap the groups, so that you'll all get to do a bit of everything," he told them.

Leaf was put into a group with four other children. She did not know which group Sarah had been put in. Sarah had made a point of sitting with Massy Douglas at the other end of the coach from Leaf. They went in another group, so Leaf did not see Sarah all day. Leaf was half glad that Sarah was avoiding her because that morning Leaf had found the best friend necklace Sarah had given her for her birthday, broken in her bed. She was dreading having to tell Sarah about it, especially as Sarah was already not talking to her.

The kids in Leaf's group were okay, except for Brian, the boy with a green flick in his blonde hair who kept mucking about trying to be funny, but most the time he just caused accidents and got into trouble.

Leaf's group went with Ben first to see the milking machines. About ten cows were squeezed into thin metal stalls.

"The stalls might look tight but it actually keeps the cows calmer, like a squeeze hug." Ben told them.

"Those tubes from the machines are attached to the cow's nipples by rubber teats and pump the milk out. It goes up the tubes and into cylinders to be boiled and sterilised, before being bottled and sold."

Ben took them back outside to where a docile cow was tied up next to a stool and a metal bucket. He demonstrated to them how to milk a cow by hand and they each had a go. It was not as easy as it looked. When Leaf finally managed to squirt some out, the warm milk hit the side of the bucket and spattered back on her face. Yuck!

"Look, machine gun boobs." Brian pulled on the poor cow's nipples and aimed, trying to squirt them all with milk. The cow mooed. One girl got it straight in her face. It was dripping off her glasses.

Next they went to feed the pigs and clean the sty. Six pigs in a pen snorted as they approached. Ben filled their long metal trough from a blue bucket of scraps. The pigs all huddled round grunting and tucked into the grub. Ben closed the eating area off with a small fence to allow the children to enter the main part of the sty with hard wooden brooms to sweep out the old straw and muck. Phew! It stank! When the sty had been washed out by hose and fresh hay laid, the children went out and Ben released the pigs back into the clean pen.

Ben took them to a smaller pen where a big sow and a little pink piglet lived. Ben introduced the pigs as Sally and her son Wilbur.

"He is so cute!" Leaf stated, reaching over the fence to scratch Wilbur on the head.

"Martha named him after the pig from her Disney DVD of Charlotte's Web," Ben told her.

"Why are these two separate from the others?" Brian asked.

"Sally does not breed well, she is too old now. The rest of her litter died during birth. So she is being sold at market tomorrow, before she gets too old to make good pork chops," Ben told them. He looked really sad.

"I grew up with this old pig. I shall miss her, but that is farming life." He wiped an eye with his sleeve.

"AND THE PIGLET IS BEING SOLD TO A RESTAURANT THAT SERVES ROAST SUCKLING PIG ON SUNDAYS,"

Wilbur Wiggins

Martha shouted across the yard.

"GET BACK TO YOUR CHICKENS AND MIND YOUR OWN BUSINESS," Ben shouted back. Leaf was very upset. Poor little piglet! They were allowed to go in the pen to pet the sow and the little piggy. Leaf instantly fell in love with Wilbur.

After cups of tea and homemade jam scones in the warm farmhouse kitchen, the groups swapped over and Leaf's group went to learn to ride a horse with Lucy. It was the first time Leaf had ever been on a horse. It was a bit scary at first and not at all comfy. It hurt trying to lift your bum in rhythm to the horse. In films it looked like you just sat on it but it was actually hard work. Leaf had muscle ache in her legs for the rest of the day. She liked stroking and grooming the horses best, while the two boys mucked out the stalls. Brian kept throwing horse manure at Tom.

Everyone washed their hands with washing-up liquid and water from the outdoor tap. Then they sat in the warm, sweet smelling hay loft and ate their pack lunches. Leaf noticed that Duncan did not have any lunch so she offered him one of her sandwiches,

"No thanks, I'm not hungry," he repudiated.

"Neither am I, so it will just go to waste if you don't eat it," she replied, knowing he was too proud to accept it. He half smiled and devoured it in a hungry fervour.

"Thanks," he said as they were leaving the hay loft. Leaf knew he had really appreciated it and it was considerate of him to thank her. She wished she could do more to help him but she did not want to make a big deal out of it in case she embarrassed him. So she just smiled.

After lunch, they swapped the groups around again. Harold

and George were indeed terrible twins. They were always up to tricks and telling tall tales.

"And in this barn we have a tyrannosaurus!"

The twins taught the group to jump from the loft onto the bales of hay below. When Leaf landed she sprained her ankle. The pain was severe but she rubbed some of the green fairy dust from her necklace onto the ankle and whispered, "Dust to dust, all life begins, wishes to ashes flown to the gods on butterfly wings. Green for healing, fairy magic known, on butterfly wings wishes are flown." Her ankle was healed before anyone noticed.

They went out to a green field to round up the sheep but really the dogs did most of the work. Mr. Wiggins showed them how to plough. After half an hour of back breaking work, they went to join Martha, but there was really nothing left to do with her because the other groups had found all the eggs and had fed the chickens and ducks five times already.

"How much does a restaurant pay for a piglet, do you know?" Leaf asked Martha quietly.

"About £30 pounds I think my dad said."

Leaf wandered off on her own and when no one was looking she poured some of the fairy dust into her hand and clenched it tight.

"Dust to dust, all life begins. Wishes to ashes, flown to the gods on butterfly wings. Green for money, fifty pounds, fairy magic known, on the wings of butterflies wishes are flown." She opened her hand and there was a fifty pound note. She wandered back and gave the money to Martha.

"Give this to your dad for the piglet. I will find it a good home but do not give the money to him or say anything until we are gone, okay," Leaf instructed her.

"Okay, I never saw your face, got it," Martha replied with a grin.

While the others were slowly making their way to the coach and the Wiggins family were still chatting with their teacher, Leaf dashed across the farm and into the pen. After a palaver of trying to catch Wilbur, she stuffed the little piglet into her empty rucksack. Trying to look innocent, she boarded the coach and took a window seat at the back. She put the wriggling bag onto her lap, and put her hand inside to comfort Wilbur with a back scratch. It did the trick, he calmed right down but every so often he would grunt with pleasure and the other kids on the back row would look at her with disgust. She had to pretend she had fallen asleep and let out the occasional snore.

Mum was waiting for her at the school when the coach arrived. She didn't notice anything as Leaf put her heavy backpack in the back of the car. Thankfully, Wilbur was sleeping quietly.

When they got home Leaf told Mum she wanted to walk Bubba over to Grammy's house and would be back in an hour. Mum felt safer about Leaf being out when she had Bubba to protect her and it was only a fifteen minute walk if you crossed the heath.

"Okay, but just give me a quick call so I know you got there okay. Don't forget. Don't stay at Grammy's more than an hour, it is getting late. Give me a missed call when you are leaving." She gave Leaf a kiss.

With the rucksack on Leaf's back and Bubba on her lead, they walked across the heath to Grammy's house.

"Grammy?" Leaf called as she walked in through the front door. She used the phone in Grammy's hallway, dialled Mum's number, waited for her to answer, said "I'm here, love you", waited for "I love you too" and hung up.

"Hello darling, what a nice surprise. Did you have a nice day on the farm? Come through," Grammy ushered Leaf and Bubba into the kitchen. Grammy sat down at the table, waiting to hear all about Leaf's day on the farm.

"Oh yes, it was great. I bought you a present. It was quite expensive but I'm sure you are going to love it." Leaf was trying to manipulate the situation. She pulled the piglet out of the bag and dumped him in Grammy's lap. Wilbur woke up and grunted at Grammy.

"But I'm Jewish, Wormy!" Grammy teased.

"That's how I knew he would be safe with you," Leaf replied with a smile, always one to appreciate Grammy's humour. Actually, as Grammy had been born Jewish it wasn't entirely a joke but now she followed Shamanic teachings and she did eat pork, especially Spanish Jamon Serrano and English bacon sandwiches.

"Well, he is rather cute. What's his name?"

"Wilbur Wiggins. He'll love your garden. They are really clean and they are much more intelligent than dogs. You can walk him and he will keep you company," Leaf told her. Grammy laughed.

"Wilbur is the name of the piglet from a book called Charlotte's Web, written by a man called Elwyn Brooks-White. Wilbur is the name I probably would have called him. Perfect!" She put Wilbur down on the floor and went to get him a saucer of milk. Wilbur followed Grammy to the kitchen wagging his tiny tail.

Wilbur Wiggins

After that Wilbur Wiggins followed Grammy everywhere and became quite well known around Hampstead. People would wave to him when they saw Grammy driving past in her Union-Jack Mini with Wilbur on a booster seat, belted into the passenger side and looking happily out the window. Wilbur even slept with Grammy in the turquoise bed as he was a very clean little pig.

Grammy bought Wilbur a blue harness and lead, and they would meet up with Leaf and Bubba for walks on Hampstead Heath. Bubba and Wilbur loved to swim in the pond there. Wilbur thought he was a dog and got on great with Bubba. He was a much loved pig. Despite Grammy having been born Jewish, Wilbur became her new best friend.

Chapter Fifteen

THE BEATLES

The 28th of July was Grammy's birthday. Grammy had asked Mum if she could take Leaf out for the day to celebrate. Leaf had just got home from dog training class when Grammy drove up in Sally, her Union Jack Mini, with music blaring out of the windows.

Leaf hugged Mum goodbye and handed her Bubba on the lead. Grammy turned the music off. She was wearing a rainbow T-shirt which read:

PLANT LOVELY IDEAS, NOT LANDMINES.

"Honey, we won't be long and I'll pop in later and have a cup of tea and a birthday biscuit with you," Grammy yelled out the window to Mum. Mum waved as Leaf got in the car and then went back into the kitchen to finish the raspberry ripple cake she was making for Grammy. Grammy started the engine and they shot off, singing along to **I Love Rock 'n' Roll** with Joan Jett at the top of their voices.

When Grammy had parked, Leaf gave her a card she had made, lots of pretty coloured feathers she had collected, and two hand-painted flower pots that she had decorated in art class at school. Grammy was really pleased and said she would grow watercress in them, and she chose two white feathers to wear in her hair that day.

Grammy and Leaf went for tea and cakes in a special café

that sold every type of cake there was. Leaf had a slice of rocky-road double chocolate ice-cream cake and Grammy had two slices of white chocolate ice-cream cake drizzled in raspberry sauce. Raspberry was her favourite flavour.

"If you have the Key on you we could go anywhere you like to celebrate your birthday," Leaf suggested. Grammy thought about it for a while, stated that as Leaf liked concerts they should go to a Beatles concert.

"Beatles?"

"The Beatles were the most famous group in the whole world when I was young. Come on, you'll love them," Grammy assured her.

"Okay, it is your birthday. Do you know where one of their concerts was held?"

"The most famous concert was the Shea concert in America."

"Okay, then let's go," Leaf said. Grammy paid the bill and they went for a walk around the block.

It was a nice quiet neighbourhood, neat modern houses with tidy lawns and not many people about. They walked up a path and put the Key in the lock of someone's green front door. At the last minute they almost got caught by a neighbour coming out of his house.

"In the audience of The Beatles Shea Concert in America, 15th of August, 1965," Grammy instructed the door before the neighbour saw them.

Suddenly, they were falling through a door and into the audience of fifty-five thousand people around a field. The security guards covered their ears and so did Grammy because as the Beatles entered the field the noise from the crowd was deafening.

"OH DEAR, MAYBE I AM TOO OLD FOR THIS NOW!"

212

Grammy shouted to Leaf.

After the cheering partially died down, the music began.

"That one on keyboards is John Lennon, the one singing now is Paul McCartney and that is George Harrison and Ringo Starr," Grammy told her, pointing them out.

The concert was actually great fun and Leaf recognised one or two of the songs, not that anyone could hear the music very well over the crowd and the vast distance between the band and the audience. The people at the front would start singing and that is how the ones at the back knew what to sing along to. Even the band could not hear themselves playing. John Lennon found the whole thing so ridiculous that he started playing the keyboard with his elbows and the whole band started laughing.

Once or twice fans ran out onto the field and were taken away by the security guards. All the women were screaming with delight, some were crying and one or two even fainted. The concert did not last long. It was over in half an hour which was about as much as anyone could take of the deafening roar of the crowd. Grammy and Leaf were jostled along towards the exit and filed out with the others.

In a back street they put the Key in the front door of a house and went back to Grammy's car in England. They had only been gone an hour in total.

"WOW! That was the most exciting birthday I've ever had. But I couldn't do it again. I prefer to listen to them on cassette or on a compact disk," Grammy admitted. Putting her foot down on the accelerator, she drove Leaf home in Sally, singing along to **I've Got a Ticket to Ride** with The Beatles.

Two nights after Grammy's birthday, two men in dark suits

with mirrored sunglasses knocked on Mr and Mrs Parker's front door. The commissioner removed his glasses.

"Good evening. Sorry to disturb you. I am Commissioner Paul Locker, Justice of the Peace of the Metropolitan police and this is detective Malcolm Shiver," stated the forty-eight-year-old man of sturdy stature with white blonde hair, fixing Mrs. Parker with his cruel grey eyes that had slit pupils like a snake and bulged out of his pale pock-marked face. Malcolm Shiver stood in his shadow, a tall blonde, square-jawed man in his late thirties with a flattened nose and pale blue expressionless eyes hidden behind his face-recognition glasses.

Both men flashed their badges at Mrs. Parker who stood in the lit doorway wearing a purple dressing gown over her porky figure and curlers in her thinning hair.

"We are following up on a robbery that occurred next door on Thursday the fourth of September last year, and we were wondering if you remember seeing anything suspicious or out of the ordinary that night or around the date in question?" inquired Paul Locker.

"There is always something out of the ordinary going on next door!" Mrs. Parker exclaimed, disapprovingly.

"I don't remember anything about that night but a week later that weird woman and her overly skinny granddaughter were prancing about the garden in long witchy cloaks summoning demons. She deserves everything she gets that woman, lowering the tone of the neighbourhood, quite disgraceful the way she behaves and brainwashing that poor underfed child. She should be locked up she should, and she always parks that unsightly car of hers in front of our house."

"Summoning demons?" inquired Detective Shiver

"Oh yes! And talking to the aliens! She was making quite a spectacle of herself, yelling something about anarchy and toads. I think she cut the girl when they were hiding under the tree. The girl was sucking on her finger when they came back out. I believe they were performing blood ceremonies and the child looked terrified out of her mind. Child abuse that is! Ought to be locked up! The woman is quite out of her tiny mind! Witchcraft! Always running about her garden, beating a drum and waving feathers around. Ludicrous old woman! Could you do something about her parking that eye-sore in front of our house?"

"WHO IS IT, NORMA?" yelled Roger Parker, heaving himself up from the sofa to find out who was rude enough to come calling at nine-thirty at night. His oversized form appearing from the living room, stomping down the hallway to his wife's side.

"Good evening, Sir. I am Commissioner Paul Locker from the Metropolitan Police, inquiring about the robbery at number twelve last September."

"Commissioner? Aren't you a bit high up in the ranks to be making house calls?"

"Yes well, it is not because we are short staffed, I can assure you. No, just setting the tone that we are serious about catching house burglars. We are tough on crime in the community."

"That is why it has taken ten months for you to come making inquiries, is it?" smirked Mr. Parker.

"Did you happen to see anything suspicious on the night of the robbery or any other nights leading up it?" interrupted the detective to alleviate the commissioner's apparent discomfort and lack of reasonable explanation.

"I saw that ruddy hippy woman going out on a foggy night in legwarmers and a leotard which was suspicious. Imagine bumping into that in an alley! She's in her seventies, you know. It shouldn't be allowed! That's an offence in itself," snorted Roger Parker.

"Okay, thank you both for your time," finished the detective. Mrs. Parker shut the door.

"That ceremony she was talking about could have been the Whiteash Initiation Ceremony for her granddaughter," said the agitated commissioner through clenched teeth, as they deviated from the Parker's front door towards the unmarked car.

"But we still do not have any proof that they are Guardians. It is all still based on vague suspicion," observed the detective.

"Talk about hostile witnesses," scoffed the commissioner, putting his glasses back on as they got into the car.

"I think we should force the information out of the child and the old woman," suggested the detective. They sat for a moment in the dark staring at Grammy's house.

"Not tonight. We'll come back. Have Dixon watch the house again. We'll return when we know the child is there. If we threaten to kill them, one of them will break and tell us."

"You do realise we will have to kill them either way."

"Dixon can kill the kid. He'll do anything if I order him to. We'll come back in a few days, when those nosey Parkers next door aren't snooping through the curtains," Paul Locker replied and they both looked back to where Mrs. Parker was having a last look before closing the drapes.

The commissioner removed his sunglasses again and massaged his temples where he could feel another headache starting. Malcolm Shiver inserted the key, started the engine and they drove away into the night.

Chapter Sixteen

THE WHITE RABBIT

Bubba was doing quite well at training classes. Grammy had started taking them so that Wilbur could attend the classes too. Wilbur loved the dogs and was quick to learn tricks and how to follow basic instructions. In fact Wilbur was the best in the class.

Leaf learnt how dogs pick up information by scent and that dogs have a much wider field of vision than humans, enabling them to see to the sides and even behind them.

"Dogs are not completely colour blind as most people believe," Maggie the trainer told them, "But they do not see colours as well as we do and sometimes have a problem telling reds from greens. They see better than us in low lighting and this makes them better hunters. When you don't see colours too well, you see movement faster. One in three men are colour blind, it is a prehistoric gene for hunting, and women see colours better because they were the berry pickers who had to see red from green."

Maggie taught them that a dog's hyper sensitivity to movement meant it was easier to train a dog by hand gestures and body language rather than verbal commands.

"Dogs are long sighted and don't focus well when things are too close to them. Up close a dog will rely on his or her nose for information. Dog's ears can hear five times further than human ears and they pick up high pitched sounds that humans cannot hear. Dogs have their own language and communicate in many different ways through gestures and stances, yawns, licking, nibbling, raising heads, lowering tails and lots of sounds. A

217

wrinkled forehead can indicate aggression, a smooth forehead shows the dog is relaxed," Maggie explained.

"When a dog wants to dominate a situation they will push their eyebrows forward and stare in challenge. Staring is usually a sign of dominance and aggression, but it could also mean that he is just confident and paying attention. If a dog looks away it shows he or she feels insecure but poses no threat. They blink a lot when frightened. In a relaxed environment a dog may stare and blink at the owner to say I love you. Ears up mean they are confident and alert. Ears back can show a dog is nervous and they want you to back off, unless accompanied by tail wagging and then it usually means friendliness."

"Dogs also show they are nervous by lifting their paw, licking their lips, tail between the legs, crouching down and eyes slightly closed. Lips are often used to show aggression. When the lips are drawn forward it means aggression. If the teeth are exposed it usually means aggression. So it would be time to back off," Maggie told them.

Leaf was pretty sure Maggie knew what she was talking about, she had been a dog trainer for fifteen years, but some dogs, especially Staffies like Bubba, simply liked smiling. Maggie certainly knew a lot about dogs, and Leaf felt she was learning loads from these classes but she wasn't sure how much Bubba was learning. After the basic, SIT, WAIT, CROSS (when crossing a road) and JUMP, Bubba did not seem to want to learn any more. She just wanted to make friends and sit for treats.

Wilbur and Grammy were getting on far better. In just two classes Wilbur had learnt SIT, LIE DOWN, ROLL OVER, WAIT, CROSS, JUMP, and now Grammy was trying to teach Wilbur to play dead when she pretended to shoot him. Next Grammy would be teaching Wilbur Wiggins to break-dance and parkour, Leaf thought to herself.

Bubba was pulling Leaf all over the place. Leaf was shouting, "HERE! HERE! HERE!" and trying to pull her back but Bubba was not listening. She had spotted a treat someone had dropped and then she wanted to play to the English bulldog on the other side of Maggie's big back yard.

Leaf told her dad that Bubba was doing well in training class. Well she had learnt sit, wait, off, and no, so she was doing okay. Who needed a dog that could roll over anyway? Dad was very pleased to hear that Bubba was doing well in training. Leaf was not pleased to hear his news. They announced it at breakfast and Leaf almost choked on her cornflakes.

"Dana and I have decided to get married," Dad told her in a please don't make a fuss tone. Leaf didn't say anything. Dana waddled out of the room so they could talk alone. She was getting so hugely pregnant.

"Well, are you not happy for me?" Dad questioned.

"Happy for what?"

"I'm getting married, Leaf!"

"Why do you have to marry her? Why are you going to tie yourself to her forever?" Leaf asked.

"Well for one, we are having a baby in four months and that is forever," her dad reminded her.

"Mum wasn't forever! I wasn't! Well you can't stop the baby now but why marry her?"

"Leaf, you are forever. Mum and I will always be family. I love Dana and she is now also a big part of our family," Dad told her.

"She is not my family! She is just your girlfriend," Leaf

screamed.

"Well now she is going to be my wife and the mother of your soon to be born sister. Go to your room if you are going to be so miserable about it." Dad pointed to the door.

Leaf lay on her bed feeling miserable. She didn't even have Bubba to hug because Dana didn't want Bubba jumping on her stomach, so she now stayed at Mum's house on the weekends and Leaf went alone to her Dad's. Leaf felt sad and wanted to go home to her mum.

There was a knock on the door. Dana popped her head into the room.

"Kan I kome in?" she asked in her thick Russian accent.

"Please yourself," Leaf answered, nonchalantly.

"I know zis verrry harrd forr you rright now, lots of big changes. Am I rright? But I love yourr farrzerr, he make me verrry happy and ve have baby. All vill be good, you vill see," Dana said, sitting next to her on the bed. Leaf tried a weak smile.

"Kome! I buy you prresent, koz Bubba niet kome herre now. I like dog. Vhen I vas child ve had big blue Grrreat Dane. You know zis? Big, big dog. I like Bubba, but forrr baby I need be karrreful. Bubba verrrry strrong, too strrong for me have herre now. So I buy you big white rrabbit. Kome see."

Leaf followed Dana down the corridor, through the kitchen and out into the garden. There was a lovely wooden hutch. Leaf opened the little door and peeked inside. Two little beady black eyes, almost hidden in a big ball of white fluff, stared back at Leaf. A little pink nose twitched and sniffed at her. Leaf reached inside and pulled out the biggest fluffiest white rabbit she had ever seen.

"You like? He Angorra rrabbet. Yourr farrzerr made kage forr two veeks," Dana told her. Leaf snuggled into the fluffy

220

The White Rabbit

white rabbit that seemed to snuggle back.

"I love him! Thank you, Dana."

"Vhat you kall him? Snowbol?" Dana suggested.

"No, Snowball is too obvious. I want to give him a proper name. Beatrice Potter gave her rabbits proper names, like Peter and Benjamin. I think I'll call mine George." Dana laughed.

"How you know he boy?"

"He looks like a boy. He is too big to be a girl. Anyway if worst came to worse, I could say it was short for Georgette."

"Courrgette. Verrrry good name," Dana joked, although her English was not that great so you could never be sure if she was joking.

"His name will be Snowball George. Do you want to hold him?" Leaf offered.

"Niet, in Rrrussia ve no play viz food. I joke! He prrretty rrrabbet but I vearr black. Hairy black drress no good look forr me. I go klean kitchen. You play." Off she went back into the house. Leaf stayed and stroked George.

Dana came out to bring some carrots and lettuce for Snowball George and Leaf happily hand fed him. Snowball George seemed very tame and after the food was gone, he hopped onto Leaf's lap and snuggled down for more nose stroking. Leaf felt happy and maybe having Dana around would not be so bad after all. She was funny. At least Leaf hoped she was joking and wasn't planning to eat George at some point.

Leaf spent the whole of Saturday afternoon happily playing in the garden with Snowball George who sniffed and chewed at Dad's plants and vegetables growing in the small square garden.

"I'll have to fence those off" said Dad, coming out into the garden to tell Leaf to come in for supper.

221

"Thanks for making the cage, Dad. It's brill!"

"You're welcome. You like your Angora rabbit then?"

"I love him!" Leaf declared.

"Good, now put him back in his hut for the night and come in and wash your hands for supper" Dad instructed.

On Sunday morning before breakfast, Leaf cleaned out George's cage and gave him fresh straw, carrots and dry rabbit food which Dana had bought. Dad said that because the garden was fenced on all sides George could be left to jump around the garden during the day but at night he must be locked up in the hut, otherwise the cold or foxes would get to him.

Leaf left Snowball George free to hop about while she went in to have some toast and honey. Dana poured her a glass of orange juice and set a plate of golden toast down in front of her.

"What does Angora mean?" Leaf asked. Dad looked up from his paper.

"It's a country or rather it was. It is Turkey now."

"Turkey? A RABBIT COUNTRY TURNED INTO A TURKEY? You are pulling my chicken leg," Leaf sniggered.

"No dummy, the country called Turkey," Dad smirked. "There is no country called Turkey," Leaf spluttered her orange juice. Dad frowned.

"Of kourrse! It Kountrry farr away frrom Hungrry kountrry," Dana joked. Leaf didn't know what she was on about but Dad laughed. They seemed to understand one another and found each other funny.

"Snowball George is an English Angora rabbit" Dad informed her, as if that was supposed to make any sense.

"Snowbol George English Turrkey rrabbet!" Dana laughed. "The pet shop owner said you must brush him a lot and cut the

222

rabbit's fur back every ninety days. If you do not, he will get fur balls stuck in his throat and digestive system which could kill him, so it is very important you look after him properly," Dad stated.

"But I'm only here two weekends a month," Leaf protested.

"I vill do it. I vill brrush rrabbet and give hairr kut and perrm vhen you arrre not herre," Dana offered kindly.

"PERM?" Leaf spluttered.

"Da nice kurrly rrabbet. I just joke, Leaf. I niet serrious," Dana laughed.

"Apparently papaya fruit is the best thing to give him to help him break down the wool he has digested. I'll buy some tomorrow. We bought you a special brush, food, straw and a bottle you hang up in the hutch for him to drink from. You must give him fresh water every day. Dana or I will do it when you are not here."

Leaf went to watch the television for a while. Dana said as long as Snowball George sat on a towel and did not get hair all over the sofa or poop that he could come in and watch TV too. George seemed to like cartoons and action films the best and he sat on his towel next to Leaf on the sofa staring at the moving pictures. It looked like he was watching the TV but it was hard to tell with all that fur hanging down in front of his face. Leaf decided to plait it so George could see more of the world around him. By the time she was finished George was covered in tiny plaits. Dana laughed when she saw George.

"Zat not Angorra rrabbet, zat Rrrastafarrrian rrabbet!" Dana laughed at her own joke but as usual Leaf didn't know what she was on about. Leaf just smiled and did not tell Dana that George had pooped about fifty times in his towel.

"It's Boy George!" Dad laughed as he came into the room. He

223

and Dana started singing a Boy George song that Leaf had never heard of. A German dad and a Russian step-mum reviving eighties karaoke Leaf found hysterically funny.

Leaf was sad to leave George when she went back to her mum's house on Sunday evening but she was happy to be reunited with Mum and Bubba.

The next weekend, Leaf was spending Saturday night to Sunday afternoon at Grammy's house. Mum dropped her off at six-thirty. By seven, Grammy and Leaf were curled up on the sofa with tea, homemade biscuits, and Grammy's tablet watching the X-Factor's top ten performances of 2013/2014 on YouTube. Grammy was crying over Nicholas McDonald singing 'A Thousand Years'.

Suddenly, there was a knock at the door. Grammy wiped her tears and got up to answer it. There were angry voices in the hall. The next thing Leaf knew was that Grammy was being forced into the living room by a three men in dark suits as Sam Bailey belted out the vocals in a great rendition of 'Who's Loving You'. Leaf dropped the tablet in fright.

"Sit down." Dixon pushed Grammy onto the sofa. He wore a dark suit and mirrored sunglasses but seemed all muscles, brutish and unrefined. He chewed gum and spoke with a cockney accent.

"I suppose you know why we are here?" said the commissioner in an upper class voice. Leaf shrivelled under his cold, snake-like stare and Grammy put her arm protectively around Leaf.

"I have no idea. How dare you just barge into my house!"

"Just tell us where the Key is and we will leave," insisted

Detective Shiver.

"Key? What key? My house keys and car keys are on the table in the hall."

"Oh come now, don't play games," Commissioner Locker smirked.

"I think you have the wrong house. I know nothing about a key. Now please leave, you are scaring the child," Grammy insisted as Dixon began searching in drawers and breaking things. Grammy winced as he threw her new ornaments from the mantel and they smashed on the floor.

"We will leave when you give us the Key."

"I told you..." Everyone was momentarily distracted by Tamera Foster's stunning voice singing a Whitney classic, the men obviously moved by her beauty. For six seconds everyone just stared at the tablet that was face-up on the floor.

The commissioner crushed the tablet with his boot.

"Take the child in the other room," he instructed Dixon. Leaf screamed as the bad man grabbed her and carried her kicking through the dining room and into the kitchen.

"Grammy..." Leaf pleaded for her to help.

"No! Don't hurt her!" Grammy cried out and she rose to her feet. Shiver pushed her back down and she fell onto the sofa and sobbed.

"We won't hurt her if you tell us where the Key is."

"I told you I don't know what you are talking about," Grammy insisted, the tears pouring down her face.

"Shiver, search the cellar," ordered the commissioner. Shiver left the room.

"If you don't tell us where the Key is, we are going to start cutting up your lovely granddaughter," hissed Paul Locker into Grammy's face.

"I cannot tell you what I do not know" wailed Grammy. They

could hear Leaf screaming and Wilbur squealing in the kitchen.

"You were seen going in through a door in 1983 but you never came out and it happened again this year. I know Leaf cannot have the Key until she is twelve but does your granddaughter have the Key hidden on her? Don't lie to me. Dixon will find out if she has. Ten year olds are rather sensitive to pain."

"Don't you hurt her!" Grammy shot to her feet and palm punched him straight in the nose. Then she got scared and lost her confidence. With watery eyes, he caught her wrist and twisted her arm behind her back. She yelped in arthritic pain. He pressed the barrel of his gun to the side of her head. Grammy closed her eyes in silent prayer.

"Do you know who I am?" the commissioner said in a threatening voice.

"No and I don't want to know. If you leave now I won't tell the police, I promise."

"I am the police! I am also a surviving member of generations of the Locker family. I, like my forefathers, have dedicated my life to finding people like you who think you are above the law, above God. If I do not succeed in wiping out the Key Guardians, then I have two sons, twins, they are only babies right now but one day they will hunt down your granddaughter's grandchild."

Grammy noticed the black tattoo behind the commissioner's ear, a flaming black sun around the cross and the nails. Detective Shiver returned without his jacket on, carrying one of Grammy's most expensive bottles of wine, and said he had searched the cellar but found nothing.

"The woman is insane! She's got a live pig just running around the kitchen. The bloody thing tried to bite me. I kicked it into the cupboard," Shiver exclaimed.

"You brute!" Grammy scowled.

"Lock the old woman and the child in the cellar while we search the rest of the house. We will deal with them later," Paul Locker said furiously. As Shiver grabbed her arm she noticed he also bore the same tattoo as the commissioner. She was escorted roughly to the kitchen. Leaf ran into her arms.

"Are you okay? Did they hurt you?" Grammy held her at arm's length to assess her.

"I'm fine," Leaf spoke bravely, "but they kicked Wilbur and said they were going to kill you if I did not tell them about a key. I told them I don't know anything about any key but I was so scared."

They could hear Wilbur Wiggins squealing inside the cupboard under the sink. Shiver opened the cellar door and ordered them down the stairs. They heard him lock the door behind them.

"Well done, Beautiful. I am so proud of you for saying nothing. Now call Flamous on your pentagram, he will get rid of them for us." Leaf reached inside her jumper for the silver pentagram, clutched it in her hand and called, "Flamous, please come we need you!"

There was a loud popping sound and Flamous appeared in the cellar.

"Good Evening, ladies. My, my, what a fine collection of wines," Flamous stated, blowing the dust off a bottle of Merlot. Leaf sneezed.

"Flamous, there are dangerous men upstairs. They are Lockers and they are searching the house for the Key. We need you to get rid of them before they find it," Grammy told him.

"Only if I can have this bottle, I do love a little drop of a good wine."

"Yes, take it," Grammy agreed. Flamous disappeared with the bottle.

227

"Come, Leaf, I need to get you out of here." Grammy pulled the side of the wine rack and it swung forward to reveal the mouth of a tunnel behind it. There was a strong stench of damp and the sound of dripping. Grammy yanked a horrified Leaf through a cobweb into the dark tunnel and pulled at the wine rack to seal the hidden escape route.

"Do you have your phone?" said Grammy's voice in the darkness. Leaf stopped frantically checking her hair for spiders and pulled her cheap mobile out of her pocket, pressing the button for the torch. It did not have a camera or any cool apps but she was so grateful for the fact it had a torch.

"Shine it up on the left wall." Leaf did as Grammy had said. Grammy reached for an oil lantern sitting on a shelf which she lit with a match from the small box beside it. The space illuminated to show a short stretch of thin concrete passage that turned abruptly left, left again and then right. It continued on down a much larger but pitch-black stretch of tunnel with no end in sight. Leaf kept her phone torch on and followed Grammy. She walked through another cobweb and ran her hand frantically over her hair.

After ten metres, the tunnel under Grammy's garden turned to the right, where stone steps rose up to a small trap door. Grammy pushed upwards and it stiffly opened to let in the cold starry night. They climbed out of a pile of leaves between the trees on the other side of Grammy's garden wall. They were in the wooded area that ran behind the gardens of Grammy's street.

Over the wall and through Grammy's bedroom window, they could see lightning striking inside the house. Someone cried out. Grammy gasped as a curtain caught fire, and then sighed as it was immediately extinguished.

"Get down!" Grammy pulled Leaf to the ground as Mrs. Parker looked out of her window to see what was causing the disturbance. Seeing nothing in the garden, she went downstairs to get a glass so she could put it to the wall to hear what was going on next door.

The lightning stopped. There was silence for a few moments, and then Grammy and Leaf heard the screech of tires as a car sped off. Flamous reappeared beside them.

"They have gone," he assured them.

"Do we have to bury any dead bodies?" Grammy asked.

"No, not this time, but they won't be back in a hurry. They didn't know what hit them!" laughed Flamous.

"Oh Flamous, thank you so much." Leaf hugged him. She was so relieved.

"You were a very brave young lady. Well, I'll be off then to enjoy putting my feet up with a nice glass of wine," he said, brandishing the bottle. There was a loud pop and he was gone.

"Grammy, how come the wizards know about the Key?"

"They are sworn to secrecy as Key Carers who protect the Key Guardians. Plus, I know a few of their secrets so they would never tell. Now, I think we deserve a nice cup of tea before we clean up whatever mess they have left for us, and we need to get Wilbur Wiggins out of the cupboard," Grammy declared, giving Leaf a kiss on the head.

The following Friday Leaf went back to her dad's. Her mum dropped her off in the evening after Leaf's singing class. She kissed Mum goodbye at the door and used her own front door key to go inside. Dad and Dana were in the kitchen.

"We have a big problem!" Dad said to Leaf. He opened the back door and pointed out to the garden. Leaf looked, and wide eyed counted fifteen baby rabbits hopping all over the garden.

"It has gone hopping mad around here!" Dad exclaimed with

229

his hands on his head in despair.

"Turrrns out Snowbol Georrrge neit boy." Dana said sarcastically. Leaf could not believe her eyes. There were so many bunnies and all so cute. Dad said they were almost two weeks old. Leaf went out to see Snowball George who was hiding from the sun in the hutch. Leaf pulled him - no - her out. She was smaller than before, not much, but definitely lighter.

"Well Georgette, this is a surprise!" Leaf stated, hugging Snowball George and looking around. She sat down on the rabbit trimmed grass and put Georgette on her lap. Some of the tiny bunnies came up and nibbled the grass around them.

"What are we going to call them all?" Leaf asked her dad.

"We can't keep them, Leaf. The pet shop has agreed to take ten next week and we will have to find homes for the rest."

"We are not going to keep any?" Leaf looked horrified.

"Ve can keep one, maybe two, but neit more, and ONLY BOYS!" Dana shouted from the kitchen. Leaf looked around. There were hairy balls of different patterns and colours, mostly white or blue grey or both. Leaf spotted one that had ears in pink or peach, she wasn't sure, but Leaf wanted that one. She reached over and scooped the bunny up and placed it in her lap next to Snowball George.

"I'll call you Melocoton. Mellow for short," Leaf said, remembering melocoton was the word for peach in Spanish. A little grey/blue bunny with a black splodge on his nose also hopped over and crawled into her lap and snuggled up to his mum.

"Okay, I'll keep you too little fellow and I shall call you Splodge," Leaf declared, not really knowing if they were boys or girls, assuming a boy might be blue but maybe not peach coloured. She hoped Dana did not notice.

The White Rabbit

At night Leaf put Mellow and Splodge in the hutch with their mum Snowball Georgette. The rest were going to be kept in a cardboard box in the kitchen. Of course by morning the kitchen was a hopping disaster.

At 10:30 on Saturday mornings, Grammy would collect Leaf in her little car, Sally. Leaf sat in the passenger seat up front, Wilbur and Bubba strapped in the back.

At dog training, Wilbur sat as good as gold listening to Maggie talk about dogs. Bubba was not behaving too well at all. She was not listening to anyone and just wanted to jump and play.

"A confident dog will walk with its head up. A weaker dog might show its throat to another dog to show that they are no threat, as if to say please don't hurt me either," Maggie told them.

There was a Boxer in the group called Morris. Morris had been abandoned by his previous owner but was now loved by Jim, his new man-friend. Morris had his tail cut off when he was a pup and his owner Jim was asking Maggie how much this would affect Morris.

"It is very cruel to cut off a dog's tail and Morris will always be affected by it. Dogs need tails to balance and communicate. A tail that is held high means confidence. Low indicates fear. A wagging tail means being happy and friendly. A tail that wags slowly is being cautious. A still straight tail means a problem. Extended and slightly curled is a warning. Without his tail he cannot communicate like a dog," Maggie told Jim and the rest of the group.

"A paw placed over another dog's neck means a challenge, to

231

play fight or a real fight or to dominate. When we hug dogs they may think we are trying to be controlling, unless the dog is used to you hugging it."

If another dog put its paw on Bubba's neck she might feel she was being dominated but at home with Leaf and Mum it was clear that Bubba knew it was hugging. Bubba slept like a human with her arms around Leaf's neck. She never seemed to be nervous when hugged. Quite the opposite, Bubba would spend all day hugging if she could. Silly dog!

"When dogs bow down they are inviting you to play. When a dog shows its belly it is usually to say, I am no threat so please don't hurt me or they are asking a human for a belly rub. If you do not know the dog, don't touch it because showing the belly could be saying back off." Maggie warned.

"The leader of a pack of wild dogs will attack the stomach on prey first because it has the most meat and nutriments. So you could scare a dog that does not know you if you touch its exposed belly," Maggie told them.

They did some more basic training that Saturday. Bubba was good at jumping over things in Maggie's back yard and seemed to enjoy it. Bubba made a new friend, a blue Pit Bull named Duncan. They had great fun play fighting and could really go for it without fear because they were almost the same weight and size. Bubba had met her match and made a real friend. Leaf decided that on Monday she would tell her classmate Duncan that her dog was best friends with a Pit Bull named Duncan. Maybe that would make him smile.

Leaf had noticed Duncan staring out of the classroom window a lot lately as if dreaming of being anywhere but school. Leaf could tell there was more to Duncan than just a shabby uniform. She had read that often people who led interesting lives

232

and achieved great things had not been popular or great students in school. The teachers had explained that Duncan was dyslexic but the children were cruel and called him stupid. Leaf had read that Richard Branson the billionaire, Agatha Christie who was one of the bestselling authors of all time, Albert Einstein the theoretical physicist, Steve Jobs the global icon of media, Leonardo Di Vinci, and Thomas Edison the inventor, were all dyslexic, and that dyslexic people have great minds for business, they question things and are full of great ideas. She did not think Duncan was a loser like the other children in her class did. She saw that he still had the potential to become something great and often wondered what Duncan thought about as he stared out of the classroom window.

That morning in the dog training class, Maggie said that it is wrong to hit or hurt a dog when they have been naughty because this causes them to lose trust and confidence in the owner and teaches them to fear.

"A dog without confidence is more likely to lash out with aggression, best to lock them outside for a timeout when they have done something bad. The same discipline training is best also for children, although you can put children on a naughty step or in a timeout chair. You can send dogs to their bed, if they have one, but putting them outside is more effective," Maggie told them.

Leaf thought about the Staffy cry when you lock them out. American Staffordshire Bull Terriers wail at the oddest high pitched sound level and try to make the neighbours believe they are being tortured. If Staffies are excited to play with another dog on the other side of the road they howl like they are being strangled. It is such a loud and peculiar sound that everyone in the street turns to see where it came from and laugh to see a

233

muscular American Staffordshire Bull Terrier talking in such a high-pitched squeal.

After the class, Grammy dropped Bubba back with Mum, and then drove Leaf back to her dad's. Leaf spent Saturday afternoon and all of Sunday playing with Snowball Georgette and the bunnies. In the evening she went home to Mum and Bubba.

Dad took the ten bunnies to the pet shop on a day when Leaf was not there, to make it less upsetting for her. They still had Georgette, Splodge, Melocoton and three more which Leaf had named Hop, Skip and Jump. Leaf had asked around at school and a girl in her class had asked her mum. She told Leaf she was allowed to have Hop and Jump. So now they only needed a home for Skip. In the end, Grammy said she would take him. It would be good company for Wilbur Wiggins she said. Not that Wilbur needed company as he went just about everywhere with Grammy.

Wilbur thought he was a dog, and within a week Skip thought he was a pig. Wilbur followed Grammy, and Skip hopped after Wilbur wherever he went. Skip loved Wilbur.

Skip was so covered in fluffy white fur that it was hard to see what he was. His ears did not stick up like Mellow's, Splodge's or Snowball Georgette's. Skip's ears flopped down like a dog's and his face was so furry that Grammy usually put his hair up in a band, giving Skip a high ponytail so that he could see where he was going.

Grammy was often seen driving through town in her Union-Jack Mini with Wilbur and Skip buckled into the back of the car on booster seats. What a sight! They were three very unusual friends

Chapter Seventeen

SAN ISIDRO AND THE BIG SUPRISE

Sarah had phoned Leaf after Eastenders and she was not in a good mood.

"You've changed, Leaf! You never spend any time with me anymore. When was the last time we hung out together? I am not lying for you anymore. I got into trouble with my mum last week. She heard me telling your mum you were in the bathroom. I hate lying, and it is like you are lying to me too. Why won't you tell me where you go? Are you in trouble Leaf? Well I'm not getting into trouble for you anymore. You don't even treat me like a friend these days, so I think we should stop being friends altogether," ranted Sarah.

"No, Sarah, please don't say that. You are my best friend. I'm not in trouble and I am sorry I made you lie and got you into trouble. I won't ask you again," Leaf pleaded.

"So you still won't tell me?"

"I can't, Sarah. I told you it is a secret."

"Whatever! Keep your secrets. See if I care, but don't involve me. If fact, don't even talk to me ever again!" Sarah slammed down the phone. Leaf stayed sitting on her mum's bed feeling crushed. She cried for a bit and then shuffled down the hall to blow her nose in the bathroom.

Leaf was on the way to her own bedroom to sulk, when she heard the phone ringing again. She thought it might be Sarah calling her back to say all was forgiven, so she ran down the hall and picked up the extension of the house phone next to her mum's bed.

235

"Oh, it's you, Grammy."

"Well don't sound so excited to hear from me," Grammy said, offended.

"Sorry Grammy, I just had a big argument with Sarah and our friendship is over forever."

"A lot can change in forever, Wormy, so cheer up. I was thinking we should go to the San Isidro Festival on Friday. It actually took place in May but that's no bother to us. It will be lots of fun, you'll love it," Grammy insisted.

"Oh, okay."

"I could pick you up after school and then we can go for the rest of the afternoon."

"Where is it?"

"Remember that lovely little town we went to with the caves?"

"What? Nerjar? In Spain?"

"It is pronounced Nerha dear, J is pronounced like an H in Spanish. But it is spelt N-E-R-J-A. Yes, it is there. I do so love that little town and they have this wonderful San Isidro Festival. All the girls get dressed up in flamenco dresses and they ride from Nerja to the caves in decorated floats pulled by tractors or big bulls or they ride on horses. There is lots of colour and music and fun. It is quite the affair. Tell your mum I am picking you up and taking you to my house for the afternoon," Grammy told her. Leaf decided that it was probably just what she needed to get her out of her losing-Sarah-slump.

After school on Friday, Leaf changed out of her uniform into jeans and a T-shirt, a hoodie and her purple DM boots. Grammy picked Leaf up, drove her round the corner and parked Sally at the kerb.

"Here, put some sun block on. We can use one of these

front doors," Grammy said reaching behind Leaf's seat for her big beach bag.

"Here's a hat and shades."

The two of them got out of the Mini wearing T-shirts, big floppy sun hats and dark glasses on an overcast day in North London.

They were in a long tree-lined road of three-story white houses. The houses all looked the same except for the doors painted in different colours. They climbed the steps up to a white front door and Grammy stuck the Key in the lock.

"The San Isidro Festival in Nerja, Malaga, Spain, the 15th of May 2015, at one o'clock in the afternoon," Grammy said hurriedly, having spotted a uniformed policeman walking down the road.

"Quick! Let's go," Grammy urged, turning the handle and practically pushing Leaf through the door.

They came out on one of Nerja's main roads in the bright sunlight. Grammy was feeling jolly.

"Isn't this wonderful Leaf?" Grammy said, waving her arms theatrically about as if to embrace it all. In her large hat and dark glasses she looked like an overdramatic film star incognito. She was wearing a long blue skirt and a brown tie- dye t-shirt which read:

THE ONLY ONES, WHO ADORE BEING YOUNG, ARE THE MIDDLE AGED! - Pam Brown 1928.

Grammy looked like a disguised ex-actress trying not to be noticed but finding it impossible not to draw attention to herself, as was her nature.

Swarms of people buzzed about on either side of the N340 and in the centre of the road to watch the Romeria pilgrimage, a procession of colourful floats, elegant horses and groomed riders in traditional Andalusian riding outfits. Girls wore long or short, straight or flouncy, spotty or flowered, flamboyant flamenco dresses of every colour.

The floats were followed by increasingly drunk crowds of locals and tourists walking up to the caves just before the next town of Maro. The whole procession was led by a statue of San Isidro, the Patron Saint of Madrid, escorted by ox and cart.

Isidro was a religious man who had lived a simple life as a farmer, working for a rich family in Madrid. Despite not having much himself, he always showed charity to the poor, whom he often brought home to be fed by his wife, Maria. Isidro was said to be a hard working pious man who took care of animals and those in need, and he prayed every day. It was thought that angels helped him to plough the fields as he always produced three times as much as other farmers.

One day, while ploughing the land with his oxen, he heard the church bells ringing for mass. Thinking he must be late, he ran to the church. When he returned all his land had been ploughed. The townspeople declared it a miracle. In 1622, Isidro was canonised as the patron saint of farmers and animals, so the townspeople of Nerja and Maro get another day off on the 15th of May and celebrate in traditional style. There is a festival every month of the year in Nerja and nearby villages but San Isidro is one of the best.

Leaf and Grammy grabbed some refreshments from a supermarket that was taking advantage of the festivities in the street and had stayed open despite the public holiday.

They followed the crowds up the main road. Every patch of grass along the way was occupied by parties of people (mostly English) barbecuing, drinking or just enjoying watching the festivities pass with no intentions of walking all the way to Maro.

Many of the floats had their own music systems. Leaf and Grammy danced along behind them, trying not to step in large piles of horse, bull or mule poo.

It was a long walk and by the time they reached the bridge and the final ascent to the cave area, Grammy and Leaf were all danced out and ready to collapse. The animals were tied to trees at the start of the surrounding woodland and the procession entered the cave car park, now filled with decorated stalls for food and drink. Parts of the space were dance areas where adolescents got down to Reggaeton, or local groups of Flamenco dancers performed on a stage.

Grammy and Leaf parked themselves on a grass patch to the left where families of different nationalities were having picnics. Children were racing around shooting each other with water pistols or eating ice-creams and towering pink, blue or yellow cotton candyfloss, like sunset clouds caught on a stick.

A blonde girl in a flamenco dress, about a year or two older than Leaf, was walking around with a big water gun asking the other children in both English and Spanish if they had seen her brother.

"Where's Fynn? Donde esta Fynn?" Then the girl walked over to her mother and asked her in German. Leaf wished she could speak so many languages like that. She could speak a bit of German, she understood more than she spoke, and she had picked up a few swear words in Russian from overhearing Dana yelling at Dad.

The grass was rough and spiky, not like soft English grass. Grammy fidgeted as she got poked in the bum. Reaching for her beach bag, she retrieved a towel to sit on, the fresh bread, the packet of Serrano ham and the now warm bottle of water. They munched hungrily and happily as they watched the horses on the other side of the wire-mesh fence and the pretty flamenco dresses swishing past.

Several elegantly dressed riders strutted into the woodland area on their shiny horses. Leaf loved all the colourful dresses and wished she was wearing one. She felt so incorrectly dressed at this event. Actually, she really wished she was wearing shorts, instead of jeans as it was so hot. She could not imagine how much the girls must be sweating in those thick, heavy dresses.

After their snack and a rest, they walked up the path through flowered terraces, passed stalls and three big dance areas where hundreds of teenagers were packed like sardines, jumping around to deafeningly loud music. Opposite, adults sat in groups at metal tables or queued for beers and pinchitos (pieces of grilled meat on sticks) at the makeshift pop-up bars.

Further up they found a play park where little kids, also dressed up in flamenco styles, were rocking and swinging, climbing bridges and changing gears in a wooden toy car or running around in gangs with water pistols. There was a picnic area with covered stone tables. On the lower terraces they recognised the entrance to the caves, closed on this public holiday. Leaf thought about how it had been when she had collected flowers there with Onga for her grandparent's funeral. She felt sad that she would never be able to visit Onga again as she did not know where their tribe had gone.

240

San Isidro and the Big Surprise

She remembered Onga waving to her from the canoe as her father rowed them away. Leaf and Onga had not had much communication between them but nevertheless they had become friends in that one day. Leaf felt extremely lonely these days with no one except Grammy and Bubba to share the secret of the Key with. Now Sarah wasn't even talking to her. Sarah was making a point of ignoring Leaf at school, like she was dead. Leaf felt isolated. She needed new friends. She wished with all her heart that other people had Keys too.

Grammy and Leaf queued up in the public toilets, listening to the women talking in Spanish as they formed an unruly line or took lipsticks out of secret pockets hidden amongst the inner ruffles under their full flamenco skirts and squeezed in for a spot in front of the mirror.

After washing their hands with no soap, the dispenser being empty, Grammy and Leaf headed towards the exit of the car park area. Along the car park were stalls set up by different bars and restaurants of the town. To the left of the exit was a huge stage area circled by chairs and drinks stalls. Here musicians and different flamenco dancing groups, from old ladies to toddlers, performed. Grammy and Leaf stayed to watch for a while, and then they headed back towards the main gate.

Outside the main gate to the left there was a restaurant with tables in the garden.

"Come, let's get a drink and sit there, I need to talk to you about something. Remember a few months ago I told you I had a big surprise for you? Well now I am going to tell you what it is," Grammy said to Leaf.

They chose a wooden table in the small garden. Leaf felt she needed to pee again so she asked the waiter the way to the bathroom. Following the instructions given in shaky English, she descended the stairs inside the restaurant and found herself in a weird empty room with a life-size statue of Jesus and nothing else. It was unnerving. Leaf wondered if she had come the right way and then she saw the door for the toilets on the other side. Jesus was staring at her when she came out of the loo, and she could feel him watching her as she crossed the room.

"I have such a big surprise for you." Grammy was grinning as Leaf walked back to her and sat at the wooden table in the sunlight. From the size of Grammy's grin, Leaf knew this was going to be good. She sucked her lemon drink up through the straw as she listened.

"I will soon be handing the Key over to you but just for the summer. You will not be able to use it...hush...all will become clear in a moment," Grammy told her, putting her hand up in the wait signal they had learnt in dog training to stop Leaf from interrupting.

"When you are twelve you will be allowed to use the Key without supervision but you must train for that privilege. You are not allowed to run off and use it willy-nilly. You are just starting out, Leaf, so go slow, be responsible and careful. You must be educated so that you do not go running off into war zones or dangerous places. Research the places you want to visit. Learn as many languages as you can. Learn as much about everything as you can. Knowledge is the Key, Leaf!" Grammy paused and looked at Leaf thoughtfully.

"Always remember to never mess with the past or the future, for the consequences could be catastrophic. Just your presence affects destiny, Leaf, so keep your visits through time brief and keep your actions small. Keep the Key a secret and don't get caught using it."

San Isidro and the Big Surprise

Leaf felt overwhelmed, excited and scared all at the same time. Even though Grammy was repeating what she already knew, Leaf could feel that it was leading up to something big.

"I have something I did not tell you before because the rules say that I must first teach you as much as I can, and I wanted to see how you got on before you knew. I didn't want you to get distracted and over excited. I was trying to make you more responsible I suppose."

"The previous Guardian of the Key, being me, is supposed to get you started with fun trips like this one, but it is not all fun and games, Leaf. Being a Guardian of a Whiteash Key is a serious responsibility. Winston Churchill said, "The price of greatness is responsibility!" The Key can bring great danger and you must be careful not to change events during time-travel or you could be messing with the destiny of the whole planet. You must be responsible and understand the consequences of actions. There is so much for you to learn. Anyway the point is...what I have not told you... is that you are not alone in this, Leaf." Grammy smiled because of Leaf's raised eyebrows and sudden alert expression.

"Every Summer for one month, there is a Key Camp Summer School held in Somerset for the children of the Key Guardian Families," Grammy told her with excitement.

"The Key Guardian Families?" Leaf was so surprised she almost snorted the fizzy lemon drink out her nose.

"In England alone there are about sixty families who have a Guardian of a Key. There were **One Hundred and Eleven** Whiteash Keys made in total." Leaf now knew why that number was special to Grammy.

"About three or four Keys have been lost, and lots have gone to other parts of the world but all the Key Guardians from all over the world aged ten to sixteen go to the Key Camp in

243

Somerset."

"So you are telling me that we are not the only ones with this secret? There are others like me?"

"Plenty! Although no one is quite like you, Leaf," Grammy said, beaming with love and pride.

"And I can go?" Leaf checked before she burst with excitement.

"I've already paid for the next seven summers, so now we just have to convince your mother. That should not be too hard as you learn lots of things there. We could tell her it is a language camp which is not really a lie because you will learn several languages there. It is a summer school camp for the month of August, so we will tell her that."

"Is it a camp just for girls?"

"No, there will be boys there too. Girls are given their Key by their maternal grandmothers but boys are given the Key by their paternal grandfathers," Grammy informed her.

"Did you go when you were younger, Grammy?" asked Leaf after a five minute silence. She had been blowing bubbles through her straw and imagining what the Key Camp would be like.

Grammy had her head back absorbing the sun but the question grabbed her attention. Grammy looked at Leaf, her eyes full of memories.

"Oh yes, I loved every minute of it. I'm sure you will too and the friends you make there will be friends for life," exclaimed Grammy, fishing a piece of apple out of her drink.

"I met my friend Hippy Millicent at the Whiteash Key Camp sixty years ago. Her granddaughter is the current Key Guardian and she was teaching at the camp last year but is now pursuing her career in law."

"Oh Grammy, I am so excited. I thought I would have to keep this a secret from everyone for the rest of my life. I was just

244

thinking I need to make some new friends. I can't wait to meet other Guardians of my age. Oh Grammy, thank you so much!"

"So you're up for it then?" Grammy teased.

"I hope Mum lets me go." Leaf frowned.

"Well, let's go home and convince her then. No time to waste as camp starts next week. I've had enough of this sangria anyway, too much fruit floating about in it, and this sun is ageing me by the minute. I'll have to use another monatomic face pack when I get back. "

They put their floppy hats and dark glasses back on, and started off down the road to find a door to get home. Leaf was ecstatic. She knew her life was about to change again and become even more exhilarating. She skipped down the hill in the sunshine, excited and eager to find out what thrilling adventures were coming next.

Drawings by Leaf Golden

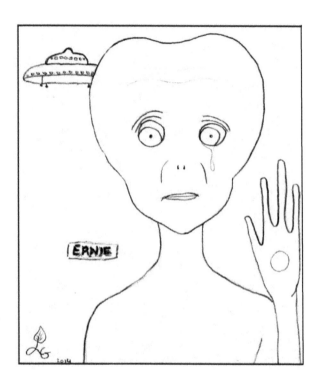